PRAISE FOR THE S.

When the D

CW01513102

"A promising first mystery of particular interes

"…an action-packed mystery that will garner mucn attention from fans who enjoy a police procedural with a twist."

— *Midwest Book Review*

"For those readers with an interest in the religion of Native Americans and specifically the Sioux, they will find tantalizing hints of these practices within the pages of When the Dead Speak. It looks like Tooley has a winner on her first novel and I look forward to her next, Nothing Else Matters."

— Leslie Doran, *Mystery News*

Nothing Else Matters

"Entertaining reading in what looks to be a solid series."

— *Booklist*

"The author, who spent six years as a casino dealer, effectively blends Native American lore with the world of riverboat gambling."

— *Publishers Weekly*

Restless Spirit

"An exciting mix of police procedure, spiritual 'intuition,' creeping suspense, and page-turning narrative."

— *Library Journal*

"Sam Casey is amazing—a beautifully described and magically interesting character…the plot, characters and pacing are all excellent."

— 4 Star Review, *Romantic Times*

Echoes from the Grave

"Author S. D. Tooley delivers this fourth installment in the exciting Sam Casey series with suavity and grace in a writing style which will rivet the reader to the roller-coaster plotting."

— *EuroReviews*

What Lies Within

"Known as one of the first to write paranormal mysteries, S.D. Tooley also writes the Chase Dagger series under the name Lee Driver. The fast-paced investigative story line grips the reader. Character driven by mostly Sam, fans will enjoy the latest Casey paranormal whodunit."

— *Midwest Book Review*

Also by S.D. Tooley

Sam Casey Series

What Lies Within

Echoes from the Grave

Restless Spirit

Nothing Else Matters

When the Dead Speak

Remy and Roadkill Series

The Skull

Written as Lee Driver

Chase Dagger Series

Fatal Storm

Chasing Ghosts

The Unseen

Full Moon-Bloody Moon

The Good Die Twice

Short Stories

Sara Morningsky, *Mystery in Mind Anthology*

The Thirteenth Hole, *Mystery in Mind Anthology*

Mysteries to Die For, a Short Story Collection (ebook only)

DESTINY KILLS

S.D. Tooley

Full Moon Publishing

This book is a work of fiction. Names, characters, places and incidents are the product of the author's imagination or are used fictitiously. Any resemblance to actual events, locales or persons, living or dead, is coincidental. Any slights of people, places, or organizations is purely unintentional.

Library of Congress Catalog Number: 2012936521

ISBN-10 0-9846357-5-0
ISBN-13 978-0-9846357-5-7

Published April 2012

Printed in the United States of America

Logo Design by Lesley Staples

Full Moon Publishing LLC
433 Mystic Point Dr.
Bluffton, SC 29909

www.fullmoonpub.com

1

"Mommy's coming, Savannah." Marti Johnson's nine-month-old daughter was a mirror image of her with big brown eyes and dark curls, although Marti straightened her own with enough chemicals to open her own lab. Savannah huddled in the middle of the crib, tiny hands slapping her legs in a baby tantrum. Marti usually timed it just right. She would shower, dress, and run a brush through her short hair before Savannah awakened. But today she was five minutes off schedule and Savannah knew it.

The infant howled when she caught sight of Marti, a baby version of a scolding. "Are you hungry, sweetpea? Mommy has your breakfast heating now." She lifted Savannah from the crib and laid her on the dressing table. After a diaper change and a quick swipe of Savannah's face with a wet cloth, Marti hoisted the infant on her hip and carried her to the kitchen where she sat her daughter in a high chair.

Both Forrest and Marti wanted a houseful of kids. They were well on their way as Marti had just learned she was pregnant again. Forrest had a great job as a bank manager, enabling Marti to quit her retail management job to be a stay-at-home mom. They had moved from a roach-infested apartment in Gary, Indiana a year ago to a beautiful condo overlooking a golf course in Chasen Heights, Illinois.

Marti placed one piece of cinnamon raisin bread in the toaster, then poured herself a cup of coffee while the television newscaster gave the weather report. Savannah entertained herself with measuring spoons, banging them on the tray and babbling in baby talk. Sunny and seventy degrees at eight o'clock in the morning. It was looking to be another great summer day.

Marti dabbed the spoon into the jar of baby food and touched it to her tongue. "Still hot, baby. Let's give it a few more minutes." She set the jar aside and placed a few Cheerios on Samantha's tray to placate her until the food was ready.

The breakfast nook was located in front of a bay window overlooking the golf course. Their building was situated at an angle which protected their second-floor windows from stray golf balls. The windows in their unit folded in for easy cleaning. Marti had affixed a bird feeder to the window where she and Savannah would watch as the finches feasted on the thistle seed. Marti set her cup of coffee down and was just ready to slide onto the bench seat when the phone rang.

"I bet that's daddy." She kissed Savannah's head and hustled to find her cell phone. She picked up a stuffed dog from the floor and placed it on the glass top coffee table. The phone continued its chirping and Marti soon located it on the couch in the living room buried under a stack of yesterday's newspapers. She smiled as she said, "What did you forget?" The smile slowly faded as she listened to the voice. Her face took on a Stepford glare as she set the phone down. Marti walked over to the door, slipped on her tennis shoes and tied them. She didn't bother to grab a jacket or her keys. Without looking in on her daughter she calmly walked out of the condo and took the stairs. Once in the lobby Marti walked past the guard without her typical sunny hello. Two people at the curb were emptying their car of groceries. Not one of them thought it strange that Marti didn't have Savannah with her, nor did they watch as she headed toward the gate. Aromas from a nearby Burger King wafted through the air. The sun was blinding, streaking between the tree branches, prompting the guard at the gate to pull a visor down on the window of his guard shed. He looked up and waved but went right back to his morning paper. He didn't follow her with his eyes to see her turn at the light and head toward the expressway two blocks away. Cars were zipping by on River Oaks Drive while joggers and power walkers maneuvered along the sidewalk. Marti was completely oblivious to the activity around her.

A patrol officer sat behind the wheel of a squad car writing out a speeding ticket for the truck driver parked in front of him. He gave more than a passing glance at the attractive woman as she walked past.

As an afterthought, he checked out her ass in the rearview mirror. But something wasn't right. For one thing, she paid little attention to cars, not looking once before crossing the side street. Her pace was determined, not a stagger to her step as if she were drunk or on drugs. When she reached the top of the overpass she turned and without hesitation climbed over the railing. He rushed out of the squad car and ran toward the woman.

"HEY!" he yelled. Either she couldn't hear or was ignoring him. She never acknowledged him nor the screeching of tires or loud horns of passing motorists who weren't quite sure what they were witnessing. The semi-driver on the expressway below didn't see the woman either until her body hit the windshield. He was going seventy miles an hour.

2

"Mister Johnson, I'm so glad you could join us today. How have you been? We were really worried about you." The woman smothered him so much with her motherly concern that he wanted to hurl. "I do hope you participate today. It really does help to get your feelings out in the open." She wove her arm through his and led him toward the group. Grace Hunt was a recovering nun who started the suicide support group five years ago after her father took a gun to his head following the news that his cancer had returned. Meetings were held once a week in the evening in the basement of the Christian Family Center. The church had been Marti's second home. She had been a choir member since they moved to Chasen Heights.

Forrest poured himself a cup of coffee and hung back by the refreshment table while other members laughed and joked with each other, everyone except Carrie. Sometimes he would catch her looking at him, as though they shared the same thought that this was all bullshit. How soon until he could smile again much less laugh? It was an effort just to put on a happy face for Savannah. He resented how most everyone in the room appeared to have moved on, but Grace had told him it takes time. After all, it had only been two months since Marti's accident. He still refused to call it suicide. There wasn't any way his wife would have taken her own life.

The group consisted of six people counting Grace. One woman shuffled over with her cane, her body as straight and thin as the cane itself. Her husband had left a note that he had had enough of life. Eighty years was sufficient. He saw and did all he wanted to do. That was five years ago. Forrest figured Velma Corbin joined because she had nothing better to do with her life.

Luke Fasula was a sulky teenager who was trying to deal with his sister's suicide. She had been teased in school because of her weight, came home, tied his belt around her neck, and hung herself from a rod in the closet. The fact that she used his belt bothered him more than the fact that she was dead. His parents and therapist were forcing him to come and it was obvious he'd rather be home secluded in his room. Even now his thumbs tapped out text messages with the speed of a drummer. He had become withdrawn and would rather spend time texting or playing video games than talking it out. His time with the shrink had been nothing more than staring sessions. Luke still felt his mom naming his sister Fatima was a disaster waiting to happen.

Ben Kowalski was an Iraq war vet who left one arm in Iraq along with a couple unit members. His best friend, Vinnie, had joined the Marines with him, came home all intact, had a wife and two beautiful girls. Even planned Ben's bachelor party and was Ben's best man. On the outside Vinnie was always laughing, joking, not fazed by what he had seen in Iraq so no one had suspected he was suffering from post-traumatic stress disorder. He left a note for his wife that said *I'm sorry* before checking into a seedy motel and blowing his brains out.

Carrie Farnswood was the most reserved of all. Although she had smiled a couple times, she wasn't at the point of laughing and joking with the rest. Her twin sister, Carly, had been one week from her wedding when she took a stroll on the beach, stripped, took the time to fold her clothes neatly, then walked into Lake Michigan. Carrie was sure Carly loved her fiancée, was excited about the honeymoon and the life she and Sean would start together. They had worked hard and saved for three years to put a down payment on her dream home. Carrie still couldn't believe Carly was gone. Being a nurse she knew the importance of a support group and of the five, she and Forrest appeared to be the only ones who still hadn't moved beyond the denial stage. Carly had died several weeks before Marti.

"Okay everyone." Grace clapped her hands as though confronting a room of first graders. "Let's get started." The chairs formed a circle with Grace at the head. Although no longer a nun, she still dressed conservatively in a black skirt, white blouse, and sensible shoes. Her hair was short and peppered with gray and her face had little, if any, makeup.

Forrest refilled his cup and doctored it with cream and sugar as he stalled for time. But Grace wasn't buying it. "Come, Forrest. We need to hear from you tonight." She patted a chair next to hers. He could feel all five sets of eyes on him.

He kept the coffee cup clasped in his hands as he took a seat. Remnants of streamers hung in the corners of the room, floating like something possessed every time air drifted from the vents. Pink and blue streamers, probably from a baby shower. He felt something squeeze his heart. "Where do you want me to start?"

"Tell us about your wife."

"Why?" The word came out without thinking, and like a row of dominoes, he couldn't halt the rest of his feelings from being exposed. "What good does it do to tell you about a woman you're never going to meet? All it does is make me miss her more. I have enough of that every day just looking at my daughter who is the spitting image of Marti." Forrest wished the coffee was a glass of scotch straight up. Now he was on a roll. "Do you think sitting around talking about the deceased makes it hurt any less or brings them back? Those five stages—denial, anger, bargaining, depression, acceptance. Hell, I can't get past stage one. How am I going to get to stage five?"

"Everyone in this room has been at stage one," Grace said in her Mother Superior voice. "Some get past faster than others. You have to accept that it takes time."

"How long? When Savannah graduates eighth grade and her mother isn't there to witness it?" Now the tears were starting and that was one thing Forrest didn't want to do in public. Look at the black man crying like a baby. Six foot, one-eighty and he's a wimp. "Or maybe when she only sees one half of her parents in the audience when she graduates college? Or how do you think it will look when she doesn't have a mother to help her pick out her wedding gown?"

The room was stunned to silence. Even Luke had stopped tapping out a text message to stare at Forrest. Grace normally had a way of keeping everyone calm, of being able to keep the group on an even keel. But today the meeting was getting away from her. She looked around the room sensing she should probably say something. But it was Carrie who was the first to speak.

"Why don't you think your wife committed suicide?" Her voice was soft but it may as well have been a clap of thunder since Forrest had shocked the room into silence.

Forrest blinked as though wondering where the sound had come from. "What?"

"You said you were still in stage one. Some people assume it means they deny their loved ones are dead. But for you and me we are in denial because we don't believe our loved ones committed suicide."

Forrest found himself shaking his head yes without even knowing it.

"Tell us about it," Carrie said, appearing to take control of the session.

Forrest took a swallow of coffee and looked around the room. Like the police, would they think he was crazy? He had thought about it every night as he rocked his daughter to sleep. "The police chalked it up to post-partum depression but I know she didn't have it. She doted on Savannah and she was pregnant again. We talked often about how we wanted to have a houseful of kids. Marti and I were both shuffled around foster homes growing up so we knew the importance of a stable family life. That morning I was already at work but I knew her daily routine. She showered and dressed before Savannah woke up. She was dressed in her warm up suit, made a pot of coffee." Forrest could see Marti dressed in her lavender warm up suit to power walk while pushing Savannah's stroller. He smiled through the tears as though sitting at the kitchen table watching her. "She always drank a cup of coffee and ate cinnamon raisin toast while feeding Savannah her breakfast. They would sit at the kitchen table by the bay window so Savannah could watch the birds." He placed his cup of coffee down on the floor. He made a motion with his hands as if it were show and tell at school. "Marti had put this suction cup bird feeder on the window so they could watch the birds. But that day," Forrest paused to take a deep breath. "That day she poured her coffee, had Savannah's jar of baby food on the counter heated and ready to serve, and then walked out of the condo, down the street, and jumped off the overpass. Savannah was still seated in her high chair. Now does that sound right to you?"

Not one person responded. Velma and Carrie had tears streaming down their faces. Grace was sniffing, trying to hold it together. Ben and Luke just stared.

"And I bet the police think you had something to do with it," Carrie said.

"What?" Luke whipped his head toward Forrest sending a curtain of hair across his forehead.

"That's what they did to Sean, my sister's fiancee." Carrie raked a hand through her blonde hair. She was pretty, with a girl-next-door squeaky clean look. If Carly was an identical twin, she would have made a beautiful bride. "They thought maybe he verbally and physically abused her, or maybe she wanted to back out of the wedding and he wouldn't let her. Even my parents thought someone had to put the idea in her head and it had to be Sean."

"Yeah. They talked to neighbors and people I work with, friends at the gym and Marti's friends trying to dig up some type of spousal abuse. But it was nothing like that. I loved my wife. I don't care what the cops say, my wife did NOT commit suicide. Yet they closed the case. They called it a suicide so it's a suicide. And then they have the audacity to suggest I just wanted the insurance money, that if they would rule it an accidental death or something, then I could have the money."

"The insurance company won't pay on a suicide," Velma said. She had a skein of yarn in her lap while her nimble fingers worked the crochet needles. "My husband didn't believe in insurance. Said it was all a scam because you don't collect unless you're dead. Isn't that ridiculous?" Velma looked around the room, expecting a reply. As usual, her sudden interruption was met with silence.

"I couldn't care less about the money," Forrest stressed.

"Wow, dude. That's deep," Luke said. "If it wasn't suicide and it wasn't an accident, what else is left?"

3

A movie played in her head, a surreal image of a vehicle disintegrating in slow motion. Shiny pieces of steel floated in the sunlight—a side mirror, driver's side door torn into multiple pieces, the windshield, the hood of the car, first flipping up then scattering into pieces. Along with the sections of the vehicle were more recognizable parts, human parts. A hand, parts of an arm, fabric that might have been a shirt, pieces of skull with hair attached. She tried to turn away but she was transfixed by the horror. Just like a transformer movie, everything started to reverse as the body parts slowly reassembled. First the body parts twisted in flight, fabric gradually attached to the human it had previously clothed. Then the car slowly reassembled—the roof, windshield, car door, side mirrors. Sam was watching everything from behind a window, and the driver in the car smiled at her, waved. And she waved back.

Sam no longer woke with a start when she had these dreams. Her eyelids snapped open and she stared at the ceiling wondering why it was becoming more consistent and why now. Doctor Talbot at Sara Binyon's, a posh retreat for people who needed a place to relax and re-tune their psyches, had been helpful during her stay after the Preston Hilliard case. For the first few months of her pregnancy with Dillon the dreams had disappeared. Then they started again, but this time with the transformer special effects. If she were still a cop it would have been mandatory that she see the department shrink. She rolled back and closed her eyes but sleep wouldn't come. The clock above the headboard said it was after eight in the morning. Saturday. Of course Jake was up early. He had a golf date.

◇◇

Lamon Robinson hauled his massive frame out of the golf cart and studied the foursome in the middle of the fairway in front of them. "May as well hold up. We're not going anywhere." He pulled an apple out of a paper bag and took a large bite. He had a linebacker-sized body and a tight-hugging Afro. His voice had a deep resonance, one that people have said reminded them of Barry White.

Ed Scofield, the desk sergeant at the Sixth Precinct, climbed out of the passenger side with a can of bug spray. "Damn mosquitos. Isn't it about time for them to hibernate or something?"

Jake Mitchell and Frank Travis sat in the golf cart next to them. Frank ripped off a piece of a power bar while Jake took a long pull from a water bottle. "Should have gotten two more egg McMuffins," Frank said as he scrutinized the power bar. "This is a poor excuse for breakfast."

The annual Gun and Hose Scramble was usually held at the Three Oaks Golf Course, but this year they were holding it at the new Lake Bluff Country Club thanks to the pull of newly elected Mayor Jeff Schuler. He was a close friend of the owner and wanted to make the golf outing between the police and fire departments an annual event.

"Listen guys." Frank stroked the soul patch below his lip. "I noticed yesterday that Justin has a kinda wiggle when he walks. You don't think I should be worried, do you?" He tossed the wrapper from the power bar into the garbage. "Do most four-year-old boys wiggle? I don't think I wiggled."

Three heads turned in Frank's direction. Jake's eyes bore a hole through his partner. "You wiggle now," Robinson said. "Besides, it is what it is. Let him be who he's supposed to be."

Ed hitched up his pants and gave Frank's comment a shrug. "Look at them pansy-ass lime green balls you use. And you wonder about your son?"

"They were on sale in the pro shop," Frank protested. "Besides, they are yellow, not green."

"Whatever." Ed sprayed his arms with the bug spray. "Take your son to Home Depot. That will man him up."

Now heads turned toward Ed who rarely laughed at his own dry humor but within seconds they were all cackling. Ed was tall and rail thin with a concave chest. As desk sergeant, he was the gatekeeper to the fourth floor at the Sixth Precinct.

They sported matching powder blue shirts and dark blue sweaters with the image of a gun embroidered on the left side of the sweater. Gun and Hose Scramble was embroidered above the gun. Their counterparts, the firemen, had white shirts and red sweaters with the same embroidery except theirs had a fire hose instead of a gun.

"Okay, who's up?" Robinson checked the score card. "Frank. Get us some good distance. We need a birdie if we plan to beat those firefighters. And you can wiggle all you want, just don't do an Ed Norton and take five minutes to prepare."

"Damn, Captain, all these orders. Do this, don't do that." But Frank was smiling. He took two practice swings, then lined up his shot. "Okay, right down the middle." He shuffled his feet, waved the club back and forth, eyed the fairway one last time, then swung.

"Whoa, what a shot." Ed shielded his eyes from the sun.

"Stay up. No, don't hook. Damn." Frank leaned his body to the right as though the movement alone could control the ball. He grimaced as the ball took a sharp turn and sailed into the trees on the left side of the fairway.

"I'll show you how it's done." Robinson grabbed a driver with a head the size of a grapefruit. He didn't bother with a practice swing. The air whooshed as the ball went sailing. The four stood in stunned silence as the ball sailed over the trees on the right hand side. "Looks like I have the longest drive so far."

"Yeah, too bad it's two fairways over." Ed pulled out a three wood, tossed a ball on the tee box, not bothering to tee it up. "Don't know how you guys can hit them drivers with those large heads. Mine's been in time out for five years." He made a quick swing and popped the ball down the middle of the fairway. "Not far but at least it's in the middle."

"You're awful quiet today, Jake." Robinson tossed his driver back into the golf bag.

"Dillon has another tooth coming in. Kept us up all night. Abby is usually able to quiet him down but he wanted me. I finally waited until Abby wasn't looking and rubbed some whiskey on his gums."

"Told you that would work," Frank said.

Jake wished he had a cup of black coffee about now. He settled a Chicago Bears baseball cap on his head, then pulled a driver from his golf bag. They couldn't ask for better weather for a golf outing. It was in the high sixties the first week of October. Shirt and sweater weather. Jake placed the ball and tee in the ground, lined up his shot, then took a measured backswing and let the club fly.

"Wow, down the middle," Ed yelled. "That's how it's done." The words no sooner left his lips then the ball took a crazy bounce and ended up in a sand trap. "Oops. Guess we all get to play in the beach."

"No. That trap has a big lip on it. Might be hard to get on the green from there."

"I agree with Jake," Robinson said. "Jake has great distance but Ed's ball isn't in any trouble. We can get on in two from where Ed's ball is parked."

"I'm going to look for my ball. The damn things cost over twenty bucks a dozen." Frank grabbed an iron and headed toward the woods. "Take the cart, Jake. I'll walk and meet you." In a scramble, the players pick the best of the four hits, then everyone plays their next shot from the same spot. For four years in a row the police department had won. Last year the fire department squeezed past.

Only the front nine of the course had been opened since the beginning of the season while a crew worked on finishing the bunkers and bridges over the ponds on the back nine. It had been completed in time for the Gun and Hose Scramble.

The two golf carts rumbled to a stop near Ed's ball. "Love the GPS they have on these carts. Look at this." Robinson pointed at the monitor hanging from the roof of the cart on the driver's side. "It even shows where the carts are in front of you plus the yardage."

"Aren't you going to go retrieve your ball?" Ed climbed out of the cart and looked toward the adjoining fairway.

"Nah. Not worth it. I'll just drop another ball."

"Hate it when they have a shotgun start," Ed whined. "We had to start on the back nine. It's like walking up the stairs backwards. My game is off."

"Is that the excuse you're going to use today?"

"Yeah, I'm sticking with it." Ed stood back and studied the yardage to the green. "What are you using, Captain? Think my five wood will get me there?"

"I was going to use my hybrid. You show us the way." Robinson dropped a tee near Ed's ball to mark the spot.

"I'll go with my five wood." Ed took two practice swings, eyed the green, then swung the club. The ball made a line drive toward the target, stopping just short of the green. "That's one way to get it there."

Jake turned in the direction of the woods. "Where the hell did Frank go? He should know better than to spend more than two minutes looking for his ball." Jake looked back at the tee area to see if they were holding up the next group. Frank emerged from the woods, breaking into a trot. "Did you find your ball?"

"Yes and no." Frank ran a hand over his shaved head and gave a sheepish grin. "It kinda rolled into this…" He rolled his hand as though he wanted someone else to finish his thought.

"Into what?" Robinson barked.

"Oh shit." Jake grimaced. Having been Frank's partner for over eight years, he half-expected the next phrase out of Frank's mouth.

"Well…it rolled into the hand of…"

"For crissake, Frank," Robinson yelled. "Don't tell me you stumbled onto another body." He held up one mitt-sized hand like a stop sign. "Don't even say it."

Scofield pulled off his hat and swiped at his forehead. "Does this mean we aren't going to get to finish?"

4

The four men clustered around the body of a woman partially hidden by underbrush. The body was deep enough into the woods that they didn't have to close the eleventh hole. They had retrieved their balls, waved the foursome behind them through, then parked the two golf carts off the fairway. If the golfers were curious what they were doing in the woods, they didn't show it. They were only concerned with their golf game.

"Did you tell Benny and the crime scene unit to take the back road?" Robinson asked.

Ed crouched down and studied the body. "Yeah. The street is only about twenty yards away. Anyone could have driven up and dumped the body. Impossible to see tire tracks in the gravel up there."

Jake used a pen and lifted a branch from a bush hanging over the body. It was clear to see that the victim had been strangled. Although the skin had started to slough off, he could still see a dark line circling her neck. She was wearing leather slacks, heels, a leather jacket and a low cut sweater. Gold bracelets were on her right wrist. What looked like an expensive watch was on her left wrist. And in her opened hand was a lime green golf ball. All Jake could do was shake his head.

"See a purse anywhere?" Jake cautiously stepped back. They had been careful not to move around too much and risk disturbing any evidence the crime techs might discover. Heads swiveled in a quick assessment of the area. The underbrush was thick. Trees were numerous enough to block out most of the sunlight. Unless a golfer was desperate enough to find a lost ball, he would have no reason to wander into the woods.

Between the thick foliage they saw several cars pull over onto the gravel shoulder. Car doors slammed and several figures emerged. Benny Lau, the medical examiner for Chasen Heights, picked his way through, his appearance visible by the colorful Hawaiian shirt he wore under his jacket. An M.E. van parked behind his station wagon followed by a white CSU van. The four cops slowly moved away from the body, careful to retrace their steps. They found a small clearing a safe distance away. One patrol car parked behind the M.E. van.

"Pretty convenient." Benny pointed toward the street. "That wasn't an easy street to find so it makes for a great place to dump a body."

"Gee, Benny, maybe we'll promote you to detective," Ed said as he swatted at the air, wishing he had brought the bug spray.

"Thanks, but I already have a job." Benny waved over his assistant who was lugging a satchel. "Joe, let's wait here until the techs are through."

Captain Robinson instructed the two beat cops to stand vigil on the side of the eleventh fairway to prevent anyone from venturing into the crime scene.

Two crime techs started photographing the area. Carol Beemison was bent over examining the area ten feet away working her way toward the victim. Her honey-colored hair was tucked under a baseball cap. After packing two years of nursing under her belt, she had switched her major to criminology. A ten-year veteran with the crime lab, she had been the only one who could put up with Hank. For her it was easy. He reminded her of her father.

"Could the killer have picked a more dense forest?" Hank Sobczak grumbled. "Who was the lucky ass to uncover the body?" Hank lasered a glare at the faces staying a safe distance away and then saw Frank. "Shoulda known it was you, Travis. You are like a human blowfly, attracted to any decomposing flesh or crime in the making." Hank had twenty years experience and counting the days until he retired. He had seen enough of what a certain element of society can do to another human being and it had made him cynical.

Frank didn't have a reply because Hank was right. Frank had a way of attracting dead bodies. "If you guys bothered to remember," Frank started, "none of this ever happened before I started teaming up with this guy." He hooked a thumb toward Jake. "I'd have to visit the cemetery to be close to a dead body. My patrol days were boring. Then I get teamed up with Mister Ex-FBI. I wonder what their body count was when he worked there."

Jake lit a cigarette and blew the smoke in Frank's direction. "Not true. My life with the FBI was uneventful. We always got our man but they were usually still standing. It's you, Frank."

"It's both of you," Robinson said. "Frick and Frack, yin and yang, whatever. The minute you two were partnered up, the whole town went to hell in a hand basket."

A golf cart rumbled up, one man behind the wheel dressed in a sweater with a Lake Bluff crest on the pocket. Jake remembered him as the starter. *Bob* was embroidered above the crest. He filled Bob in on what was happening and asked him to notify the owner that they would need to speak to him. Bob turned the cart around and headed back up the fairway. It wouldn't take long for word to spread now that a course employee had been told about the body.

"Well, that's it." Robinson waved his hands in a give-up gesture. "We'll have to leave it up to our other CHPD foursome to reclaim our crown. I'm headed back to the office to field calls from the chief and mayor. So much for a quiet weekend. Jake, Frank, let me know what Benny says. Make sure he gets to the autopsy before next year. And you." He pointed a finger at Scofield. "You head back to man the phones. I'm not taking the calls from the press." As Robinson and Scofield sped away, Jake and Frank turned their attention back to the body.

Hank pulled off his gloves and made a quick phone call. He snapped the phone closed as he approached. "No footprints, weapons, zip-nada on the evidence except for some cigarette butts. Even the shoulder of the road over there is gravel. Can't see a tire tread mark if we wanted to. We didn't find a purse anywhere in the area." He slapped the gloves against his thigh as though they were to blame for his crappy day. "So much for getting my grass cut."

Carol patted her partner on the back. "Be thankful she wasn't buried in a sand trap. Then we'd have to sift through every grain."

"As long as Benny is busy, why don't we go to the club house where there's food, hot coffee, and a groundskeeper or two?" Frank suggested to Jake.

"Hey," Hank yelled, holding an object in his hand. "Want your golf ball back?"

5

"Damn, this place must have cost a mint to build." Frank gawked at the bronze statue of a golfer in the lobby. A plaque was affixed to the statue announcing that it was donated by Connor Revere, the owner of the golf course. Those participating in the scramble had been directed to the pro shop upon arriving so they had yet to see the club house. The locker rooms were in the lower level, complete with a fitness center in an adjoining room. Adjacent to the locker rooms were separate men's and women's lounges complete with card tables, wide screen television sets, book shelves, and a juice bar. Walls were decorated with framed pictures of famous golf courses, such as St. Andrews in Scotland and Augusta National in Georgia. The sports motif carried through the building in shades of hunter green and burgundy in the men's section and mint green and pale pink in the women's section. The owner spared no expense from the plush complimentary robes to the well-stocked countertops with toiletries. Massages could be scheduled by appointment only, as well as manicures and pedicures.

Of course, everything came with a price. Although the course and facilities were open to the public, one could receive unlimited golf and use of those complimentary amenities for an annual fee of ten thousand dollars.

On the main level was a dining room large enough to hold wedding receptions complete with a gazebo outside for the ceremony itself. Tables dotted a tiled patio under an overhang should people want to eat outdoors. There was also seating in the bar with enough television sets to show every conceivable sporting event. The pro shop had a small restaurant and Nineteenth Hole lounge.

A man, tall and tan with hair too perfect, glided down the hallway toward the lobby. A paisley print ascot peeked out from under his shirt.

A stocky man dressed in a dark blue uniform emerged from a side door and joined him.

"Gentlemen. Connor Revere." He clasped each of their hands in a strong grip. Revere was almost eye level with Jake's six foot two inch frame. "Manny Ruiz is my grounds foreman," he said as he nodded toward the man in the uniform. "He can answer any questions you might have regarding the back nine." After introductions and handshakes around, Connor led them to his office. Once the waitress brought in the cups, carafe, and a tray of dainty desserts that looked leftover from an elaborate banquet, they settled back for the interview.

"I can't believe this is happening," Connor said as he filled cups with coffee and passed them across the table. "First day the back nine is open. This is the kind of publicity I don't need. Have you identified the body?"

"Not yet. We do know it's a woman," Jake said. "Do you have anyone on your staff who has been missing?"

"To tell you the truth, I don't know everyone on staff. I have a restaurant manager, bar manager, pro shop, cleaning crew, grounds crew. I sign the checks but I am embarrassed to say I haven't met everyone. We hired far more than we needed before we opened and then weeded out those that weren't a good fit."

"If needed, once we have an estimate of the age of the deceased and a composite picture, we'd like to check her description with employees who are no longer employed," Jake said.

"So you are confident she was connected to Lake Bluff?" Connor's well-groomed brows knitted.

"It's a place to start," Frank said. "That fairway is close to the back road. Anyone could have dumped her body." Frank turned to Manny. "When was the last time anyone worked on the back nine?"

"We had to rush to get done in time for today's tournament. Joe and Fritz were working up until late yesterday," Manny replied. "I did a final ride through this morning." Manny had a full head of salt-and-pepper hair. His hands were calloused and his skin tanned a deep brown. Tan lines could be seen at his neck and forearms. "We didn't detect anything unusual. Uh, we would have smelled something, right?"

"Do you live on the property?" Frank asked.

Connor interrupted before Manny could reply. "I assure you my employees were all checked out before I hired them. I doubt anyone associated with this course had anything to do with the body. I'm sure they would all submit to lie detector tests if needed." Connor grabbed the carafe and refilled his cup, then slid the carafe across the table to Jake. "How soon til your people are through out there? I certainly want to make sure you complete your investigation but I also have a tournament, ribbon cutting, and banquet to attend."

"They should be done today. As soon as our medical examiner determines time of death, we will need to interview everyone who had worked that day." Jake's phone rang. He excused himself and walked over to the window. The office was large enough that Jake didn't need to leave the room. He listened for several minutes, then hung up and returned to the conference table but didn't sit down. "That was our medical examiner. He estimates the deceased to be about one hundred and thirty pounds, between twenty-five and thirty-five years of age, brown hair. Sound like anyone you know?"

"About half my waitress staff."

6

"Okay, honey." Sam wiped the tears from Dillon's face. "Look what Mommy has." Sam held her son's hands as she placed the tip of the banana popsicle in his mouth. Dillon clamped down on the cold treat, unable to break it off. Tears puddled in his soft brown eyes. It tugged at Sam's heart and she wished she could take away every pain and discomfort. Dillon was six months old and already had two front teeth. The third one appeared to be more troublesome than the first two.

"That should numb his gums a bit." Abby's colorful skirt brushed against the tops of her moccasins. Even though she no longer lived on the Eagle Ridge Reservation, Abby still dressed in traditional clothing. Her squash necklace had been made with great skill by Alex Red Cloud, a friend and protector, as were the turquoise bracelet and rings she wore.

Dillon's chubby hands and feet pumped as he reached for the popsicle Sam held. "Go ahead and let him hold it," Abby said. "We'll just dump him in the tub afterwards."

Sam winced at the thought of sticky fingers on the high chair tray. Every day was a new set of changes she had to get used to. Marriage, baby, new job, although more like partial retirement, something she had no problem getting used to.

"How long does Jake's golf game last?" Abby grabbed a mist bottle and proceeded to mist the plants in the window box behind the sink. The kitchen was Abby's favorite place in the house. It was bright and airy with an island counter and stools. Counter space was plentiful since Abby loved to cook most meals from scratch.

"I'm not sure. It's really a stupid game, chasing a little white ball around the grass. Last time I think it was four hours to golf and six hours to eat and rehash every shot each of the guys made. I'm sure Alex will be happy when golf season is over with."

Abby glanced out of the window where Alex was trimming back the perennials. He had appeared on their doorstep over ten years ago, claiming that the spirits had sent him to protect *wicasa wakan*—Abby, who was believed to be a medicine woman. Jake felt Alex was a bit smitten with Abby, but he would never tell him that. Alex still practiced Native American customs, preferring to keep his gray hair in either a ponytail or pigtails. Weather permitting he slept in the tipi he had erected in the back acres of the estate near a sweat lodge which he also built.

"I thought Alex was going to have a heart attack when he saw Jake and Frank chipping golf balls into the bird bath. As if that wasn't bad enough, Jake taught Poco how to fetch the golf balls if he missed the bird bath." Sam had to smile at the friendly barbs Alex and Jake tossed at each other. Alex had always felt Sam should marry someone from the reservation, but Abby had to remind him that Sam was only half Lakota and Sam had a hard enough time being accepted at the Eagle Ridge Reservation.

Dillon rubbed his eyes smearing popsicle juice on his face. He was the spitting image of Jake from the broad shoulders to his chiseled features. And thank God he had Jake's hair and not hers. Although Sam had Abby's cheekbones and olive complexion, she had her father's blue eyes and his curly hair which looked more like a burlap rug if she didn't lather it with conditioner. Only by keeping it long was she able to tame it. Even now she had to wear it up in a banana clip to keep Dillon's tiny fingers from getting tangled in the curls.

"Nap time, sweetie?" Dillon whimpered and held his hands up. Sam backed away from the sticky fingers. "I think I'm going to need a shower after bathing him."

"I'll clean the high chair and floor," Abby offered.

Alex slid open the screen door, kicked his moccasins off on the door mat outside, and stepped into the kitchen. Dillon held out a sticky hand in Alex's direction. "*Hau*, little one." Dillon made a gurgling sound that Alex took as "hi" in return. "Boy, what have you been eating?"

"Popsicles." Sam held up the dripping yellow treat before returning it to Dillon's mouth. "We are going to go jump in the shower."

Alex's dark eyes danced as he broke out in a wide grin. "Just heard on the radio that they found a body on the golf course where Jake is playing today."

Sam had to laugh. "Of course. Frank is with him."

"Talk to me." Captain Robinson dropped a paper bag smelling like sauerkraut on his desk. He unscrewed a cap on a water bottle and motioned to the two chairs in front of his desk.

"Is that a Reuben sandwich from Eli's Deli?" Frank asked.

Robinson inhaled deeply and smiled. "And it's all mine."

"We gotta go eat something." Frank rubbed his stomach while eyeing his partner.

"Then you better talk quick." Robinson tore open the bag and unwrapped the sandwich.

Jake filled the captain in on their conversation with Connor Revere, the owner of the golf course, and Manny, the grounds foreman. "We haven't received Hank's report yet nor has Benny started the autopsy, although he does estimate she's been dead for at least a couple weeks."

"So in other words, we've got zip," Robinson said around a mouthful of corned beef.

"Not quite." Frank followed the route of the sandwich from Robinson's mouth down to the stained bag. "We are printing out a list of missing women who might fit her description. We'll start with Chasen Heights and then expand the search if we don't get any hits."

"And crime techs are checking the cigarette butts for DNA. Benny will try to get a composite so we'll have something to show to Revere's employees." Jake checked his phone for missed calls but there weren't any.

"What's your feeling about this Revere guy?" Robinson pulled on a string of sauerkraut and dangled it for a few seconds for Frank's benefit.

"He was very cooperative."

"Very rich," Frank added. "Kinda the Donald Trump of the Midwest."

"Oh he runs in an elite circle." Robinson crunched on a kosher pickle, then pointed it at the detectives. "I do need to caution you that your Trump Light is a very close friend and contributor to our newly esteemed Mayor Jefferson Schuler."

"I thought his name was Jeffery?" Frank said.

"Yeah, but that Tom Lukavich guy who ran his campaign is now his chief of staff. He thought Jefferson sounded more mayoral."

"If Revere is a close friend of Schuler, does that mean we tread lightly?" Frank asked.

Robinson let out a deep, full-throated chuckle. "Hell, no. Lean and lean heavy."

7

"How come she isn't more, you know, soupy?" Frank asked, glad Benny hadn't started the autopsy until well after he had eaten lunch. In fact, the body reminded him of the show, *The Walking Dead,* the way the mottled skin hung like crepe paper.

"Temperatures have been cool at night and the body was hidden somewhat, not a lot of scavengers except for the typical bugs. The skin that was clothed, especially with leather, decomposed much slower than the exposed skin." Benny had a smorgasbord of organs sitting on a side table. He moved the microphone hanging from the ceiling to one side. "She has never been pregnant, no healed bones or fractures from her youth. I'd say she's between twenty-five and thirty-five years of age. Been dead for about two weeks, definitely a homicide. She was strangled, quite violently, too. Cracked the hyoid bone." Benny pointed at the deep purple marks around the neck. "Killer could have used a rope or belt by the looks of the markings."

"She must have done or said something to make him angry enough to overkill. Any other marks on her body?" Jake studied the body, looking for tattoos.

"Nothing." Benny pointed at the fingers. "Nails have already sloughed off so no luck getting any scrapings."

"Sexual assault?" Jake asked.

"No. I have dental X-rays for you if you ever get to the point of needing a comparison. She has all of her own teeth, very few fillings, only one root canal." Benny turned one of the victim's feet in his direction. "I'd say she either was a runner or had a job where she was on her feet all day. A lot of callouses on her feet. Might have been a waitress."

"Maybe at the Lake Bluff Country Club," Frank said.

8

Captain Robinson wasn't a morning person. He cradled his thermos of hot coffee between his hands as he lumbered to his office. God help the employee whose desk resembled a dump site because it would be Robinson's ass that would be chewed out by Chief Murphy.

There had been changes to the fourth floor at Precinct Six. Mayor Schuler, having won a very tight race for mayor with Police Chief Dennis Murphy, decided to play hardball with the chief seeing that the city council refused to back the mayor's replacement for Murphy. Now he was stuck with his adversary until the next election. Sam Casey had been a thorn in Schuler's side during the election process. She had helped to clear Murphy's name in a murder case, a charge that knocked Murphy's name right off the ballot. Trying to revoke Sam's consultant job with CHPD was a non-starter. She was too damn good at what she did. But Schuler could do the next best thing. He decided the Sixth needed a larger conference room so he had a wall knocked out to expand the current conference room. Unfortunately, that wall had separated Jake's and Frank's offices. Now they were out in the open, amid the noise and congestion where desks were butted against each other in pairs around the room. Along the outer walls were a copy room, file room, two interview rooms, and a break room. Jake and Frank had desks butted against each other outside the captain's office.

"JAKE!" Captain Robinson bellowed. "Why the hell have I got pigeon poop on my window sill?" His linebacker frame filled his doorway.

"They ain't pigeons," Frank said. "They are mourning doves."

"I don't care if they are protected bald eagles. What are they doing on my window sill?"

Jake turned from his computer and didn't even try to keep the smile from forming. "When they moved me from my office, they had to look for a friendly face and they found yours."

Robinson wasn't buying it. "They got other window sills to pick from but for some reason mine has sunflower seeds scattered on it."

"Blame Sam. She was worried they wouldn't get fed so she told them to go to your window."

"She told them?" Robinson was skeptical. He had heard rumors that Sam had a way of talking to the doves, that when Murphy was still captain Sam had told the doves to fly into the office and make a deposit on Murphy's desk. But Robinson had considered it all myth. Now he wasn't so sure. "I don't suppose if I say no that Sam is going to have them leave a gift on my desk."

Now Jake couldn't stop the smile. He was a witness to Sam speaking to the doves in her native language and witnessed the doves obeying her commands. "I wouldn't try it if I were you."

Robinson saw Scofield motioning from his desk near the elevators. He sighed inwardly and motioned for Scofield to send the visitor down to his office. Jake had little problem reading the visitor. He moved slowly, as though in pain, but Jake didn't think it was a physical pain. He gathered the man was around thirty, in good shape, and probably had a desk job because of the suit he wore. Jake caught Frank's attention and lifted his brows in question. Frank shrugged.

Jake's intercom buzzed. He looked up to see Scofield on the phone. "What have you got?"

"A possible I.D. for your victim. Vi Lasky owns a six flat on Escanaba. She wants to report a missing person. Says she hasn't seen one of her tenants in two weeks. Got alarmed 'cause her tenant always pays her rent early. This month she's late. Vi let herself into the apartment to find a cat, against rules, naturally, but it had eaten what it could from a bag of cat food it rummaged out of a pantry, and Vi also saw it turning off the damn water faucet so it had food and water."

"Did she give a description?"

"Says she's about five foot six and has brown hair. Also says she is a waitress at a sports bar."

"Is Vi home now? Get her address. We'll drop by to talk to her and take a look at her tenant's apartment. Maybe there's a photo in the apartment."

"Will do."

"Got a lead?" Frank asked.

"Yeah, sounds like a good one." Jake grabbed his jacket and they headed for the elevator.

"I don't want to be a pest," Forrest said. "I just need…"

To talk, Robinson thought in his head. He felt for the man. Robinson had lost his own wife years ago leaving Robinson to raise a son and daughter on his own. Forrest was having a hard time accepting the fact that his wife had committed suicide. Maybe there was something in Robinson's eyes that told Forrest he shared the same pain—the loss of a loved one.

"How is that support group going?" Robinson poured Forrest a cup of coffee from the carafe on his desk.

"Okay, I guess. It's just kind of hard to relate. I feel like I'm not at the same point as the rest of the group."

"And where is that?"

"They seem to accept it. It's just me and one woman who feel suicide wasn't in the nature of our loved ones. I know…knew my wife. She would never have committed suicide." Forrest had told himself to hold it together. How could his suspicions be taken seriously if he was always breaking down? "God, I'm sorry. I told myself to stop doing this, stop blubbering." He pressed the heels of his hands to his eyes, then took out a hankie and blew his nose. "I keep reading the autopsy report."

"Not a good thing, Forrest. You gotta let it go."

"I know, I know. But the tox results. People kept suggesting she was on drugs, but she wasn't. I just can't wrap my head around what was going through her mind with a hungry baby still sitting in her high chair."

"How's the job, Forrest? You have a little girl to think of. You can't risk jeopardizing your financial future by spending all your time going on…"

"Wild goose chases?" Forrest finished the sentence for him.

"Put yourself in my detectives' heads, Forrest. You read the police report, all the eyewitness statements. What other explanation could there have been?"

Forrest stared at the steam coming off the coffee while his eyes filled. "You know a day doesn't go by that Savannah doesn't ask for her mommy. The one day I dread is when Savannah no longer says her name or looks around the condo for her. How do I keep Marti's memory for her? I should have taken more pictures, you know?"

Robinson didn't have any answers for him. The case was closed, ruled a suicide. He couldn't assign any man hours to the case again. Tonto and Cochise, the two mourning doves, pecked at the window and damn if it didn't feel as though they were talking to him. He opened his desk drawer and pulled out a business card.

"Why don't you give her a call? She's an outside consultant we use from time to time. She'll look into it as a favor to me. She won't charge you. If there's anything worth finding, she's the one who can do it. But you have to promise me. You focus on your daughter and your job and leave the worries to Sam Casey."

9

The demure woman moved as though she had Red Bull in her veins. Short gray hair was neatly trimmed, nails polished. They had obviously interrupted her exercise routine as she was dressed in a jogging suit and jacket. Either that or she had a closet of track suits in an array of colors.

"Can I get you gentlemen anything?" They could smell heavenly odors coming from the kitchen. Frank looked ravenous. It wouldn't be the first time a lonely, elderly woman devised any means for company. "I have chocolate chip cookies made. They're still warm."

"Sure," Frank blurted before Jake could stop him.

She looked expectantly at Jake. "Coffee, if you have some fresh." Jake figured the missing tenant wasn't going to be showing up any time soon and the cookies definitely sounded good. Vi appeared delighted as she clapped her little hands. "God, why did the plot of *Arsenic and Old Lace* just pop into my head?" Jake moaned as Vi scooted off to the kitchen.

She poked her head around the door frame. "If you are interested, I left Donna's application with her personal information on the coffee table in front of you. That is my tenant's name. Donna Oberweiss."

"Huh." Frank appeared impressed and grabbed a seat next to Jake on the couch. Vi's furnishings were early garage sale, although for some reason, or by sheer luck, everything seemed to go together. The area rug had a dizzy pattern of flowers and swirls. Somehow the floral upholstered chairs didn't clash. They had just enough of the same colors as in the rug to appear a distant relative. The couch they sat on had those curled feet from an era where kings had a lot of numerals after their names. There was a mixture of wood tones that seemed to complement each other. Vi's selection included light and dark wood, oak, mahogany, cherry wood, you name it. A chess set was on a square table near a front window.

The chess pieces were in the shape of Star Wars characters, probably a collector's item.

"Here we go." Vi hefted a tray onto the coffee table. "There's cream and sugar and plates for your cookies. Help yourself."

A small tan head poked out from between Frank's feet. "Whoa!" He lifted his feet and a cat scurried out.

"There you are." Vi lifted the cat into her arms. "This is the little stowaway rascal I found in Donna's apartment. I'm going to go out and buy cat food later on. In the meantime, I gave it one of my cans of tuna. I don't allow pets but now I'm stuck with a cat, unless one of you..."

"No thanks," they replied in unison.

"You will notice that Donna moved here from Indianapolis five years ago. She has a license from some beauty college to be a cosmologist. She told me she was waitressing and bartending to pay for school but the money in those jobs paid far more than she could make as a skin care specialist." Vi was babbling. Either she was nervous or starving for company.

They perused Donna's application while they ate and drank. "She lists a Marian Oberweiss as next of kin," Jake said.

"Her mother still lives in Indianapolis."

Frank asked, "Have any of her co-workers or her boss called looking for her, that you know of?"

"I called Bailey's, that's the restaurant where she works. It's one of those sports bars. Anyway, I called after I couldn't reach her at home. It wasn't like her to miss a rent payment. She has always been one month early, like clockwork. Anyway, I called and asked for Donna but was told she wasn't working that day. When I asked when she would be working next I was told they weren't allowed to give out that information. So I asked for the manager but he's never returned my call."

After one more cup of coffee and three more cookies, Vi lead them to the apartment on the second floor. "I took the liberty of being nosy when I checked out the apartment earlier," she said as she used her master key to unlock the door. "The milk was long past the due date, cheese was growing penicillin, her mail had piled up in her mailbox, and I'm surprised the mailman didn't point that out. Oh no, he just keeps cramming it in there." The apartment smelled musty and stale with a hint of food well past its prime.

Frank asked, "Would she have told you if she were going out of town, maybe to visit her mother?"

"No, at least she never did before. I don't really pry but my tenants are good about letting me know if they are going to be gone for a while. Usually they want me to pick up their mail or watch for any deliveries. Donna never told me she was leaving town. Hope I'm not being worried over nothing."

"You are one nice landlady to have," Frank assured her.

"I just treat my tenants the way I would like them to treat the place if they actually owned it. I figured if the hallways are unmarred, vacuumed daily, flowers in the alcove, they will make an effort to keep things nice. But don't pat me on the back too quickly. I have been taken to court for evicting a woman and her three horribly bratty kids. They tore the place apart. I was told I was discriminating against mothers. She won but I hit her with a fifty thousand dollar suit for damages, the exact amount she was awarded in court. It was a wash. Charges were dropped all around."

Vi picked up several magazines lying on the floor and fluffed up a pillow on the couch. "Sorry, this is just nervous Nellie hands finding something to do. That and the realization that a dear tenant is missing."

Jake walked over to a long table against the wall. There were framed photos of an attractive woman on a beach with a male friend. "Is this Donna?"

"Yes. And that's her boyfriend Ron, I think."

"Did she have a lot of boyfriends?" Frank asked.

"I don't watch who comes and goes out of the apartments," Vi sniffed, although they wouldn't doubt if she kept a diary. "After the lawsuit it was pretty hard to be selective when renting. It doesn't seem to matter, I've learned over the years. Single people have too many parties. Married people have too many fights or too many kids. The elderly, well, who wants to live somewhere where the only vehicles that make daily stops at the building are ambulances? My husband, rest is soul, could write a book about all the characters we've had over the years."

"You have been very helpful, Vi," Jake started.

Vi hesitated, then asked, "You don't think anything bad happened to her, do you?"

Jake flicked his gaze to Frank, letting his partner switch to his pastoral mode. Frank said, "We treat all missing persons as just that. We'll give her mother a call just to make sure she didn't make a quick trip home, and we'll take her photograph to route through the system."

Vi gave a nervous smile. "Okay then. I'll leave you to your work. Just close the door when you are through."

Once Vi left, they set to work inspecting the rest of the apartment. The building was old but in a good way. The woodwork and molding were solid wood, not the plastic used in some newer buildings. Walls were solid and soundproof. Ceilings were at least twelve-feet high with ceiling fans in the living room and bedroom.

Frank stood in the center of the living room, hands on his hips. "If Donna is the victim, her apartment doesn't look like the crime scene."

"Check the bathroom for a hairbrush so we can have a sample of her DNA for comparison." Jake held the photo of Donna in his hand. "Maybe if she is our victim, we can find out where lover boy was the day she was killed."

10

Sam flipped through the nightgowns on the rack. Nothing was calling out to her. Although she had more than enough tasteful nightgowns, she was looking for something a little warmer as winter approached. But a flannel nightgown buttoned up to the neck was not her cup of tea, not that she would ever find one at Jackie's Boutique.

"Hey girlfriend, I have got just the thing for you." Jackie sashayed over on five-inch Jimmy Choo heels.

"Sorry, thongs are not my thing."

"Oh, pulleeze. Give me credit for knowing my Sam." Jackie smiled her Whitney Houston smile, revealing a mouth of veneers that were blinding.

"I actually came in looking for bras."

"Honey, I don't sell training bras." Jackie cackled, one hand flashing long talon nails pressed to her chest. Even the clerk behind the counter couldn't keep from laughing.

Sam pointed at her chest. "Do these girls look like training bra material?"

"Well, honey, you're still nursing. Of course they are going to be a little swollen."

"I dried up and stopped nursing weeks ago but the girls won't go down. I could swear my little girls are growing up."

Jackie's smile faded. Much to Sam's surprise, her friend reached out and grabbed a breast in each of her hands.

"Hey!" Sam slapped her hands away. "What are you doing?"

"Girlfriend, you are pregnant."

"What!? No way. I just haven't started my period yet. I have been nursing you know. Besides, you can't get pregnant while you're nursing."

Jackie folded her arms under her massive chest, long talons tapping impatiently. "Sez who?"

"Jake. Frank told him."

"Wait." Jackie's eyes narrowed and she cocked her head in thought. "You mean Jake 'keep her barefoot and pregnant' Mitchell? That Jake?"

Sam thought for a moment. Had she read about it or did Jake tell her? Maybe Abby? She should get her period soon, right? "I read it somewhere, too," she added as though trying to convince herself.

"Honey, you are looking at a woman who was conceived while her mama was breast feeding."

"Me too," the clerk added.

"No, you have to be wrong. I'm just growing, that's all. Some women do get bigger after a baby." A web of fear clawed its way up Sam's spine. She couldn't saddle Abby with another baby, nor Jake. The hell with them. She couldn't saddle herself with another one this soon.

Jackie steered Sam toward another rack. "These bras just came in. They are Vera Wang's latest in a variety of colors. Why don't you select a couple different sizes and go try them on. There are also some new lounge suits, nightshirts and nightgowns from Karen Neuburger." She weaved through the racks until she came to a display of sleep tees. She held one up. "Now on nights that are frigid you can turn on that fireplace of yours and snuggle up to that hunk of a husband you have. These tees are easy on, easy off." Jackie loved to see Sam blush. "Go, have fun, try everything on."

Sam grabbed several selections and headed to the dressing room. She hung the garments up on the hook, meanwhile shoving Jackie's words out of her head. Sam wasn't feeling any morning sickness. But then she remembered how Abby had made hot chocolate this morning, and for the past week Abby has made sure Sam had a glass of orange juice with her breakfast, something Sam neglected to do on a routine basis. And what was with the vitamin pill Abby placed next to Sam's plate every morning? Was Sam projecting some motherly glow she herself didn't see?

Sam dismissed all thoughts and quickly stripped off her sweater and bra. The Vera Wang bras were keepers as was the lounging suit. She looked at herself in the mirror. It hadn't taken her long to get back to her pre-pregnant size. She studied her face. Was she breaking out? No, complexion was still clear, eyes bright. Were her cheeks flushed? Did she have that certain glow people said pregnant women have? "Stop it," she scolded herself. She gathered up her purchases and headed for the register.

"You must be new," Sam said.

"Calista Carr. I don't know a thing about fashion but Jackie liked the sound of my name." Calista wore her flaming red hair in a Buster Brown hair cut. Her peaches and cream skin accented her Kelly green eyes. She had never seen eyes so vibrant and assumed they were contact lenses. For claiming not to know a thing about fashion, Calista looked dressed for a runway.

"Don't let her fool you." Jackie sidled up carrying a plastic bag in her hand. "She has a flare for style and an eye for color."

"Is that all for you, Sam?" Calista took Sam's purchases and ran the scanner across the tags.

"I don't think so." Jackie placed the bag on the counter in front of Sam.

"What's this?"

"A little something you can do for me."

Puzzled, Sam opened the package to find a pregnancy test. "Oh, stop, Jackie." While Sam was in the dressing room Jackie must have sent Calista two doors down to the pharmacy.

"It will take you all of a few minutes. Come come." She dragged Sam to the back of the store and up the stairs to Jackie's living quarters. "Let's just get this over with before you have a chance to change your mind."

"You know this is utterly ridiculous."

"Then prove me wrong."

Sam smelled fresh cut flowers from the vase on the table. Jackie's condo was tastefully decorated in black enamel, chrome and glass. Red throw pillows and a red love seat added a contrasting color. "Whoa." She paused in front of a huge painting of Jackie wearing nothing more than a white thong, white hooker heels and white feathery wings. Sam remembered this portrait. In order to keep a suspect occupied in an art class so Sam could snoop in his dorm room, she had talked Jackie into modeling for the class. Jackie was able to keep the best of the portraits as a gift for Lamon. "I think I'm scarred for life."

Jackie picked up a remote and pressed a button. A sheet of paneling with a landscape painting on it dropped down from the ceiling, concealing the portrait of Jackie. She flicked a hand through her head of Donna Summer hair. "I do like Lamon to see every morning what he'll be missing during the day." She and Captain Robinson had been dating for almost a year.

Sam shook the image of Jackie's gargantuan breasts out of her mind and headed off to the bathroom. After several minutes she heard nails rapping on the door.

"What's taking you so long? Don't you go flushing those results down the toilet, sugar."

Sam came out of the bathroom with the results behind her back. She didn't have to say anything. The results were written all over her face, if one could interpret fear and denial as a positive sign. "You know these tests are not always accurate."

Jackie waved her hands in a gimme gesture. Sam whipped the test strip from behind her back. "Are you happy?"

Jackie squealed with delight but Sam still wasn't smiling. She shoved another package at Sam. "I knew you wouldn't believe the results so I had Calista buy three tests. Here's number two."

"I don't have to go."

"Take it with you."

"No!" Sam pushed her hand away. "I don't want Jake to see it."

"Tomorrow at nine o'clock sharp you be back here for test number two."

Sam's phone rang. She checked the screen but didn't recognize the number. She held up a finger for Jackie to be quiet. "Sam Casey." Sam listened as a man with a very nice voice told her he was given her number by Captain Robinson.

They walked into Robinson's office to find him tossing sunflower seeds onto the window sill. "Don't say it," Robinson grumbled.

"Didn't say a word," although a chuckle was leaking out from Frank's throat. "It is hard not to warm up to the little guys. Think it's those beady little eyes."

"Well, those beady eyes give me nightmares about being pecked to death. I should bring in Cleo, Jackie's cat, and set her out on the window sill. See how quick these feathered rodents come around."

"So why the change of heart?" Jake slapped his notepad on the desk and took a seat.

Robinson cranked the window shut and sighed. "I'm embarrassed to say they saved my ass earlier." He sank into his plush, custom-made chair.

"Have anything to do with your visitor?" Jake remembered the look on the captain's face when Scofield had announced a visitor.

"Forrest Johnson. His wife committed suicide two months ago and he is having a hard time accepting it. He was in here just about every day after her death trying to convince us not to close her case."

"Who worked it?" Frank asked.

"The baby dicks." Andy Brainard and Maury Jackson were referred to as the baby dicks behind their backs. They were the youngest detectives and booted up the ladder faster than one could say Master's degree. "I personally made sure Andy and Maury had a good case. The two were sympathetic to Mister Johnson's feelings but after coming here four days in a row to rehash the case, I took him under my wing, thought maybe hearing it from a higher up would convince him."

"It didn't?" Jake asked.

"Nah. All it did was cut down his visits to twice a week. I got him hooked up with a support group but it's tough. He's got the cutest little girl, too. Breaks my heart." He flicked his gaze to Jake and was almost guilty when he said, "I tossed him Sam's way."

"Sam will have to reach deep for her inner bitch to keep from having her heart strings tugged."

Frank chuckled. "I don't think Sam has to reach that deep."

This made Robinson bark out a laugh, a little too long and a little too loud. Jake didn't have a retort. "What did you find at the apartment?"

Jake filled him in on Vi Lasky's tenant, how the photo does show a similarity to the victim's age, size, and hair color. "We dropped off the hair brush at Benny's and Donna's phone book had a number for a dentist. Benny is going to contact the dentist to get a copy of the X-rays. Vi said Donna drove some type of sports car but it wasn't parked anywhere near the building."

"Probably missing, too," Robinson said, "unless she did take a drive to Indy. If Benny does give us a positive I.D., then head over to that place where she worked and talk to the manager and anyone who knew her, see if we can run down the boyfriend."

11

At nine the next morning Sam found herself in the condo of Forrest Johnson. "Shouldn't you be at work, Mister Johnson?" Sam accepted a cup of tea as a girl not quite a year old slapped a spoon on the tray of her high chair.

"My assistant knows where to reach me. I have a meeting at eleven so we have time." He sprinkled several Cheerios on the tray in front of his daughter.

"She's beautiful. How did you come up with the name Savannah?"

"That was where Marti and I had our honeymoon. Savannah was conceived during our trip."

Conceived…that word conjured up the results of pregnancy test number two Sam had taken at Jackie's before her meeting with Forrest. Sam still had test number three to take but right now her own doubts were wavering.

"Captain Robinson faxed me the police report last night." Sam pulled a file folder from her tote bag. She had read the interview with the guard at the gate, the patrol officer who had been writing a truck driver a ticket, and several motorists who had witnessed Marti climb over the railing and jump, without any hesitation. Not one person had been near her so she hadn't been pushed nor had it appeared that she had been running from someone.

"I don't see any interviews with any of the residents. There are a lot of units in this building. I'm surprised someone didn't see Marti that morning."

The gated community consisted of condominium buildings assembled along the seventeenth and eighteenth fairways. It was an older public course hampered by flooding since it nestled next to a creek. Underground parking was available with additional parking in the lots outside.

"The police interviewed just about every person in the building." Forrest's eyes reflected a hint of anger. He had strong features, an athlete's body, and only one scar along the side of his neck that looked like a knife wound. Captain Robinson had filled Sam in on Forrest's background, how he had escaped the gang life and shuffled through several foster homes. "Mostly their questions were about how well Marti and I got along, had they heard a lot of fighting, had I ever struck my wife in public." His large hands clenched and unclenched. He flicked his gaze to Sam. "Even now I can see you studying the scar on my neck. But it's okay. I know spouses are the first ones police look at. This scar is a reminder of my youth that I'll carry with me my whole life. I refused to join a gang when I was in high school. A guy by the name of Duke called himself King Cobra. He was the gang leader and tried to get his hooks into Bobby, my foster brother. I was reaching Bobby, getting him to go to school every day, stay on the straight and narrow. But the gang life was like a siren song and Duke wouldn't let up. Tried to enlist both of us. Dummy me tried to get Duke to find another path in life. When a rival gang member tried to kill Duke, I threw myself in front of him and ended up with a broken bottle slashed across my neck." Forrest touched his neck as though making sure the scar was still there.

"Almost bled to death but Duke was safe. He was grateful enough to let me go. But the next time I saw Bobby, he was in the morgue, killed by a rival gang. Bobby was only fourteen years old. Cried like a baby at his funeral. Duke said he'd make it up to me one day. He's in prison now, although I hear he still has a way of controlling his gang. Marti and I were childhood sweethearts. All we talked about was escaping our neighborhood when we grew up. Go somewhere we would be safe from crime."

Sam had to force herself to hold it together as she watched Savannah eat the last of her Cheerios, her big brown eyes framed in feathery lashes looking to her father for more. Her little hand was held out, palm up. Forrest obviously didn't know what to do with the little girl's hair. It stuck out in a halo around her head.

"Tell me about Marti's routine."

Forrest refilled his cup with coffee and painted a picture for Sam of a loving mother who set an alarm to be sure she had her pot of coffee going while she showered. She shaved her legs in the shower, washed her hair and put tons of conditioner on it, brushed her teeth, used very little makeup, was usually through before Savannah awakened. Then she would change Savannah, place her in her high chair and heat up a jar of baby food in the microwave while her own cinnamon raisin bread was toasting. She would sit in the same alcove where they were now seated. While Marti fed Savannah, the two would watch the finches in the bird feeder. Then Marti would put Savannah in her stroller and they would take the walking trail around the back of the course.

"And that day?" Sam had already read it in the police report but she wanted to hear it from Forrest.

"That day, her coffee was poured and the cup was sitting on this table, a piece of toast had popped up in the toaster, the jar of baby food was on the counter next to the microwave, Savannah was in her high chair crying, and Marti's purse and keys were on the table by the door."

"You don't think she ran down to check the mail?"

Forrest shook his head. "The keys to the mailbox were on her key ring still in the tray on that table." He nodded toward a long sofa table that butted against the wall by the front door.

"And the phone?"

"There weren't any calls on our home phone that morning, either in or out."

"And her cell phone?"

"Her phone?"

"Can I see her cell phone?"

Forrest left the room. Savannah stared at Sam with apprehension. She looked around the room. Was she still looking for Marti? Sam walked over to the counter, grabbed the box of Cheerios and sprinkled more onto Savannah's tray. She returned the box to the counter just as Forrest returned.

"Hey, baby girl. You wrap someone else around your finger?" He kissed Savannah on the top of her head. "Here's Marti's phone. I had been meaning to cancel the service on it but it's going to expire at the end of the year anyway so I kept it in a drawer."

"Who watches Savannah while you're at work?"

"We have a day care on the first floor of this building. Our Association approved the use of one of the rooms that used to be the sales office. It's pretty big, been child-proofed, and a registered child care educator happens to live in the building. Several retired residents volunteer some days to help out."

Sam checked the phone. She turned it on and a picture of Forrest and Savannah came into view. But then the picture slowly faded and one word appeared on the screen—*destiny*. It faded just as quickly and returned to the picture of Forrest and Savannah. Was it part of the phone's wallpaper? Sam turned the phone off, waited a few seconds and turned it back on. Only the picture of Forrest and Savannah appeared. She waited a few seconds. Had her eyes played tricks on her? She dismissed it and clicked on calls to check the history. The last call received was the same day Marti died. "Did the police check this number?"

"They said it was probably a wrong number. They couldn't trace it and it only lasted a few seconds. We both were always getting telemarketing calls, even though we are on the do-not-call registry."

"Can I take the phone with me?"

"Why? I mean is there something not right?" He leaned forward, eyes full of anticipation.

"Please, Forrest, don't get your hopes up. All I know is something doesn't sound right. I'm not sure exactly what but I know a woman with a loving husband and a beautiful baby just doesn't walk out of her house and jump off of an overpass. The police look at the evidence and all the evidence points to suicide, cut and dry. Logically that's all anyone can assume. I don't deal in logic. Actually, logic is one of my least favorite words."

12

By noon Benny had confirmed through dental records that the deceased was Donna Oberweiss. He had yet to get DNA results but the hair on the brush Vi provided was a match to the hair on the body. The deceased was thirty-two years old, single, and had worked at Bailey's Sports Bar for the past five years. They had called ahead and were told Ron Daly, the night manager, wouldn't be in until three o'clock. Jake informed them it was a murder investigation and they would stop by at one o'clock and expected Ron to be available. Frank wondered if Ron Daly was the same Ron who had dated Donna.

After a quick beef sandwich at Popolano's, they headed to Bailey's across the street from Community Hospital. "I hope that isn't a bad sign," Frank said. "Do their ads say, 'Eat here. We can get you to the hospital quick?'"

Bailey's was a large and boisterous sports bar. Men were clustered around the horseshoe-shaped bar ogling the scantily clad waitresses more than the television sets. A railing separated the bar area from the restaurant section. Sports motifs such as canoes, tennis rackets, and jerseys hung from the ceiling or were posted on the walls. A young girl Jake felt like carding greeted them in satin shorts and a sequined tank top that bared her midriff. A navel ring had a charm dangling from it but Jake tried not to figure out the image on the charm.

"Table for two?" The girl's name tag said Kristen.

"Ron Daly is expecting us," Jake said.

"He's not here." She inhaled long and slow, giving a slow rise to her ample breasts. Jake figured her response was standard.

Jake flashed his badge. "Yes he is."

Her baby blues widened and she made a quick one-eighty and headed to the bar. The bartender looked them over, then picked up the phone.

"Who says the economy is in the tank," Frank said.

"It's called plastic." Jake watched as Kristen returned and put on her best model smile. Another hostess took her place as Kristen motioned for them to follow.

"He must have just come in." She appeared to put an extra swing to her walk as she flipped her hair over her shoulders.

They walked down a hall past the kitchen, the restrooms, and into a back office. The man behind the desk had his feet propped up, legs crossed at the ankles. As he yammered on the phone, he motioned with one hand for them to enter but he never stopped talking. Kristen quickly left and closed the door behind her.

Frank took a seat while Jake surveyed the neat office, the certificates on the wall, the large safe on the floor, and two computers on the desk. Frank and Jake locked eyes, each realizing Ron was the boyfriend in the picture with Donna.

"How's Phil doing? I haven't seen that ass in a year. He still married to the rich fat lady?" Ron didn't appear to be that tall, taking into consideration the length of his legs. He had the 'didn't have time to shave' look going and was dressed in nouveau rich with a pair of loafers that looked made of some type of reptile skin.

Frank brushed a hand against the sports jacket lying across the back of the chair next to him. After the last two times Frank went dumpster diving in his thousand dollar suit and Salvatore Ferragamo shoes, he finally succumbed to Jake's urgings to dress down. Now he shops for Henley pullovers, casual slacks and casual shoes, the same as Jake. And he leaves the expensive clothes for nights out with his wife. It still didn't stop him from pining for the expensive threads.

Ron turned slightly toward the window, ignoring the detectives. "Hey, did I tell you I'm going to Cancun next week?"

Jake had had enough. "No you're not." He reached over, pulled the cell phone from Ron's ear and snapped it closed.

"Hey." Ron pulled his feet off the desk and sat up. "What the hell?"

"Donna Oberweiss was murdered and you are looking like a good suspect. Talk." Jake remained standing, arms crossed, nailing him with a laser stare.

"I uh. Donna?"

"When is the last time you saw her?" Jake could tell Ron was a player. With all this young meat working for him, he probably took a different girl home every night.

"Not for a while, a week or two."

"Can you be more specific?"

"Not really. I can tell you that she hasn't received a paycheck in two weeks because she didn't put in any hours."

"Was she on the schedule?" Frank asked.

"She was a no show." Ron flipped through his log sheets. "Yeah, no call/no show. My girls are allowed one incident and then they are fired. There are too many hot chicks out there looking for work. I cut my losses and move onto the next."

"That how you treat them in your personal life?" In Jake's mind, Ron was inching his way up the suspect ladder.

"I don't date the hired help. It's against the rules."

"Yeah," Frank said with a chuckle. "Tell me another one. We saw a picture of you and Donna in her apartment. And I saw your eyes crawling up Kristen's satins when she walked in here."

"Hey." He splayed his hands and grinned. "No harm in looking."

Jake was tiring of the little dance Ron was performing. He could imagine him going home with a different girl every night. "How long did you and Donna date before you dumped her?"

"What are you insinuating? Am I a suspect?"

"Are you guilty of something?" There was a sharp edge to Jake's words and he did little to hide his impatience. "I'll ask again. When is the last time you saw Donna?"

"I told you. Two weeks ago."

"How did you leave things with her?"

He seemed relieved when his phone rang. "You can see yourselves out." He reached for his phone but Jake was quicker.

"Let's go. We're finishing this conversation downtown." Jake grabbed Ron's arm and hauled him to his feet.

"HEY!"

"I think maybe lover boy needs to I.D. the body," Frank suggested. "That way he can get a good look at his handiwork."

Ron struggled against Jake's strong grasp. "Hey, you think I killed her?"

Jake grabbed on tighter. "I think I'm going to enjoy frog-marching you out of here."

Ron finally agreed to continue the interview at the precinct but insisted on driving himself.

He opened the newspaper but his eyes stared over the paper and at the street. Like clockwork, every Tuesday at two o'clock she arrived. After her session she always walked across the street to Java the Hut, a Starbucks-type coffee house. It was large enough to accommodate those who sat for hours on their computers and office workers who slipped in for a morning hit or a lunchtime break. Java the Hut also sold healthy sandwiches, some godawful alfalfa sprout and cream cheese creations that were more for West Coast tree huggers than the meat-and-potato Midwestern connoisseur.

As always, she had a paperback mystery in one hand, a wallet in the other. She would order the tomato and cucumber on a croissant, a cup of caramel mocha Java and sit by the window to read. Sometimes she would see a friend and he would overhear how her sessions went. She had a pretty face, actually beautiful. Her features were Latino. He had even heard her talk to one of the workers behind the counter in Spanish. Raven hair with a hint of auburn worn long was one of her best features. Her lips were a close second. A natural cherry color, full and luscious. But she had just one flaw. From the waist on down her petite body expanded to a hefty size sixteen, forcing her to shop in the large women stores. He had found pictures on her Facebook page, pictures from her slimmer high school days. She knew and he knew that there was a size seven inside her skin screaming to be set free.

Although he made sure to keep his exposure at a minimum, he prided himself in doing a thorough research. He knew she worked at one of those boutiques that sold body lotions and spa creams, a place where few men entered so he would only watch from the safety of his car. She lived in an apartment on the outskirts of the shopping center and in nice weather walked to work. She favored bold colors, her size be damned, took in a movie once a week, usually a chick flick, did her grocery shopping at Jewel on Saturdays after work, preferred Dairy Queen frozen yogurt, and went to one of those ten dollar quick cut hair places. Currently she had two male friends but not one ever stayed overnight.

He buried his face in the newspaper as she entered the coffee shop and looked around. He avoided eye contact, not wanting to draw attention to himself. If she were to strike up a conversation, maybe sit with him, customers might remember. And he couldn't have that.

Her name was Tamara Rios and she was his next victim.

13

"Oh, no. It's trouble with a Capital T."

"Nice to see you, too, Benny." Sam studied the scenic posters on the wall of Benny's office. Lush forests, angry volcanos, sandy beaches, waterfalls with abundant foliage and brilliant floral displays. Sam doubted she would ever see Hawaii in her lifetime. She and Abby were not fond of flying. "New shirt?" Benny had a closet full of colorful Hawaiian shirts at home and in the office.

"Tea?" He raised a cup toward her.

"No thanks. I've had my quota for the day." She glanced through his glass walls to the examining room across the hall. "Anything interesting come in?"

"Trolling?" Benny couldn't help but feel pride at his best student. Although Sam was never trained in forensics, she was the one cop who spent the most time picking at his brain when she was a recruit.

"You know me, always inquisitive." Sam held up Marti Johnson's cell phone. "I just came by to find out who you believe is your best electronics criminologist."

"What are you looking for?"

"To pick your brain but first I'd like to find out what calls have been erased on this SIM card."

Benny picked up his phone and dialed. "Connie, is the Beast working today?"

Sam felt her eyebrows crawl up her forehead. *Beast?*

"Good. I'm sending someone over for a quick analysis." Benny hung up.

"Beast?"

"You'll see why when you meet him."

Benny escorted her to the elevator and told her to take it down to the basement. The elevator doors opened and she took a quick step back. Benny hadn't been kidding. One of the hairiest men she had ever met stood by the elevator looking eerily like Benicio del Toro's character in the *Wolfman* movie. Beast had curly hair, a trimmed beard and eyebrows that look like miniature hedges.

"Sergeant Casey?" He held out a hand displaying knuckles in need of a wax job.

"Wow, now I understand the name." She grabbed the hairy mitt and shook it.

"Believe it or not, the rest of my body has hardly any hair on it, except for the tops of my feet." He led her down a dimly lit hallway to an office that was barren except for the wall of shelves and equipment.

"Do they keep you hidden down here for a reason?" His face looked youthful but the skin crinkled around his eyes when he smiled.

"They let me out of my cage twice a day." When he smiled she noticed his incisors were exceptionally long, almost vampire teeth.

"Are those real?"

"Yes, unfortunately. I really don't have to do much when it comes to Halloween." He flicked his gaze to the dim ceiling lights. "Bright lights hurt my eyes." He put on a pair of sunglasses and flicked two more switches on the wall illuminating the room.

"You must be a blast at parties."

"Halloween is my favorite time of the year. Now, what have you got for me, Sergeant?"

"You can drop the sergeant. I'm not a cop any more. Just Sam will do." Although she had to remind people from time to time, they still referred to her former rank. "And I assume Beast isn't your real name."

Beast gave a crooked grin. "Ya think? My birth certificate says Tuggy Boonstra."

Sam wasn't sure if he was kidding. Who names their kid Tuggy? "Were you named after Tug McGraw?"

"My Scottish grandfather. Now you know why I prefer Beast."

She handed him the cell phone. "Can you do any magic with this and tell me the history? I need to know what calls were erased, what time they came in, where the calls came from, all the pertinent poop." Sam wrote her cell phone number on the notepad and scribbled her name under the number.

Sam left Beast and returned to Benny's office. It was empty but she made herself at home by checking the contents of his refrigerator. He sometimes kept candy in it next to specimens, something guaranteed to quickly kill any appetite she might have had. Nothing, not even a cookie crumb. She walked across the hall to see Benny in the viewing room with a woman in a wrinkled trench coat, a scarf around graying hair, sobbing softly. Sam couldn't see the body on the gurney. She waited for the sobbing woman to pass. She was consoled by a young man, possibly a son. Once they left Sam motioned to Benny. He pressed a button and a buzzer sounded. Sam walked into the morgue and over to the body.

"Oh, god. That poor woman had to look at this?" Sam couldn't pull her eyes from the body.

"The mother insisted on seeing her daughter."

"Is this the woman they found at the golf course?" Sam was glad she hadn't eaten anything recently. Strong stomach or not, the queasy feeling never goes away. She gladly accepted the mint Benny offered.

"Yes, the one Frank's golf ball rolled up to during the scramble."

"I bet he won't want that ball back." Sam focused on the bruising around the neck. "Strangulation?"

"Overkill actually. And it didn't have to be some oversized wrestled, either. Anger can make even the meekest man a very dangerous one."

An assistant in blue scrubs appeared and pulled the sheet over the remains. Benny nodded for him to return the body to the cooler. They stood vigil, the room quiet except for the cart's wheels. For a brief moment Sam's dream flashed in front of her eyes. The explosion, car and body parts, all in fine detail floated in slow motion. A chill swept over her body but she chalked it up to the temperature of the room.

"You okay?" Benny opened the door and led her across the hall.

"Of course." But Sam wasn't so sure, because along with the chill and the images from her dream was that same word whispered in her ear—*destiny*.

Sam drove home, confused by not once but twice encountering the same word associated with two unconnected deaths. What did it mean? Clues were never clear to her. With her mother, it was different. Abby's powers were with the living. She could touch someone and sense things about them. With Sam her powers were with the dead. She could touch the deceased or something the killer touched and pick up clues about the case. It didn't always work and neither she nor Abby could predict when or how it would happen. Jake was skeptical and probably would always be, but he had also been a witness to some of the cases she had solved and reluctantly admitted that there was more happening than his logical mind could explain.

She checked her cell phone. There was one missed call. Sam waited until she was parked in her driveway before accessing her messages. The call was from Beast. The four-second call Marti Johnson received came from a disposable phone. "Can't trace the call," Beast reported, "but someone definitely called that number at eight forty-five."

Right before she walked out of the condo and jumped off the overpass, Sam thought.

"Let's go over it again." Jake leaned his hands flat on the table, his face just a foot from Ron's.

"Aw, jeez. You are like a broken record. Can't you see I'm sick?" Ron held his stomach. After seeing Donna's body he had rushed to the bathroom holding a hand against his mouth. He had spent ten minutes in the bathroom until Jake told him he didn't have to I.D. the body.

"One last time and then you either arrest me or I'm walking out of here. Donna broke up with me the day before she was a no show at work. We argued about my dating other waitresses. I reminded her we weren't exclusive, she knew that going in. She was pissed, I was an ass. I deserved the drink she poured over my head. I figured she was pissed enough to not even turn in a resignation, just leave me high and dry. But I did not kill her." Ron pushed away from the table and stood. "So now I'm leaving unless you'd like me to puke all over your table."

"You owe us a list of everyone who worked with Donna. And you could help out by having them stop by to give a statement. I don't want to have to chase them all over town," Jake reminded him.

They watched him leave then made their way to a second interview room. The outer office was a buzz of changing shifts and until the larger break room was completed on the first floor, the fourth floor was the gathering place for all departments.

Frank checked his watch. "I don't think he killed her."

"Me neither. Maybe her mother and brother can shed some light on the case." Jake opened the door to a weeping mother and consoling brother. Marian Oberweiss dabbed at her eyes with shaking hands and tried to rearrange her face into a smile. She squeaked out an "Eddie" as she introduced her son.

Frank reached across the table and shook the brother's hand. It was the hand of an office worker, a number cruncher for a major food chain, according to Vi. "Our condolences on your loss." He gave a nod to the mother who stared vacantly at the table. "I'm sorry you put yourselves through the ordeal of trying to identify your daughter. We do have sample DNA from her apartment."

Marian stifled another sob and all her son could do was wrap an arm around her shoulder.

"I didn't want her to see the body." Eddie's face was still flush from the ordeal. "I don't know how anyone could recognize that…" He took a gulp of water and apologized. "Mom thought there might be something she could recognize. I can't say positively that that was my sister, but Mom did recognize the leather jacket as the one she bought Donna last

Christmas." He fumbled in his pocket for a piece of paper. "The desk sergeant said you needed information on her car."

"Her landlady said she drove one of those sporty things, as she called it, but wasn't sure of the make or model," Frank said.

"I put the down payment down on a used Camaro for Donna when she graduated college. The car had sentimental value, like keeping the first dollar you ever made." Marian wadded up the hankie again. "I haven't seen her much less talked to her since last Christmas. I didn't even know she had a boyfriend. How horrible is that?" Marian said with a sob.

Jake asked, "When you did last speak to her, did she say if she had any problems with a stalker or a former boyfriend?"

"No. Everyone loved Donna. She had such a wonderful personality." Marian sobbed quietly into her hankie.

"No mention of anyone named Ron?" Frank prodded.

Eddie shrugged. "To tell you the truth, Donna didn't date anyone seriously and when she did date, it didn't last long."

14

"You have got one helluva mother-in-law." Scofield dug into the box of fry bread, freshly made that morning. He placed two on a paper plate, then licked powdered sugar from his fingers. "You'll be happy to know the first floor break room has been completed so now we have our break room to ourselves."

Abby knew Jake would have a long day of interviews and prepared a five course breakfast and sent him off with a thermos of coffee, a cooler with his lunch containing two meat loaf sandwiches and a large box of fry bread. She always packed a sandwich for Frank.

"I am going to marry that lady when it's legal to have two wives," Frank said as flakes of powdered sugar dusted his shirt. Fry bread was a Native American treat of fried airy dough dusted with either granulated or powdered sugar.

With a piece of fry bread hanging out of his mouth, Scofield handed Jake a stack of pink message slips. "You have around twenty people stopping by starting at around eleven. Since they work the night shift you really didn't think they would be sitting at our doorstep at eight, did you?"

"That's fine. We're going to go back to Donna's apartment and look through it again so her relatives can clean it out." Jake thumbed through the messages. Although they had the computer system, Scofield still preferred the age-old message pad. Scofield was of the mindset that the department was one good computer crash away from losing everything.

The elevator doors opened and Robinson stepped out, umbrella in hand, tie hanging around his neck. He took one glance at what Jake held in his hands and said, "My office, now, all three of you."

"Me too?" Scofield said.

"No, that box of Abby's specialty."

By the time Jake made it down the aisle, half the box had been relieved of its contents. Lamon closed the door behind them and used the mirror hanging on the back of his door to tie his tie. It was like tying a ribbon around a tree trunk, his neck was so large. He never bothered to button the top button on his shirt either.

Frank relieved Jake of some of the items in his arms. He set the cooler on the floor, the thermos on the desk and the box next to the thermos. Robinson grabbed a cup from his back credenza, blew dust out of it, then held it out for Jake to fill.

"What's on the agenda for today?" Robinson picked through the box and grabbed the biggest piece of fry bread he could find. "Damn, stuff still feels warm." He licked his fingers as Frank tossed him a napkin.

"Marian Oberweiss confirmed that Donna owned a seventy-five white Camaro convertible," Frank said. "There's an APB out for it. It's too old of a model to have a GPS so we can't track it that way."

"Wow. Like to have that car. What else?"

"The brother looked pretty broken up. And I don't think he had it in him to kill a garden snake let alone his sister. And what reason would he have?" Frank sank into a chair in front of Robinson's desk.

"Are they staying in town?" the captain asked.

"Until the apartment is released and they can go in and clean it out. Forensics is going through it now." Jake checked his watch. "We're going to make a stop there before all of our interviews start. Donna's co-workers should start streaming in here around eleven."

"Don't waste time interviewing any employees at the golf course. Concentrate on the ex-boyfriend. What about video from Bailey's?"

"Ron is supposed to be searching through them to find the ones from the last few days Donna worked." Frank pulled out a wet wipe from his pocket, ripped it open and wiped the sugar from his hands.

"Did Sam meet with Mister Johnson?" Robinson asked.

"She didn't learn anything knew. Went over the timeline with him, reviewed the police reports, brought home a number of photo albums. Oh, and his wife's cell phone. She had Beast look at the SIM card. It appears the last call the wife received was that morning and it came from a disposable phone."

While Abby's favorite room was the kitchen, Sam's was the Florida room. Here she could look out on the acres of blooms in the spring and summer, and the foliage in the fall. In the winter there were several bird feeders Alex kept filled for those birds that didn't pack up and fly south for the winter. And although the Florida room may be her favorite room, her favorite spot was still one of the window seats in the dining room. They were cushioned and roomy enough to stretch out. It allowed the sun's rays to warm her on chilly days and gave her a front row seat to the flag stone patio and all of its décor.

On the window seat past her feet Dillon was napping in his carrier, a thin blanket over his chubby body, his carrier turned so the sun's rays weren't hitting him full force. She opened the wedding album. Here was an example of a beautiful wedding put together on a shoestring budget. Marti's wedding dress, a simple cream-colored sheath, hugged her slim figure in all the right places. She wore a choker of lace and pearls and long lace gloves. On her head was a simple headband of tiny white roses, identical to the ones in her bouquet. Forrest was dressed in a dark suit, cream-colored shirt and a gray striped tie. One rose was pinned in his lapel. The happy couple beamed for the photographer. Not an expensive studio photo either. A friend, possibly, had taken the snapshots but he did a good job. There were church photos with a scattering of friends and a female pastor where the happy couple took their vows. The reception looked as though it were in the church basement or rec room. Then the photos switched quickly from the reception to a southern location with moss draping tree limbs like gauze fabric. Marti stood in front of a sign that said *Welcome to Savannah*. Forrest had mentioned that they had honeymooned in Savannah, Georgia.

Sam set aside that album and picked up the next. It opened with pictures of Marti in various stages of pregnancy to delivery. An exhausted

Marti, damp hair clinging to her forehead, beamed as she held her baby girl, a tiny pink ribbon affixed to the top of the baby's head. Another picture with a beaming Forrest. Sam hadn't known she was crying until the first tear hit the plastic sleeve of the album. She sniffed and swiped at her face only to open her eyes and find Abby standing over her holding a tissue and a cup of hot chocolate. Sam had barely heard the soft ruffling of Abby's long skirt.

"Sad case?" Abby handed the cup of hot chocolate to Sam and then sat down next to her. "I remember reading about that one in the paper."

"Heart-wrenching. He was so in love with his wife. And you should see their baby, Mom. She is adorable. Forrest says she still wakes up looking for her mom and now he has to struggle to raise her alone plus try to deal with why his wife committed suicide."

"Do you believe she did?"

Sam sighed and took a sip of the hot chocolate. "My head looks at the evidence and tells me she did. My heart looks at these photos, at her husband and baby, and just knows there is something not right. Something drove her to do what she did but I'm clueless as to what that could be."

"Did you pick up anything when you visited her husband?"

"Thought I did. Now I'm not so sure. It was just one word but I thought maybe I was imagining it."

"That's all our clues ever are, Samantha. Images, whispers, feelings. That's the only way the spirits have to pass on messages to us. Listen with your heart, Samantha."

15

Frank snapped his phone shut. "That was Hank. He left here five minutes ago. Said place is clean. No blood, lots of prints, mainly Donna's, and a lot of cat hair. She didn't even own a computer. He added that it was a total waste of his time and to thank you."

"Bite me," Jake said. He took Hank's barbs in stride.

Frank headed to the bedroom while Jake stayed in the living room. He found an appointment book in the secretary but other than notations of birthdays and lunch with someone name Alyce, there wasn't anything noteworthy. He did jot down the last time she had lunch with Alyce. It would have been the day after she dumped a beer on Ron.

Jake moved to the kitchen where there were articles pinned by magnets to the front of the refrigerator. Most were coupons for water, soda, cereal, and feminine products. One article on decreasing wrinkles had been ripped from a magazine.

"Anything?" Frank asked as he entered. "Bedroom doesn't have much. No male toiletries in the bathroom. No guns under the pillow or flowers pressed in a diary."

"She was supposed to have lunch with Alyce on the day after she gave Ron the heave ho. Have to see if Alyce is one of the co-workers coming in today."

There was a knock on the door. "Sorry to bother you," Vi said, a hankie pressed to her nose. "Donna's mother is on the phone. Wants to know when she can clean out the apartment." She mangled the hankie in her hand as she dabbed at her red eyes.

Jake didn't want to release the apartment until the case was closed but since it obviously wasn't the scene of the crime he saw no reason to hold onto it. "Tell her she can have it now."

Vi nodded and left.

Jake checked his watch. "Let's give it another half hour and then get back to the precinct."

"Did you find something?" Forrest answered Sam's call on the first ring. She could hear voices in the background. He was obviously at work and although she had told him she would update him daily, she hadn't expected him to jump on the phone as though she had discovered headline breaking news.

"No, I'm sorry, Forrest. I just wanted to let you know I found out Marti took a call seven minutes before the incident." She didn't feel comfortable saying she died or before she jumped. "It was from an untraceable number and it only lasted four seconds. Do you recall her receiving previous such calls?"

"No, not at all, other than telemarketers. Both of us would listen for a few seconds until we realized it was a computer talking and we'd hang up."

Sam doubted telemarketers used disposable phones. "Did your wife have any problems with anyone where she used to work or anyone in the building?"

"No."

"The fact that this person didn't call your home number and only Marti's cell phone tells me this was personal."

There was silence for a few seconds. "I think I know where you're going with this because the police went down that road, too. No, my wife was not having an affair. No, my wife wasn't being blackmailed over something lurid in her past and suicide was her only way out to spare me." Forrest spoke in a hushed tone.

"Do you recall any hang-up calls to your home phone in the days leading up to Marti's death?"

"No, but I was at work every day and there weren't any such calls when I was home at night."

"Thanks, Forrest. That's all I needed to know." She hung up before he could hand her another string of denials. It was hard enough getting to the truth if she had to listen to a loved one paint a flowery picture of the deceased. But she did know of one loved one who might be able to tell her more without opening her mouth.

It was almost nap time at the day care center. Sam had to show her credentials before entering. It was nice to know they didn't let just anyone in. Several seniors, both male and female, were holding children in their laps, some reading, others rocking. A young woman dressed in an outfit of bold geometric designs appeared to be in charge. Sam didn't think she was much older than twenty-five. How convenient to be able to take an elevator to work every day.

"The poor thing. I have to fight back tears every day when Mister Johnson brings Savannah in." She held out a hand to Sam. "I'm Trina Miller. I was about ready to put everyone down for a nap."

"Can I hold her?"

"Of course." Savannah was sitting in a puddle of building blocks, intent on fitting a square one into a star-shaped hole. Trina cooed something to Savannah, then lifted her in her arms. "Here you go." Savannah took one look at Sam and raised her arms. Savannah had a good memory.

Toddlers were curled up on blankets dotting the floor like postage stamps. Some seniors started filing out while others cradled infants and looked for vacant rocking chairs. Sam chose one by the window while Trina chose a glider across from Sam.

"Here." Trina placed a hand-sewn doll into Savannah's arms. "She never goes anywhere without it. Mister Johnson told me it is one of Savannah's favorites. Her mom made it for her."

Savannah wrapped both arms around the doll and yawned. Sam wasn't sure what she expected by being close to Savannah. It wasn't like the child could tell Sam anything that happened the morning her mother had died, although it would have been nice.

"You seem to have a lot of kids to take care of," Sam whispered to Trina.

"It seemed the more word got out, the more residents pulled their kids from their current child care facilities and signed up for mine. Now I need help but at least I have enough money to hire someone. "

"Your prices must be right."

"They are very reasonable because of a grant I applied for to help defray the costs."

Savannah gave one last yawn, then her eyelids blinked slowly. On the other side of the room one toddler kept sitting up and walking over to the toy chest. An elderly woman coaxed him back to his blanket. She gave a wave to Trina before dimming the lights and leaving the room.

Now that the noise was reduced to a few sighs and soft clatter of toys clutched protectively in toddlers' hands, Sam could detect faint music in the background. Whatever the room had been used for previously, it had been completely transformed. Bright letters of the alphabet were on one wall. Pictures of various animals were in an alcove labeled The Farm. A side room, probably a kitchen, had counters and a sink. Trina obviously had the children well-trained since there were very few toys left on the floor.

"How is she doing?" Sam asked, with a nod toward Savannah.

"The poor thing. Her eyes light up when Mister Johnson stops by to pick her up but she still seems to look past him as though her mom might have come, too. It's heartbreaking."

"Had you met Marti?"

"Yes. She was so bubbly and fun-loving. A great mother. She would only drop off Savannah when she had errands to run or a doctor's appointment so I didn't see Savannah every day." The child in Trina's arms was asleep, as was Savannah. The room was a buzz of deep breathing and soft snores. Trina looked from Savannah's face to Sam's. "Why do you think she did it? Why do you think she gave up on life?"

That was one question Sam didn't find hard to answer. "I don't think she did."

16

"That jerk cheated on everyone. I swear it was part of his interview process." The young blonde who had been the hostess the day they visited Bailey's did another long inhale to push her plump mounds above the top of her low cut sweater.

"So how many dates did you have with him?" Frank asked.

"Dates? I should be so lucky. We just did it in his office. I didn't even get a pay raise."

"Hey, everyone did it. The place is like a game of spin the bottle, see who you go home with next." Vaughn was one of the nightshift bartenders, a little too young for a receding hairline, but had great taste in clothes. Several times Frank had asked him where he bought his knit shirts, shoes, and did those linen slacks wrinkle? Vaughn's nails were buffed to a shine, or was that nail polish?

"Donna had been around the block a few times. She knew Ron used his status to get any girl he wanted. And Ron played favorites. If Sallie wanted the weekends off or Renee needed a holiday off, all she had to do was walk into Ron's office and close the door. He was such a slut."

"Donna didn't take shit from Ron." Rose crossed her legs, letting her short skirt ride up even higher.

Frank pulled his eyes from her tanned legs. "Were you working the day Donna dumped a beer over Ron's head?"

"No, but wish I had. I would have made it a pitcher."

"Did anyone ever threaten to bring harassment charges against him?" Jake asked.

"If you just breathed a word of it you suddenly found your hours cut to one day a week."

Jake checked his watch. One more interview left. Where Jake felt he had just been beat up and left on the side of the road, Frank looked more like he had just watched four hours of reality TV and salivating for three more.

"Let's get this over with." Jake opened the door and was pleasantly surprised to see someone who didn't look like a member of the *Jersey Shore* troupe. "You talk, I'm too tired."

Alyce Walker was closer to Donna's age, more in her thirties, whereas most of the other female employees were in their early twenties. Alyce was a bartender and relieved about it, too. "Can you picture this chubby body in one of those skimpy outfits? Donna still had a nice shape. She started out bartending but thought she made better tips showing off her cleavage."

"When was the last time you saw Donna?"

"We tried to have lunch once a week, usually on a Thursday. It just so happened to be the day after Donna dumped the beer on Ron's head."

"How mad was Ron?"

"Oh, royally pissed. No one embarrasses Ron in public." Alyce pulled out a pack of cigarettes, but when Frank wagged a finger at her, she put it back into her purse. "If you think he had anything to do with Donna's death, no. Not Ron's style."

"Is his style to hire someone?" Frank asked.

"Nah. He's too cheap. Ron always had another conquest on the line. Donna knew the score. She was more mad at herself. She had a history of picking players and she was tired of it."

"Any old boyfriends come back into her life recently? Maybe hang around the bar while she was working?"

"She told me her last serious boyfriend was in high school. He died in a car crash. She said he was the love of her life and there would never be another one like him."

"But no one stalking her, someone who felt she was the love of his life and he couldn't live without her?"

Alyce shook her head. "Wait. There was someone. A day before the beer incident, she was pissed royally at a customer who had her take back his steak twice. Said it wasn't cooked to his specifications. He even grabbed her arm. She wanted to make a scene but knew when it's the customer versus the waitress, the customer is always right. The ass didn't even leave her a tip, as though she did the cooking."

"Did she mention a name, maybe off of his charge card?"

"No. He paid cash. By the end of the night, she had shrugged it off. Besides, two days later she was more worried what she was going to do for a living, even thinking about going back to doing facials."

By the time they finished the interviews Scofield informed them that Donna's car had been located in the back parking lot of the Motor Inn off the expressway. Her purse and keys were in the car and the doors were locked. "Suey is going through it now," Scofield said.

Jake and Frank drove over to the crime lab. It was in the same building as the M.E.'s office and attached by a skywalk to Headquarters where Chief Dennis Murphy called home.

"Want a cup of stale coffee?" Frank stood in front of the vending machine studying the different flavors.

"No thanks. I'd rather drink motor oil than anything out of that machine." Instead, Jake shoved money into an adjoining machine for a bottle of water.

"I agree. Think I'll take a pass."

They headed toward the garage bay where cars were towed for examination. Soo Long and one other crew member were dressed in white overalls, one person leaning half into the trunk, the other person in the front seat. They could see a beam of light as flashlights were aimed at the upholstery and trunk area. Jake and Frank stood behind the barricade and watched. The larger of the two, Soo, was nicknamed Suey for his affection for Chinese food. It helped that his family owned the Red

Dragon Restaurant. Suey saw them, straightened, and pointed, a motion that either told them to get lost or to go to the room behind the wall.

They left and walked across the hall to a tennis court-sized room divided into three open cubicles. A young woman of Asian descent looked up from what she was doing, then waved them over.

"Sergeants. You are way too prompt. We have not finished processing yet." Her name tag said *Anya*. "I have already dusted the wallet and contents for fingerprints." She had the drivers license, charge cards, and various other cards laid out on the counter. Processing was easy these days. Once the items were dusted, Anya only had to scan the images using a hand-held imager which immediately searched the database for possible matches. "She had money in the wallet as well as charge cards." The purse was small, hardly enough room for the wallet, lipstick and keys. It was a shoulder strap bag and Jake was immediately suspicious of the strap.

"I see your trained eye looking at the strap. I did pick up skin samples. Doctor Lau is comparing to the victim now. This crinkly type leather is impossible to get prints off of. I should be done with the articles soon so the victim's family can have the possessions back."

Anya saw a green blinking light on her desk. "Suey says you can go back there now."

The garage bay smelled of dirt, grease, exhaust and chemicals, with one distinct underlying odor of soy from Suey's daily lunch. Suey struck a Superman pose with his fists planted somewhere in the vicinity of his hips. His white jumpsuit was stained and worse for wear.

Jake stuck his head in on the driver's side while Frank checked out the passenger side. "What can you tell us, Suey?" Jake didn't see any obvious blood stains but he did see scratch marks on the head liner.

"She kept this baby clean. No takeout boxes or cig butts. No nooky in the back seat either, if you get my drift." Suey wiggled his eyebrows. "Sweet ride. Based on the nineteen-seventy redesign. Twin exhaust tail pipes, maple wood grain."

"When you're done drooling, can you tell us if she was killed here?"

Frank saw the same marks on the liner.

"Oh yeah. Found a broken nail on the floor on the driver's side, vic's hand prints on the side window where she pounded on it, scratch marks on the liner. Anya found skin samples on the purse strap so I'd say the killer hid in the back seat and nailed her from behind. Somehow got her purse, maybe reached over the console and grabbed it from the passenger side. Then wrapped the strap around her neck and pulled. Easy for him to stay out of her grasp while she fought. I'd say he pulled her back far enough to keep her hands from reaching the horn. Found shoe marks on the dashboard under the steering wheel where she possibly tried to reach the horn with her foot."

Jake scanned the back seat, checking the print powder on the door handles. "Anything usable from the back?"

"Nah. Killer used gloves so the skin samples on the purse strap might only be hers. There are some prints we can run but the ones on the door handles are smeared. Lots of prints, maybe from friends who sat in the back or guys servicing or washing the car, but this guy seems too clever to have left any residue. I'm hoping for hair samples, but I'm not holding my breath."

Jake straightened and stepped back from the car. "What about the golf course? Hank find anything usable?"

"Leaves, bugs, cigarette butts, mainly Winston, gum wrappers and miscellaneous garbage."

"You matched the DNA?" Frank asked.

Suey rolled his eyes. "Oh, sure. We had it done right after the commercial break, like on *CSI*."

"Updates. Make it quick. Jackie's making her mama's meatloaf recipe for dinner and I expect to eat it hot." Captain Robinson perched one hefty cheek on the corner of the desk next to Jake's. All Robinson had to do was jam a fist under his chin and he would be a live impression of *The Thinker*.

"The co-workers know nothing, saw nothing," Frank offered.

"Ron Daly, the manager, would make a great suspect if we could only narrow down the time of death," Jake said. "He and the deceased have a history. "

Frank spun his chair around to face the captain. "Alyce Walker, the bartender friend, said Donna had a problem with one of the customers. It isn't unusual for customers to make complaints but this one returned an expensive steak twice. This was two days before Donna was killed."

"May be nothing but see if we can catch the altercation on the video." Robinson swiveled his head in Jake's direction. How an obviously non-existent neck could hold up such a massive head was anyone's guess. "Anything else?"

Jake stifled a yawn. It had been a long day with nothing to show for it. "According to her bank records, Donna had an ATM card. It wasn't in her purse nor her apartment. I'm hoping someone is waiting for things to cool down before using it."

"Okay then. Get some sleep and we'll start all over again in the morning."

He walked past several tables not making eye contact, and slipped into a booth right behind her, his back to Tamara. The friend with her was someone he had seen a few previous times coming out of the gym. He knew a lot about Tamara just by watching and following a discreet distance behind. Tamara hit the jogging trail three times a week. The other days she went to the gym after work, always trying to lose weight.

He ordered coffee and a piece of apple pie ala mode while the women chatted incessantly about the movie they had just seen. A couple nights a week, usually Wednesday and Friday or Friday and Saturday, Tamara would stop off at a bar with a friend. A couple times she had been alone, scanning the room as though looking for someone. She would sit at the bar, wave off any conversation with strangers, but she was always polite about it.

His pie came and so did Tamara's order. They were splitting a club sandwich. How unlike Tamara to be eating this late. Eyewitnesses would be hard pressed to remember him. Some days he dressed like a banker, others like a landscaper. He liked the outfit he was wearing now—dark blue shirt and pants with a fake name embroidered above the pocket. If anyone was asked if Tamara ever spoke to someone at Java the Hut or shown any interest in her, the police would receive all kinds of descriptions. He wore a baseball cap. He had brown hair, maybe. Blue eyes, no brown (depending on what contacts he used). He was dressed nice, dressed for work, wearing grubbies, worked at a gas station. "I'm not sure officer but he looked rich, wore a Rolex, didn't wear any jewelry, gold chains, had to be a gang-banger. Unshaven, clean shaven, he was around twenty-five officer, I'd say thirty-five, no, he had gray hair, he had a limp." He could be whatever he wanted to be. He was a chameleon. A very deadly chameleon.

17

"Hi, babe." Jake leaned over and kissed Sam on the mouth. Being married to an ex-cop, he never had to explain why he was late or even apologize for being late.

"Frank hasn't found any more dead bodies, has he?" Sam scooped out a spoonful of pecan praline ice cream from the bowl, but Jake intercepted her hand and shoved the spoon into his mouth. "There's lasagna in the fridge. If you don't want something heavy for dinner, there are some chicken pinwheel thingies mom made."

"Any quiche leftover from this morning?"

"There's that, too. And a salad." Sam flicked off the television set and followed him into the kitchen. The clock on the stove said it was almost nine-thirty.

Jake pulled the quiche from the fridge and set it on the counter. After cutting a piece and sliding it onto a plate, he covered it with wax paper and placed it in the microwave. The refrigerator was well stocked, certainly not like his bachelor days. And Abby was one helluva cook. It was too bad her talents hadn't rubbed off on her daughter. There were some things Sam was really good at making but other things everyone would just as soon she not step into the kitchen. Once the quiche was heated, he added a tossed salad, squirted Italian dressing over it, then stood at the counter to eat while Sam sat across from him.

"How's your case going?" Sam licked the spoon, scraped remnants from the bowl and had to refrain from licking it clean. A sickening thought crossed her mind. This was how she acted when she was pregnant with Dillon. She calmly placed the spoon in the bowl and refrained from looking to see if Jake caught the similarity.

He told her about the cigarette butt found under the victim but so far they didn't have a DNA match. "I still think Collin Revere could be a person of interest but I need to get his DNA somehow. Unfortunately, he is a heavy contributor and close friend of the mayor."

"Ooooh, I'm loving it already. It will look bad if the mayor tries to influence the department or even throw accusations at Murphy. Although something tells me he is enough of a snake to accuse Murphy of orchestrating a set up. If Revere's a smoker, anyone could have thrown his cigarette near the victim, someone with an axe to grind."

"You are already arguing his case for him." He stabbed the last of his salad, then wiped his mouth with a napkin.

"It's my crystal ball, sweetheart."

He grabbed her empty bowl and his plate and placed them in the sink. "Where's Abby?" After running hot water over the dishes, Jake opened the dishwasher, placed the dishes inside, and closed the door. He ran the dishrag under hot water, washed the island counter, rinsed the dishrag, wrung it out and draped it over the sink. Sam wondered if she should feel guilty that her husband was neater than she was.

"Upstairs talking to Cora on the phone." Cora Chasing Hawk was Abby's closest friend back at the Eagle Ridge Reservation. She was also a member of the tribal council and filled Abby in once a week on the latest happenings back home.

"How about the case Captain Robinson gave you? Suicide, wasn't it?"

"Everything points to it." Sam had the word on the tip of her tongue and Jake must have read it.

"But?" he prompted.

"I don't know. She had everything going for her. I don't know the inner workings of her mind. Maybe her husband didn't either. It just seems all wrong."

"Maybe you're looking too hard."

"Maybe. Beast did discover Marti received a phone call right before she left her condo. It was from a disposable, lasted all of four seconds."

"Telemarketer?"

"But do they really use disposables?" Sam thought back to that one word she had heard—*destiny*. "Anyway, I'm going to go curl up with the latest Mo Hayder mystery and I'm sure you are going to read the paper and wait for your guy O'Reilly to come on."

"You got it." Jake gave her another kiss.

Sam watched him leave and pondered grabbing another scoop of ice cream, but stopped herself. Instead she made a cup of hot tea and carried it to the Florida room where she would have some peace and quiet. As she walked through the dining room, she glanced at the photo albums on the table, the one album still open to the picture of Marti in the hospital room beaming as she held her baby girl. *It was wrong, it was all wrong,* Sam thought. But so far she didn't know how to prove it.

18

The next morning Jake and Frank made a trip to the Lake Bluff Country Club. They had reviewed the list of past and current employees but had not found Donna's name.

Collin greeted them in his customary golf attire. "Gentlemen, please have a seat." He motioned to the chairs in front of an ornately carved desk. All of the desk accessories were of the same dark wood and there was an expensive-looking crystal golf ball that served as a paperweight. "I hear you have identified the body."

Jake set a photograph on the desk in front of Collin. "Donna Oberweiss. Do you recognize her?"

Collin shook his head. "Sorry. She doesn't look familiar."

"Here's an extra copy. It would help if you could post it somewhere, have your employees take a look. They might remember her stopping in for lunch, maybe even applying for a job here. She has been a waitress for a number of years."

Collin studied the picture, his trimmed brows furrowed. Jake thought he was either putting on a good act or he was truly trying to jog his memory and be of some help. "I'll certainly have everyone on staff take a look. I understand she was strangled. A horrible way to die." He set the picture down, then poured himself a glass of water. He held up the pitcher but the detectives declined. "Unfortunately, I didn't even do the interviewing of all the applicants. I was mainly concerned that the grounds crew was top notch. I knew what questions to ask them to verify they knew what they were doing. But kitchen staff, waitresses, pro shop, I left that to others. I hired the managers but let them pick their staff."

This got Frank's attention. "You have a very good grapevine, Mister Revere."

"Right to the mayor's office. He was concerned the minute he heard about the body being discovered, especially during a police and fire department golf outing. So I asked him to keep me updated on the case and he has. Trust me, I haven't told anyone, not even my wife."

"Is she a golfer?" Jake asked, trying to keep the conversation light.

"Just now taking it up. She was always a tennis player but the principle of the swing is basically the same. She says she likes the size of the tennis ball better," he added with a smile. Behind Collin on his credenza was a photo of an attractive blonde woman with a son and daughter in their teens.

"Does she stop in on occasion? Might she have had the opportunity to run across the victim?" Frank flashed a congenial smile that didn't say, "Did your jealous wife kill your girlfriend?" But they already knew a woman couldn't have had the strength needed to strangle the victim as Donna had been strangled.

"I doubt it. She will be in today and she will see the photo on the board so I'll definitely ask her."

Jake patted his pocket, then turned to Frank. "Damn, left my cigarettes in the car."

"Here." Collin opened his desk drawer, pulled out a pack of Winstons and shook one out. "Take one of mine. Smoking is only allowed in the bar, though. And, of course, outside."

"Well, that was as smooth as the wax on your '57 Chevy," Frank said as they headed to the parking lot.

Jake checked the cigarette. "Same brand found near the victim." But, as Sam had said, anyone could have picked it out of the trash and tossed it there. He was still waiting on a report from the telephone company to see if Donna made or received any calls to Collin Revere.

"Hey, Sam. How's it going?" Benny signed a report on a clipboard, then led Sam into his office.

"Fine. Captain Robinson asked me to follow up on a closed case."

"Closed one?"

"Closed in the department's eye. Not so closed for the deceased's husband."

"Forrest Johnson. I remember that case." He walked over to a wall of filing cabinets and pulled out a drawer. "Hope you don't want to see autopsy photos because they weren't pretty. She was hit by a truck doing seventy. Broke just about every bone in her body, collapsed her lungs, ruptured organs, you name it."

"I just want to read your report. Please, no photos."

Sam reached into the pocket of her tunic top and pulled out a packet of crackers, then stared as though wondering how they got there. Did she grab them on her way out this morning? Was she going through pregnancy motions without realizing it? She hadn't even had a twinge of morning sickness but for some reason she had grabbed the packet before leaving the house. Was it something to curb her hourly hunger pains? She quickly tossed them into the garbage can next to Benny's desk.

"Here you go. She was just twenty-six years old. I'm sure what you are looking for is the tox screen."

"Any drugs at all in her system?"

"Nothing. No stomach contents either. She hadn't had breakfast much less a cup of coffee."

"What about any bruises?"

Benny stared at her over the top of his bifocals. "Did I mention she was hit by a truck?"

"Other bruises. Maybe older, maybe healed fractures."

"You looking for spousal abuse?"

"I'm looking for a logical explanation."

"This," Benny waved the file folder, "is the logical explanation. Your specialty is finding the illogical. I read the police report thoroughly as well as the eyewitness reports. Everything just seemed too surreal about the case. She didn't stagger when she walked. She moved with a purpose, the one beat cop and several onlookers reported. I even did a second tox screen to pick up any anomalies but that came back negative too. Wish I could be of more help."

An Asian woman in a lab coat walked in with a package. "Excuse me, Doctor Lau. This is the evidence bag from the Oberweiss case."

"Thank you, Anya." Benny placed the bag on his desk. It contained a purse, wallet, as well as credit cards and a driver's license. He pulled latex gloves from a box on his desk, and slipped them on. Then he opened the bag and spilled out the contents.

"Nice purse." It was a small shoulder bag in a leopard skin pattern.

"That strap is what was used to strangle the victim."

"The killer used her purse?" Out of instinct, Sam grabbed a pair of latex gloves and slipped them on. This was Jake's case. She shouldn't be injecting herself into it but if she could glean any insight that would help him, she doubted he would mind. There was a faint rush of sounds as Sam closed her hand around the purse. Benny's voice faded into the background as he described the Camaro and Suey's findings. But Sam paid little attention because as her fingers clasped the strap of the purse, the strap that the killer had slipped around Donna's neck to strangle her, Sam heard a whisper, just one word, but it was clear and distinct— *destiny*.

19

He scanned the newspaper for an update on the body found at the golf course. Other than a brief mention on page eight that the body had been identified and asking anyone who knew the victim to please contact the police department, there was little else. He saw little indication that the police had followed the bread crumb trail he had left. But that was probably one clue they would normally leave out of a press release. These cops weren't bungling idiots. They already located the victim's car. The motel wasn't that far from that seedy bar. Made it convenient. He wondered what else the cops were holding out from the press. They hadn't arrested the bar manager so there was still hope. He would have to be a little more patient. And patience had always been his strong suit.

Maybe he should take a side job at the police station. That might be a bad move though. They probably run background checks on all employees. Would be nice to read the reports on the investigation, find out exactly how much they knew, if they had any suspects. On the television set in the break room was another commercial that served only to anger him more. Those two smiling faces. They should be selling used cars with a line of bullshit like that. He returned his attention to the newspaper. If the police didn't get a break soon, he may have to accelerate his plans and that wasn't good news for Tamara.

"HEY! Isn't your break about over?"

He glared at his supervisor with the bad hair piece, always keeping tabs on him. It bothered him but he didn't show it. Cooperative, team player, hard-worker, were all descriptions he wanted people to use when describing him. He calmly folded his paper, stood up, hitched his gun belt, and went back on duty.

◇◇

Sam studied the tiles on the ceiling of the examining room as a nurse entered pushing a cart. She should have never let Abby talk her into seeing a doctor so soon. She couldn't be any more than a few weeks pregnant.

"I don't understand why you want an ultrasound. It's too soon. Besides, with Dillon you didn't do an ultrasound until twenty weeks."

Glasses hung from a chain around Doctor Allison Greene's neck. She slipped them on then pulled the sheet down to Sam's hips and the gown up to just below the breasts, exposing her abdomen. Sam estimated Greene to be around Abby's age and she always smelled like Ivory soap and lavender. Sam winced as the cold gel hit her skin.

"It's not too soon for someone fourteen weeks pregnant."

"What? You must be mistaken. I'm not that big. I don't have the same symptoms I had with the first." Sam stared at her abdomen, wondering at what point did it start to resemble yeast raised bread. The slacks she had worn today had always been a little big on her and she disregarded the fact that they now fit, thinking they had shrunk in the dryer.

She turned her focus to the floral wallpaper and bamboo picture frames. At least Doctor Greene gave her patients cloth gowns rather than postage-size paper gowns. The nurse, whose name Sam believed was Livie, didn't look a day out of high school. Maybe she wasn't a nurse. They called them medical assistants these days.

"Just relax," Doctor Greene said, noticing Sam had clenched her hands into fists. "You haven't had any morning sickness?"

"Not even queasy. Does that mean anything?"

"If you mean does it determine boy or girl? No. Doesn't mean a thing. How's your appetite?"

"Ravenous. No wonder I crave ice cream." It wasn't hard for Sam to avoid the monitor. She figured if she didn't see the little fingers and toes it would be easier to deny the pregnancy. Thoughts of the outfits she purchased recently and would now have to stay in her closet for another year sickened her. And having finished nursing she had been looking forward to really tying one on, something that would probably make her sick seeing that she hadn't tied one on in over a year.

"So if I'm not twenty weeks yet, why the ultrasound?" A nervous twinge settled in Sam's stomach. Something was wrong, had to be.

She saw Livie glancing at the monitor, then her eyes widened and her mouth formed a small oh. Livie quickly pressed her lips together and turned away. Sam went back to counting the tiles on the ceiling, her mind running through a list of things that could be wrong.

"You can get dressed now." Doctor Greene handed the transducer to Livie, then turned back to Sam. "Get some prenatal vitamins and I'm sure you know to eat healthy. "I'd like to see you again in two months."

"So the baby looks okay?" Sam slowly sat up and studied the doctor's face.

"They look fine."

Sam power-walked the asphalt path around the property, iPod plugged into her ears while Pink sang in her ear. *They.* Doctor Greene had said *they.* Sam still didn't believe it and had to see the photos for herself. In less than six months she will have three babies in diapers. If she didn't have morning sickness before, she was going to have it now just thinking about it. But it hadn't kept her from stopping off at Panera's for a cinnamon scone and iced tea before heading home. She refrained from telling Jackie she had scheduled a doctor's appointment nor had she called her after to tell her she was having twins. Sam needed to digest everything first, then find a way to tell Abby and Jake.

She slowed as she approached Alex's ranch-style house. Planters on the porch held brilliant fall mums in full bloom. She passed a timber framed structure layered with blankets, a sweat lodge that Alex had constructed. She pulled the ear buds out cutting off Pink, then turned off the iPod. The scent of wood burning filled the air as smoke drifted from the apex of a thirty foot tall tipi. The hide skin had been tanned to a silky finish. Alex sometimes slept in the tipi located a short distance from his house.

The doorway flapped open and an Irish Setter bounded from the tipi. Poco was Alex's dog, a gift from Jake as an apology for something Jake still hadn't quite figured out, probably for injecting himself into their lives.

"Hey, Poco. How are you?" She rubbed Poco's head as its tail thumped wildly. "I know what you're after." Sam reached into her pocket and pulled out two dog biscuits, treats she always carried whenever she visited Alex. "Where's Alex?"

Poco bounded back to the tipi and Sam followed. The odor of wood burning was second only to the cherry scent from Alex's pipe tobacco. Hides and blankets covered all seven hundred square feet of ground. Bowls, cooking pots and utensils hung by ropes nailed to the timbers that stretched to the peak. Alex sat cross-legged on a blanket several feet from the fire, dressed in a denim shirt and jeans. Smoke trailed from his pipe as his dark eyes studied her.

"I wondered when you would show up."

"Were you expecting me?" Sam took a seat on a blanket several feet from him. Poco plopped down between the two of them.

Alex tried to look stern but he wasn't pulling it off. A hint of a smile lit up his eyes.

"Mom told you."

"That you are diluting the gene pool again? Yes, she did."

Sam sighed. Even though Alex always thought Sam should marry Lakota, she knew Jake was growing on him and Alex was enjoying teaching Dillon all about nature. She had seen him point out the various animals and insects to the infant, even though Dillon didn't understand a word he was saying. But Alex was gearing up for when Dillon could talk and understand.

"I don't know how it happened," Sam said.

"Ummmm." Alex stoked his pipe, the cherry scent filling the air. "I thought your mother had a talk with you when you were in your teens."

Sam narrowed her eyes. "You know what I mean. It wasn't exactly planned. And besides, I was nursing. You can't get pregnant while you're nursing."

"Too much information, thank you." He eyed her suspiciously through the haze. Alex always had a way of reading her. "There is more. Is everything okay with the baby?"

"Actually, it's babies."

"Oh." After a few seconds Alex's eyes widened and he blurted, "More than one?"

"Two. I haven't told Abby yet, nor Jake. I'm still angry with him for telling me I couldn't get pregnant."

Alex got a chuckle out of that. *"Iye sni."*

"No, he is not dumb. He's just naïve when it comes to marriage and women and kids. I think Frank told him I couldn't get pregnant."

"Don't tell him until the baby is born. I'd love to see the look on his face."

"It will be hard to keep that a secret with Abby buying two of everything. I will have three babies in diapers, Alex. I don't think Abby and I will be able to handle it."

"Hire one of those nannies, maybe bring one of the women down from the reservation who is good with children. Cora might know of someone."

"That is an excellent idea, Alex." She leaned across Poco and kissed Alex's cheek.

"Now, why are you really here?"

Sam knew Alex had a talent for talking to the animals. She remembered the look on Jake's face after he caught sight of a squirrel scampering up to Alex where he sat by the pond and holding out its injured paw. She also knew Alex had a way of talking to the spirits, finding out what was happening in their world just as they told him things about his. In their Native world, Alex would be known as a shaman.

So Sam told him about Marti Johnson, her alleged suicide, the body found at the golf course, and the one word that swirled around in her head—*destiny*. "There isn't any reason those two cases should be connected."

"And yet they are. That is the only reason the spirits are revealing the word to you. You must listen to them, not your doubts." He narrowed his eyes as he studied her closer. "There is something else."

Sam took a deep breath. She hadn't even told Abby or Jake about her dreams returning, but Alex had always been a good sounding board. When she finished telling him about the dreams returning and how her father's death was being played out in slow motion, Alex stared off, as though listening to voices she couldn't hear.

"It is a message. You must pay attention to what it is showing you. There is a reason that these dreams are being presented to you in a different way." He shook more tobacco into his pipe, then held a match over the fire's flame until it ignited. He puffed several times as the tobacco caught fire.

Sam sighed. "Why isn't it ever simple?"

"Because life isn't simple. If the only way people died was by natural causes, life would be very simple. But it isn't like that. There is a lot of evil in the world and people find different ways to commit their deeds as well as conceal them."

That night, the dream returned, but this time Sam focused on every detail. Was there more to her father's death than the investigation revealed? Had something changed? Was there perhaps a different car? Another passenger in the vehicle? But there wasn't. Only her father and Melinda were in the car. She watched as their bodies exploded, while car and body parts slowly tumbled, scattering in various directions. Was she supposed to be looking at a serial number? A sign near the street? A witness the police hadn't interviewed? Then her eye caught several sections of the car, narrow and identical in size and structure, the scene freezing in place and the debris forming a frame around something. Like a zoom lens the image in the frame enhanced. *Click...click.* The sound of a camera shutter, of the zoom feature bringing the image into focus. A forest, leaves tugged from their branches by the wind and drifting in all directions. *Click...click.* The image grew in size, enhanced again by the zoom lens. There was something dark hanging from the tree like a piece of tanned hide. Sam awakened and cursed silently. She didn't have a chance to see the final image.

She rolled over and stared at Jake's back, watching the rise and fall of the sheet that covered his body. Maybe the dreams started up again when she became pregnant, as if that should have any bearing. Abby had once said her powers might be enhanced when she was pregnant, but how and why? Maybe it was time she kept her appointment with the psychologist Doctor Talbot had recommended. She rolled back and closed her eyes but sleep wouldn't come. This time she was thinking of a woman strangled and another jumping from an overpass.

20

The next morning Sam searched her rolodex for the card Doctor Talbot had given her. Over breakfast she had shared her dreams with Jake and Abby. Abby wasn't concerned but Jake had those worry lines forming between his eyes. He had asked twice if she wanted him to accompany her to the therapist, but she assured him she was a big girl.

After Jake left for work and Abby left for the grocery store with Alex and Dillon, she called Doctor Evan Collier's office and was lucky he had an opening at ten o'clock. Then again, if he were good she should have had a two-month wait. Dismissing the idea that this therapist graduated at the bottom of his class, Sam confirmed the appointment and soon found herself in a waiting room that looked more like a resale shop. There was pottery in shapes of cups, vases, pumpkins and other seasonal and holiday-type decorations. There were leather belts and wallets stitched and anagrammed by hand. Sam checked the door to make sure she was in the right place.

"It's part of their therapy," a woman said as she set a cup of tea on the coffee table. She reminded Sam of Margaret Thatcher on a good hair day. She even had a British accent.

"Hope I'm not that bad off," Sam whispered but it didn't go unheard.

"I'm Maggie and you must be Samantha Casey."

Sam forced an apologetic smile and plopped into the lush leather couch. "Nice purple couch." She ran her hand across the creamy leather.

"It's eggplant," Maggie said. Her eyes settled on the small medicine bundle hanging from Sam's neck and the third earring of beads and feathers resting against her left shoulder.

If one could dismiss the therapeutic attempts at artwork, one could see that the office and waiting room were prime candidates for a home decorating magazine. There were art deco paintings, dark cherry wood, bronze statues, and collector books. She could swear he had an authentic set of Mark Twains.

"Doctor Collier must have a gay friend. The décor is impressive."

Maggie's half glasses slid down her nose. "Doctor Collier did the decorating."

"Oh, well." Sam snapped her mouth shut but Maggie wasn't finished. "He's my son."

Sam nodded toward a picture on the wall of a man wearing horn-rimmed glasses and a bow tie. Threads of gray wove through his hair. "You don't look old enough to be his mother."

"That's my husband…was my husband. Nathan passed away earlier this year. He had always planned for the business to be called Collier and Collier. Unfortunately, Nathan died the day after Evan graduated."

"The shrink I'm seeing just graduated from college?" Sam couldn't hide the shock in her voice.

"Yes, I am a baby doc." The side door closed and Sam stared at an Adonis in a charcoal gray suit that sculpted his body. Shoes were gray animal skin of some type, maybe ostrich. The shirt was pink and the tie a lavender and gray.

"Do you always dress to match your décor?" Sam could feel Maggie shooting her daggers.

He reached out a hand to her. "I'm Doctor Evan Collier and you must be my ten o'clock." He held the door open and motioned her inside another room that was a centerfold for *House Beautiful* magazine. Sam took in more eggplant and lemon yellow with a splash of gray in the thin shade screens on the windows.

Maggie set a silver tray with a tea pot and cups on the coffee table. "I selected Li Zhi Hong tea for you today, Doctor Collier."

"Thanks, Maggie."

Maggie finished her fawning and gave Sam one final stern look before leaving.

"Listen," Sam said. "The tea tastes wonderful but I have a feeling you aren't up to speed on my case. I was supposed…"

"Yes, you were supposed to meet with my father but cancelled your appointment, several times. I have studied your file and spoke personally with Doctor Talbot at Sara Binyon's." Evan set his cup on the coffee table, then took a seat in one of the leather chairs. "I graduated first in my class and learned quite a bit from my father."

"I'm sure you did but I have shoes older than you."

He smiled revealing dimples and teeth that were blinding. "Why don't we start." He pointed toward the couch. "And I doubt you have shoes thirty years old."

Sam relented and took a seat. "Well, the tea is good. Maggie doesn't have anything to eat, does she?"

Evan reached over and pushed an intercom button. "Do you have any more of that cake left, Maggie?"

Evan hung up before Maggie could respond. One minute later Maggie returned with another silver tray and set it on the coffee table. A piece of chocolate cake was on each plate along with monogrammed paper napkins and silverware.

"Wow, thanks, Maggie." Sam grabbed a plate and dug in.

"Are you eating for two?" Maggie asked.

"Actually for three," Sam mumbled around the frosting.

Maggie was all smiles now. "Well congratulations. Can I get you more tea?"

"I'm fine, thank you."

Evan waited for Maggie to leave, then turned to a fresh page in his notepad. "Yours is an unusual case and it must have been a terrifying experience for a five-year-old."

Sam remained silent and continued eating. She was hoping she didn't have to re-tell the story of how she witnessed her father and Melinda being blown to bits in a car bomb, nor how she was catatonic for two years afterward. The case she had worked when she was still a cop involved the man responsible for her father's death. He tried to kill Sam with a car bomb but instead killed Don Connelley, the chief of police who had been a close friend of the family as well as her godfather.

That incident left her catatonic again and was how she ended up at the Sara Binyon Retreat.

"You promised Doctor Talbot that you would continue your therapy when you returned home."

"If I needed it. I didn't need it."

"Until," Evan prompted.

Sam took her time finishing the cake, savored the fluffy frosting, then wiped her mouth and took a sip of tea. Her obvious attempt at stalling wasn't lost on him. He started tapping his pen.

"The dreams started up again, but they are different."

"How so?"

Sam described the slow motion images and after everything was obliterated it all reversed, again in agonizing slow motion.

"How often do you have them?"

"First it was once every couple weeks but lately a few times a week."

"What do you think triggered it?"

"I'm looking to you for that answer."

"Has anything happened in your life, any changes?"

"Other than job, marriage and a baby, soon to be plural?"

Evan flashed his pearly whites again and scratched something on his notepad. "What about people connected to the case that started the dreams in the first place? Have you encountered any of them?" Sam shook her head no. "Can you remember when they started?"

Sam thought about the first time the new dream version began. Was it before or after Dillon was born? For lack of an answer she let her eyes crawl over the artwork on the walls. There was a picture on the back credenza of Evan and another man in a canoe. The man was also an Adonis but with surfer blonde hair and biceps the size of her thigh. She could feel Evan's gaze delving into her psyche. The aroma from the tea was intoxicating so she refilled her cup from the tea pot.

"Are you avoiding the questions or you just don't know?"

"Why don't you tell me exactly how much you know about my case?"

Evan stood and stripped out of his suit jacket. He walked over to a panel and slid it open to reveal a closet. "You were five years old when your mother took you to your father's office so you could say goodbye before he left on a trip." Evan paused with the jacket in his hand. "Who exactly was Melinda Casey?"

"Abby was a surrogate. Melinda couldn't have children and Abby had been living with them since she was a teen. There were problems on the reservation." Problems Sam preferred not to go into so she ended her response at that point.

"Nuff said. Anyway." He hung up the jacket on a satin hanger, taking time to button the buttons. Then he slid the closet door shut. "Your father was a reporter working on a story on a prominent state representative. You were waving from the window when the car exploded. You watched everything. Very traumatic for an adult, let alone a child. It's no wonder when someone tried to kill you in the same manner that you would be traumatized again."

Sam realized he had memorized her case but just hearing it was making her relive it again. It didn't seem to bother her as much as she had thought. She had heard it often enough while in therapy at Sara Binyon's.

"I'm impressed. You're not just another pretty face."

This brought a tinge of blush to Evan's cheeks. "I have an eidetic memory. But memorizing words isn't enough. I have to try to look behind the words for the meanings, to understand the cause and the reaction. Have you read anything in the newspapers or perhaps a similar occurrence that might have been reported in the papers?"

Sam had thought about it extensively, tried to think back to the first time she had the dream, but not one thing came to mind. "There hasn't been anything on the news or in the papers. And I haven't seen anything in the police logs."

"What about Preston Hilliard? Has there been any reports on him?" Representative Preston Hilliard had been behind the death of Samuel and Melinda Casey and was currently behind bars.

Sam shook her head. "Nothing, and believe me, I make sure I'm updated on his condition and if he's moved to another prison."

"How do you feel after the dream? Anxious, fearful, unable to cope?"

"No. Not even a twinge. It's just not a pleasant sight to see body parts flying around in slow motion and then, like a broken toy, everything reassembling…the car, the people. I sometimes feel like it's a message."

"What kind of message?"

Sam took another sip of tea and studied the tiny crumbs of cake left on the plate. Would it be uncouth for her to lick the plate clean? "Very subtle since I can't seem to grasp its meaning."

"Think back to when you first had the dream so we might be able to determine a timeframe. Had Dillon been born then?"

"Yes."

"Had you just finished a case?"

Sam remembered it had been summer because they had slept with the patio door open and the birds were shrieking at four in the morning. The temperature hadn't dipped below eighty during the night but there had been a breeze that sifted through the patio window and up to the opened skylight. "I remember walking down the stairs a bit groggy and seeing Alex in the foyer. He had brought in the flag. Yes. It was the day after the Fourth of July and we had left the flag out overnight."

"So the first week of July. Maybe what you can do before our next session…"

"Next?" Sam had hoped this would be a one day deal. "You can't fix things in one session?"

"Did it get broken in one session?" Evan scratched more notes. Sam tried to read upside down but Evan stopped scratching and stared at her. "What day is best for you?"

"How much notice do you need of a cancellation? I'm working a case."

"I can always come to you. I'm not tethered to this office, you know. We can meet in the park, maybe for lunch. I find that clients are more relaxed in their own comfort zone. Now what I was saying before you interrupted was I would like you to go through the newspapers one week before July fourth and see if anything jogs your memory. Do you think you can handle that?"

21

"So he was drop dead gorgeous?" Jackie sat lotus style, each foot on the opposite knee.

"Very. Real runway gorgeous. How the hell do you sit like that?" Sam adjusted the pillow under her rear. As a child, she had been laughed at on the reservation because she was the only one who could not sit Indian style. Her knees would always point toward the sky and nothing she did would get them to lie flat. To even feel comfortable in this position she had to sit on a pillow.

"I have always been flexible, sugar. Now, tell me more about this doctor of yours. I may have to dream up some syndrome."

"Relax. He had a picture of himself with another guy on a canoe trip. Both very buff in bathing suits, all tan and all smiles. He is definitely gay."

"What? Like two friends can't go canoeing?"

"There wasn't one picture of a wife."

"Ladies, please. You must clear your minds and concentrate." Evie, the shapely Swedish yoga instructor, walked the floor. "Okay, center of the mat. Let's get into our Sphinx pose. Watch the position of your hands. Your forearms should be on the mat, head high, eyes straight ahead. Now push up into the *Bhujangasana*, the cobra pose. If you feel any pain in your back, then lower the position until it feels more comfortable."

"God, I'd rather sweat in a sauna than put my body through this." Sam pressed her hands against the mat and pushed up. In a weak moment Jackie had talked her into taking yoga classes at a local fitness center. Sam was thankful they had their own room rather than in the gym where a walking track on the second floor circled the room. Sam envisioned men pausing to stare down at them when they were in their downward dog position.

"Thank Evie for those well-toned arms and legs of yours," Jackie whispered.

"Thank you," Evie said, having overheard their conversation. "Okay, relax and take one deep breath and exhale. Evie pushed a button on the CD player and an Enya song started to play. "Corpse pose, ladies. I'm sure this is your favorite of the session." Evie's lithe body stretched out on the mat at the front of the room. The women followed suit, lying flat on their backs, arms stretched out to the side. "Be aware of your breathing, slow, in and out, and relax."

"How did Jake take the news about the baby?" Jackie whispered.

"I haven't told him yet."

A soft laugh started in the back of Jackie's throat. "Sounds like you are cooking something up."

"There are some things I haven't even told you."

Jackie whipped her head around and scowled at Sam. "I don't want to hear that you are holding out on me, girl. Now give it to mama."

Sam shrugged. "I think I'll make you suffer a bit. Serves you right for making me take that pregnancy test."

"Yeah, like not taking it was going to change the outcome."

"Ladies." Evie made a shushing sound as she lifted her head to see who the culprits were.

Jackie waited for Evie to lie back down, then whispered, "What else is there to know other than you are having a baby?"

"It's plural."

"What's plural?"

Sam gave Jackie a withering glare and waited for the news to sink in.

"OH MY GAWD!" Jackie shrieked.

"Ladies!" Evie saw several heads lift from their mats and turn in Jackie's direction. With the way Jackie was screeching there could be a mouse in the room as far as they could tell.

"My girl here is having twins," Jackie said. She jerked to a sitting position and applauded. "I know just the thing too." By now the corpse position had been abandoned and the other participants were joining in the applause. "You know I have this girl crush on Jessica Alba, that actress who played *Dark Angel*. Well, she went through HypnoBirthing for her pregnancy. You need to check that out. Makes labor pain free."

"I heard of that," one woman in a one-piece leotard outfit said. Now that the entire class had been jarred from their closing relaxation session, they joined in the conversation.

"Supposed to work."

"The therapy clinic by the hospital does that."

"My sister's friend swears by it," another said.

Evie gave out a sigh and sat up.

"Let me find the right time to break it to Jake first," Sam said. She glanced at Evie's look of frustration. "Okay, I'm ready for the corpse pose now."

22

Jake drew a line from Donna's name to a rectangle box centered at the top where he had written "Baileys." Under her name was a timeline tracking Donna's location from the last time her landlord and co-workers had seen her. After her lunch with Alyce, they were unable to track Donna's movements. The whiteboard looked very empty.

"I don't like to see all that empty space." Robinson frowned from the doorway. "Any action on her ATM card?"

"Nothing yet." Although Donna's wallet had contained credit cards, her bank did confirm she had an ATM card which had yet to be located.

Frank rubbed his eyes with the heels of his hands. "You think that board looks anemic, try staring at these tapes from the restaurant. Nothing but loud drunks during Donna's shifts. Would have helped if that asshole manager had written dates on the damn things."

"What about the DNA from the cigarette butt?" Robinson nodded toward the entry on the board listing the items found at the dump site.

"Suey said it wasn't a match to anyone in our database," Jake replied.

"So Rob the bar manager/ex-boyfriend is our best bet, our only best bet. Don't like those odds."

"Except we don't have an exact day or time of Donna's death. Back to square one." Frank popped out the CD, and shoved in another one.

Sam wasn't sure if this was such a good idea. It felt so intrusive listening in on other people confessing their inner most fears and worries. Forrest had wanted Sam to sit in on their support group meeting. He thought it would give her a better perspective. Of what exactly, Sam wasn't sure. Forrest had introduced her to Grace Hunt, the group leader, and although Grace said she was more than welcome to sit in the group circle, Sam preferred to hang back by the refreshment table. A cup of hot tea sounded good about now with temperatures outside plummeting to forty, not to mention the cakes and cookies sitting out in trays that were screaming her name. She dragged a chair next to the table to make her presence as obscure as possible.

Grace forced a teen named Luke to put his cell phone away. He responded by sulking and crossing his arms. An elderly woman, however, wasn't forced to put away her crochet needles and yarn, probably because she was able to talk and pay attention without looking at what her hands were doing. But more pouting and pointing from Luke forced Grace to ask Velma to put her crocheting away.

Sam wasn't sure how valuable a support group could be. Abby would probably say talking always worked wonders. She felt for Ben, the former Marine who had lost a close friend and fellow Marine to post traumatic stress disorder. Sam wasn't even part of the group but already she was depressed. She lost count of the number of cookies she ate as she listened to each of the members talk about what was new in their lives, how they were coping. And then Grace turned the evening over to a young woman whose twin sister had died just before her wedding. She vaguely remembered Forrest mentioning her.

"It feels like it happened yesterday," Carrie started. She was sitting to Grace's right so Sam had a clear view of her from where she sat. Sam grabbed another chocolate chip cookie and wished she had brought a Zip Lock bag. "She had just come from the dressmaker's several hours beforehand. Carly had a final fitting for her wedding dress. She was so excited. Her next appointment at one o'clock was at the hairdresser's. She was going to take her headpiece and experiment with hair styles. Everything was going as planned. And then…" Carrie paused and swiped at her eyes. "My mom is still having a hard time dealing with it. She wants the police to question Sean more. She still feels he had something to do with Carly's death. But I just don't see it. He is so broken up over her death."

"So was that Peterson guy who killed his pregnant wife," Velma offered. "He was even talking to his girlfriend on the phone while at his wife's funeral. How weird is that?"

"Sean wasn't like that. He was devoted to Carly."

"So was that Peterson guy."

Sam had to agree with Velma. No matter how well you thought you knew someone, they sometimes do things that are completely out of character.

"Maybe you wanted him for yourself." Luke scowled from beneath bangs in need of a trim.

Carrie gasped and turned on the youth. "How can you say that? You don't know a thing about me."

"I know you are quick to anger. Look at you now. Pretty quick to anger if you ask me."

"I am not."

Grace straightened in her seat and flashed a stern look at the youth. "Luke, you are just lashing out because your parents thought you ridiculed your sister too much. Not one of us knows what went through our loved ones' minds when they decided to take their own life. There's no reason why we should lash out at each other. Now, Carrie, tell us about the police investigation. Did anything turn up?"

"Nothing. They checked her financial background in case she was being blackmailed. They checked any records of stalkers, health problems. They practically turned her life and my family's lives upside down before concluding it was a suicide. That and the fact that witnesses saw her undress and walk into the lake. Not one person was near that she could have been arguing or fighting with. Didn't even have her cell phone on her. She had left it at home after her call."

Sam stopped in mid-bite. Didn't Beast say Marti's cell phone records showed she received a call right before walking out of the condo and jumping off the overpass? She jotted down notes as Carrie's voice changed to nothing more than white noise. Sam had to get Carrie alone to ask her more questions.

Twenty minutes later the session broke up. Sam waited for most of the people to leave before approaching Forrest and Carrie. "Would you two like to go somewhere quiet for coffee? I need to ask both of you some questions." They agreed to meet at Round the Clock, a twenty-four hour restaurant.

Ten minutes later they were huddled in a booth by the fireplace. Although they had arrived in separate cars Sam had the feeling there was a bonding happening between Carrie and Forrest. Whether it was shared grief or something deeper, Sam wasn't sure. Forrest explained to Carrie that he had hired Sam to find out the truth behind Marti's death. A waitress came by and took their orders. Forrest asked for coffee. Carrie and Sam each ordered hot chocolate with whipped cream.

"Carrie, could you explain exactly what happened the day Carly died? I want to know every detail, the time of day, who else was in the house, what she was wearing, what were the last words she spoke and whom she was talking to." Sam set her tote bag on the table and rummaged around for a pen.

"Wow, Sam. Do you always carry?" Forrest nodded toward her gun which was just visible inside her bag.

"Hubby's orders. Don't leave home without it." She tucked it back safely into the tote bag.

Once the waitress deposited their orders Carrie spoke. "Like I said, I haven't lived at home since I graduated from college. But my mom has repeated the story so many times that I practically have it memorized. Carly was up at seven. Mom was up at six with Dad. She made him breakfast before he went to work. Mom and Carly had breakfast together at seven-thirty. They were going over the seating arrangement for the reception."

"Did your mom and sister get along?" Sam asked.

"We all did. I didn't move out because Mom and I fought, if that's what you're asking. I wanted to live closer to the train station. I work in Chicago so a friend and I rent an apartment together."

"Male or female?" Sam asked as she jotted notes. She saw Forrest's eyebrows jerk up. "I'm just trying to get a picture here."

Carrie waved her off. "Female. Don't worry. The cops asked the same question." Carrie ate the whipped cream off of the hot chocolate with a spoon, then took a sip before continuing. "Carly and Mom left at ten-thirty for the final fitting. Carly was so thrilled she was able to lose twenty pounds for the wedding. The dress fit perfectly. Later she was going to go to the hair dresser to try out different hair styles with her head piece. She was a fanatic about details."

"Would you call her obsessive compulsive?"

"Oh, no. Only with the wedding. She wanted everything just right but Mom was really good at keeping Carly centered."

Sam felt as though she were back in yoga class but bit back a retort.

"Mom made Carly understand that things were going to go wrong. It's Murphy's Law so she shouldn't sweat it. It might rain on her wedding day. The flowers might wilt, the limo could break down. Mom was one stress-free lady so if you are asking, no, Carly was not despondent because someone cancelled at the last minute and it threw off the seating arrangements."

Forrest sat back and listened. Sam could see in his eyes he was reliving Marti's last day, how her morning routine might have worked. He pushed his cup closer to the edge when the waitress zipped by with the carafe.

"What time did Carly plan to leave for the hairdresser?"

"About twelve-thirty. Thing is, Mom wanted to go with. Around noon Mom was in the kitchen reading a book and Carly was in the living room going through more RSVPs. Next thing Mom knew, she heard the door close and saw Carly's car backing out of the driveway."

"You had mentioned a phone call during the session." When Sam mentioned this, Forrest suddenly looked up.

"Right. Mom said she heard the phone ring. It wasn't the home phone, it was Carly's cell phone. When Mom walked into the living room to ask who had called, that is when she saw the car backing out of the driveway. Carly left her purse with her driver's license and her cell phone on the couch."

Sam thought Forrest was going to launch himself over the table. His body kept rocking back and forth. "Do you know who called?" Forrest asked.

"We didn't think about it. The police checked phone records but didn't find anything. They said the call never connected or some such thing." She looked from Sam to Forrest. "Why? Is that important?"

"Marti received a call, too," Forrest replied. "At least according to the phone records it lasted four seconds. The call was from a disposable phone."

"Like something drug dealers use?" Carrie looked at Sam. "Carly wasn't into drugs."

"Neither was Marti, but it certainly makes me suspicious when two people receive a call and soon after they commit suicide. Did your mother catch any words of the conversation?" Sam asked.

"No. She didn't hear Carly say anything but hello and then Mom heard the front door close."

"What does it mean?" Forrest asked.

"I'm not sure but I don't believe in coincidences."

23

He slipped the frozen dinner into the microwave and pressed the button. A steak dinner would taste good about now. Although his mother, rest her nagging soul, would have told him to give it a rest, he preferred to let it boil and fester. It kept him focused to remind himself of what he was missing out on. *Mamby-pamby*. That was what his mother called him. *No ambition*. That's what his ex-wife had said. He had hopes and dreams. He had been the brains behind the entire concept but now here he was, living in a one-bedroom apartment above a café.

The microwave dinged. He pulled out the dinner and set it on a plate. After grabbing a beer from the refrigerator, he carried his meal to a table in front of the window where he liked to watch the comings and goings across the street. The lasagna didn't smell half bad, not as good as the Italian restaurant by the mall but it would do. No ambition. How wrong she was. He had lots of ambition, but more important, he had patience and planning. His number one rule was to keep his hands clean. He wasn't a violent person. Murder had never been in his plans, at least not by his own hands. If only the bitch at the restaurant had been a little more cooperative. He had been at the restaurant the night the customer had given her a hard time. What a perfect time to tie one of them to the deaths. So he followed her, tried to get her patterns down straight. When she walked into a seedy bar on the outskirts of town, he grabbed a stool next to hers to strike up a conversation, work his magic. But something went horribly wrong. He should have known waitresses who can remember the food and drink orders of eight people at a table without writing anything down, might not be the best targets. How stupid. The few times he had eaten at Bailey's he had never looked the same. Stupid, stupid, stupid. How foolish he had been to not change his eating habits. Whether steak or hamburgers, he always ordered a side of horseradish, and she remembered that.

His hand shook as he stabbed at the lasagna, remembering the night he followed her to the seedy bar. If he had frequented Bailey's more often he would have known of her relationship with the manager. He would have heard the other waitresses talk about the public argument the two had had, how she had poured the beer over his head. Now the newspapers were hinting that the manager was the number one suspect in her murder, not the customer who sent his steak back twice.

It wasn't often that he encountered a woman who didn't succumb to his talents. Instead, she had turned to him and said, "What kind of line of bullshit is that? What are you trying to pull?" And after a pause, she had said, "I remember you. You always ordered a side of horseradish."

She was a little tipsy when she left that bar. For being so smart, she hadn't locked her car doors. If only her memory hadn't been so good. Oh well. It still worked out for the best.

Sam climbed off the elevator, gave a wave to the night shift desk sergeant and marched down the aisle to Jake's desk. He was pounding away at the keyboard while Frank was leaning over Jake's shoulder. Takeout boxes from a Chinese restaurant littered the desks. The night shift had a skeleton crew and it was obvious the skeletons were either out to dinner or on the streets. Robinson was tidying up his desk. Sam could see a fortune cookie clamped between his lips.

Frank straightened as Sam approached. "Hey, Sam. What brings you out?"

"Had to meet a client." She zeroed in on her husband who raised his eyebrows and cocked his head as his way of asking, "what kind of trouble are you in?" She was getting good at reading his body language.

"You mean you aren't tethered to the stove?" Frank stifled a chuckle.

Sam's eyes flashed like electric sparks as she pointed a finger at Frank. "Don't even talk to me." She reached into her purse and flung a piece of paper at Jake. "Same to you." She turned and marched back to the elevator and never looked back.

"What was that all about?" Robinson closed his office door and lumbered over to Jake's desk.

Jake studied the fuzzy picture, turned it several ways and cocked his head. "What the hell?"

"That's a sonogram," Frank said. "Sam's pregnant?"

Jake studied it closer, looked at the elevator as the doors closed, then back to the picture. "Why are there three legs?"

Robinson pulled the photo from Jake's grasp and let out a huff of breath. "Actually, there are four legs, four arms, and two heads, you ass."

Frank nodded in agreement. "Either Sam is having an alien or she's having twins. But why the hell did she look at me as if it's my fault?"

"Shit. You told me she couldn't get pregnant while she's nursing."

Robinson pointed at the numbers at the top of the photo. "Hell, she's fourteen weeks pregnant. Did you know this?"

"Would she have flung it at me if I knew?" Jake leaned back and washed his hands over his face. "Damn. I need a drink." He stood and pulled his jacket from the back of his chair.

"Uh uh." Robinson tsked. "If I were you, I'd head straight home."

Sam stroked Dillon's back as he slept soundly against her chest. She was huddled on the window seat in the nursery. The room was dark except for the constellations on the ceiling formed by glow-in-the-dark stars. Abby and Alex had worked extensively on the nursery, adding a scenery of animals behind a picket fence and a life-like painting of a tree in the corner with a bird house hanging from a hook in the ceiling. Sam had left all the decorating up to her mother.

Abby folded the freshly laundered blanket and placed it in the bottom dresser drawer. "So you never stayed to witness Jacob's reaction."

"No. I figured he needed time to let it sink in. He probably needed a stiff drink, too."

Abby studied her daughter, then sat on the window seat across from her. "You are worried."

Sam smiled as she watched Dillon's bud lips suck on his thumb. She inhaled the clean bath smell of his skin and hair. How precious. How innocent. "I just wanted a little more time to spend with Dillon before I had to split my attention with another baby. Or in my case, babies. I don't want him to feel short-changed."

"It will be good for him to have kids to play with, Samantha. Women throughout life have had children just a year apart."

"Yes, but they weren't married to someone already damaged from a bad childhood."

"Jacob can handle it. There are enough of us here to help manage the chaos." There was a gleam of excitement in Abby's eyes. She brushed stray hairs from her face and tucked them into the knot at the nape of her neck. "I have spoken to Cora about recommending someone to help out. Of course she will make sure any applicant has some medical and child care training. I don't want to entrust my grandchildren to just anyone. We can remodel the basement to make it resemble more of an apartment."

"I don't know, Mom. No matter how much training that person would have, it would still be a stranger under our roof."

"Think about it. Talk it over with Jacob." Abby rose from the seat and reached for her grandson. "Let's get Dillon into his crib."

Sam relinquished custody with a sigh. "The problem is I would feel like a complete inept mother if I had to rely on some nanny to help out."

Abby placed Dillon in the crib and covered him with a light blanket. She kept her voice low so as not to awaken her grandson. "Perhaps you might think differently, Samantha, when you have three babies and suddenly an enticing case is dumped in your lap and you wished you had some spare time to help out a spirit who only has you to rely on."

Abby always had a subtle way of making sense. Sam lightly touched the dreamcatcher hanging over one end of the crib. It was believed a dreamcatcher would trap bad dreams and only let in the good dreams. Feathers hung from the bottom of the art piece but it was hung high enough that when Dillon was able to stand, they would be out of his reach. Jake appeared in the doorway. If it wasn't for the lighting, Sam would swear his face was white.

"How long have you been standing there?" Sam asked.

"Long enough."

Abby patted his arm as she walked out of the room.

"Yeah, wonder of wonders." Sam tucked the blanket around her sleeping son. "Isn't he adorable?"

"We do make cute babies."

"Spaced a few years apart would be nice, like maybe ten years."

He circled his arms around her and kissed her forehead. "Frank offered his apology."

"Right, like that's going to get him anywhere."

Jake moved his lips to her mouth and let them hover. "Frank also said you can't get pregnant when you're pregnant."

Sam struggled not to smile but it was hard. Jake's hands were exploring and his tongue was tasting the corner of her mouth. *Damn him!*

24

"Okay. You've had a chance to digest this mess." Robinson raised a beefy arm at the whiteboard. "What have you got?" Robinson closed the conference door to the hustle and bustle in the outer office. The detectives eased into the chairs as the captain remained standing.

Jake passed a report to Robinson. "Suey faxed this over this morning. DNA on the cigarette found at the scene is inconclusive, although somehow Revere's name still made it into the papers. I think we have a leak."

Robinson gave the report a cursory glance, then tossed it on the desk. "That should make the mayor happy, although he's still squealing like a baby that we are even talking to his Number One contributor."

The door burst open and Chief Dennis Murphy occupied the doorway in a black suit, black shirt that could only be silk, and a white tie.

They stared for several beats until Robinson said, "Sorry, your boss Capone died years ago."

Murphy closed the door, not even a hint of a smile on his face. "Where's the coffee?" He pulled out a chair and sat down, careful to check the chair first for dirt. "Our illustrious Mayor Jefferson Schuler, would you believe that shit? He suddenly isn't Jeffery anymore. Jefferson sounds more formal. Anyway, Schuler is pissed that we are questioning his numero uno contributor about a murder." He filled his cup and set the carafe in the middle of the table.

"The body was found on his property," Jake said.

"Doesn't matter to him if she was found in Revere's bed. Fill me in. I don't want to look like an imbecile when he stops by my office later this morning." Murphy eyed the notes on the whiteboard.

Jake and Frank ran down the entire case, all the co-workers, the apartment where the victim lived, comments from her closest friend, but absent a positive time of death makes it hard to peg the bar manager as a suspect. "The body was found on golf course property and a cigarette near the body was the same brand Revere uses."

Murphy dismissed it with a wave of a hand. "A good defense attorney would say the wind blew the cigarette there or someone could have planted it. What else have you got?" The silence in the room told him all he needed to know. "Go back to Revere. Hell, make a trip every day for that matter just to make sure he gets the message he's on our radar. Get a list of current and ex-employees with a grudge. Go at it from that angle while I teach our esteemed mayor basic detective work one-oh-one. The ass." Murphy left in as big of a rush as he had entered.

"Wow, back so soon."

"Miss me?" Sam placed Carly Farnswood's phone on Beast's desk. She was tempted to use a flashlight to find her way around his basement lair. "I have another phone I'd like you to check." Beast grabbed the phone with a hairy mitt and popped out the SIM card. "I have a few minutes if you'd like to stick around."

"Sure." Sam watched as Beast shoved the SIM card into a device no larger than an iPad. A series of numbers and codes showed up on the screen. Against the corner of the lab was a desk. Sam didn't see any family pictures or personal items. In the garbage was a fast food bag, remnants of his breakfast. Sam envisioned Beast arriving at work before daylight and leaving after dusk, either because the sunlight did bother his eyes or maybe he didn't like being stared at because of his appearance.

"The last call received lasted around four seconds." Beast tapped a few keys on the keyboard. "It came from another disposable phone, just like before. Anyone can buy a prepaid phone as well as cards at a number of outlets. Customer pays with cash so there's no way to trace who purchased it."

"Interesting."

Beast pulled out the SIM card and handed it back to Sam. "What kind of character are you dealing with here?"

Sam thought about that for several seconds. Two suicides, both receiving phone calls prior to their deaths, both calls from disposable phones. Were those calls from two different people or one? "I think we are dealing with someone very clever and very dangerous."

25

"Nice." Sam looked around the quaint bistro. The interior resembled a grotto with cobblestone floors, archways and a stone fountain in the corner of the room. Some guests were coping with the crisp sunny air by huddling around cups of hot coffee outside on the patio. Vines with tiny pink flowers crawled the walls on two sides of the room. White enamel tables had floral designs etched on the glass tops, their matching chairs more fitting of an upscale ice cream shop. She changed her opinion to an ice cream shop in Monte Carlo.

"I take it Café Fleurs Grotte has something to do with flowers." Sam took a seat, thankful she decided against jeans and instead had chosen wine-colored gaucho pants, matching leather boots, and a wine and cream cable-stitched tunic top with crocheted roses. How fitting.

Evan Collier nodded in agreement. "Fleurs Grotte is flower grotto in French. You need to take a second language. It opens you up to a whole new life."

"Thanks, but I have a second language. It's English. The first language I learned to speak was Lakota." Her eyes drifted to the ceiling where a maiden in a strapless orange gown sat holding a huge book while surrounded by a pool of flowers.

"It's a replica of Michelangelo's Libyan Sibyl named Phemonoe, believed to be a prophetic priestess." The man who had sidled up to the table spoke in an accent that sounded like French. He wore a tight shirt that fit him like a second skin. With the beret he was wearing Sam expected to see him paddling a tourist canoe in Venice. Thinking the word canoe made her re-examine his sun-streaked hair and the rippling muscles. He was the man in the picture in Doctor Collier's office.

"Sorry. I bet you own this place."

Evan introduced Sam to Christian Didier. "Christian learned to cook in Paris and Rome. Went to school in England and the United States. We met when I spent one college summer backpacking across Europe. He's never quite lost his French accent even though he was born in Kansas."

"Kansas? Like the U.S. Kansas?"

Christian pulled out a chair and sat down, taking time to hand each of them a menu. "Same. My father was in the military and was stationed in Europe for years. He met my mother in Paris during leave. He brought her to Kansas to meet his parents. After I was born, we were off to Europe again."

Sam motioned toward the walls and ceiling. "And the fascination with grottoes?"

"I fell in love with Bernard Palissy's grotto he designed for Catherine de' Medici's chateau in Paris. The gardens were beautiful. Soon I found myself seeking the grottoes at Twickenham in England, then Painshill Park, Clandor Park, and at Wilton House. Evan and I even visited the grotto at Lourdes." He pointed to several items on the menu. "I like to include flowers in some of my recipes."

"Flowers?" Sam had visions of grazing on dandelions.

"I grow my own in the greenhouse in our backyard." Christian reverted easily into his lecture mode. "Carnation petals have been used since the seventeenth century to make Chartreuse, which is a French liqueur. And they work wonderfully in desserts. I use the leaves and stems of the Crown Daisy in my Oriental stir fries. The shoots of day lilies are a great substitute for asparagus."

Sam flipped open her menu. "Please tell me this isn't a vegan restaurant, not that I have any problem with people grazing on whatever they want to eat. I just like a little meat and fish every now and then."

"Most of the flowers are used in salads or to flavor fruit dishes or sauces, although lavender does make it into my breads and cookies."

"You do have that fabulous lavender beef," Evan reminded him.

"Oh, I did get your tea, Evan. I have Li Zhi Hong and Prana Chai."

"The Li Zhi Hong would be great."

"Make it two," Sam said. "Is it hot or iced tea?"

"Whichever you prefer. The iced tea will have impatiens flowers floating on top."

"Make it two iced teas," Evan said.

"Now, may I recommend the crespeou." Christian pointed at the menu.

"What is it?" Sam wasn't one to eagerly try a dish she couldn't pronounce.

"Think of it as omelets with different fillings layered on top of each other like a layer cake. Then it is sliced. Makes a colorful presentation. We also have the Croque-Monsieur, more like a toasted ham and Swiss sandwich."

"Why don't you just call it a ham and cheese sandwich." Sam looked up to see them staring at her.

"You have to understand that Sam is very direct," Evan explained. "I was warned that she has a tendency to speak first and analyze later."

"I already had breakfast. Do you have something light but fattening as hell?" Sam asked.

"Sure. How about cinnamon orange popovers, miniature brioche rolls, mini crab quiche, choux a la crème."

"Crème puffs," Evan interjected.

"Tartes aux fruits."

"Fruit tart. I got that one," Sam said.

"Religieuse," Christian continued.

"Chocolate éclair."

"It's shaped to resemble a nun," Christian added with a smile.

Sam wondered where someone would get a cookie cutter shaped like a nun.

"Profiteroles." Christian wiggled his eyebrows as though that were the most enticing item on the menu.

"Baked puff pastries filled with cream," Evan clarified. He turned to Christian and said, "I'll take the mini crab quiche and a couple of the nuns."

"Just give me two of the mini crab quiche and one of the cinnamon orange popovers."

Christian gathered up the menus. "I'll get that tea right out. If you need anything else, mademoiselle, just let me know."

"Merci beaucoup," Sam said. "See. I know three languages." She could see Christian smile as he turned away.

"So, Sam. Why did you need a second session so quickly? Did you have a chance to go through those newspapers as I had suggested?"

"Oops. Not yet, but I will. Actually, I wanted to pick your brain on a case I'm working."

"You want to pick my brain at one hundred twenty-five dollars for a fifty-minute session?"

"Guess we have to eat fast."

Christian set two glasses of iced tea on the table. He was true to his word. Violet-colored impatiens flowers were floating on the surface of the teas. "Looks colorful." Sam waited for him to leave before continuing. "Can you give me some insight as to why someone would want to commit suicide?"

Evan stopped stirring his tea and looked at her sharply. "I thought the dreams didn't…"

"Whoa, not me, Doc. As I said, I'm working a case. A young woman left her baby in a high chair, a jar of baby food on the counter, walked out of her house, down the street and jumped off the overpass."

"That's tragic. My god, Sam. You work these kinds of cases, no wonder you have nightmares."

Christian returned with a tray and set their plates on the table. "Smells good," Sam said. And it did. She suddenly wished she had asked for a half dozen of the mini quiche.

"Can I get you anything else?"

Sam watched a waitress breeze by with a loaf of heavenly smelling bread on a wooden cutting board. "What's that?"

"That's my lavender hazel nut bread. Would you like some?"

"Please." Sam was feeling the waistband of her Gaucho pants nipping in protest.

Once he left, Evan continued. "What exactly do you need to know, Sam?"

"The why would be good. Other than the most common—depression. But I have to tell you, my client's wife was not depressed."

"Some people are very good at hiding their depression. Was she on any kind of drugs?"

"No. Tox report came out clean."

"So she wasn't schizophrenic." Evan paused while a waitress set a cutting board on the table.

She set a small cup next to the cutting board. "This is hazelnut butter for the bread. Can I get you anything else?"

"Everything looks wonderful, Leesa. Thanks." Evan cut into the crab quiche and took a bite. He mulled over Sam's question, then pointed the fork at her. "People sometimes do something completely out of character and then suffer from such extreme remorse they commit suicide on an impulse."

"She wasn't haven't an affair, if that's what you are thinking." Sam savored the flaky pastry surrounding the quiche.

"Gambling problems? Maybe she lost their savings and was afraid to tell her husband."

"No again."

"And she wasn't recently diagnosed with some fatal disease that she didn't want to share with anyone."

"It's a puzzle, Doc. That's why I came to an expert." She slathered butter on a slice of bread and bit into it. "Ummm, is that marvelous or what."

"Christian is a fabulous cook. I thought he should have opened a restaurant in Chicago but he said the rental prices were exorbitant."

Sam shoved one empty plate away, then grabbed the orange popover. "What about a brain tumor? Wouldn't that alter someone's behavior?" Sam waved the idea off with her fork. "Scratch that. It didn't come up in the autopsy. She didn't have drugs in her system or tumors, and the family doctor they use said she was in perfect health."

"Postpartum depression," Evan said with a shrug. "That's the only thing it could be. How old was her baby?"

"Nine months."

"It's a possibility. And it isn't anything you would find in an autopsy."

"I don't know." Sam licked crumbs from her fingers and pushed her plate away with a sigh. Everything had tasted heavenly. She had gained forty pounds with Dillon and wasn't eager to see how much she was going to gain with twins. "Everything I have read about PPD says there are warning signs. You just don't wake up after nine months and decide you have zero feelings for your baby. She was pregnant again but was thrilled at the prospect."

"Some women become overwhelmed. What about that mother years ago who drowned each of her children in the bathtub. I believe the oldest was seven."

"I think that one was more getting back at her husband who wanted a divorce."

Evan set his empty plates on top of each other and shoved them to the side. Immediately a busboy appeared and swept up the stack. "What about family history? Do you know anything about her parents or grandparents?"

"Actually, no. Her husband did say they were each raised in foster homes so I assumed there weren't any extended family members. Now I have a similar case. This one a young woman drives to the beach, strips, takes time to fold her clothes neatly, then walks into the lake and drowns. A woman just one week from her wedding. Again, no drugs or abuse involved, and no explanation as to why."

"I think we may need more than fifty minutes."

26

"Detectives. You are back." The look on Connor Revere's face as he rose from his desk was more like "I thought I got rid of you for good."

"Just one more question." Jake pulled folded sheets of paper from his pocket and pressed them open. He handed the pages to Revere. It was a listing of employees who had been hired since the course opened. "You said you didn't do all the hiring. What about the firing? Anyone on this list who might have an axe to grind?"

Revere took his time studying the list, then shook his head. "Sorry, not one name sticks out. But in all honesty, everyone I have hired loves it here. Those who didn't work out received a small severance and they were thrilled with it. I haven't received any threatening phone calls nor has any former employee stormed in here waving a gun. You guys are barking up the wrong tree, as usual."

If Revere thought his brash comment was a hint the detectives were dismissed, he was sorely mistaken. "What about this one?" Jake pointed at a name on the page. "CiCi Tyler."

"Sounds like a stage name," Frank said with a chuckle.

"She," Revere cleared his throat. "Miss Tyler misread my casual, friendly demeanor as wanting more than an employer/employee relationship. She threatened to tell my wife, go to the press, walk naked down the street carrying a sign, the whole nine yards, if I didn't, well, you get the picture." Revere grimaced as though it was beneath him to carry on with the hired help, but his eyes bounced everywhere except on Jake's face. Jake was sure it was a case of unrequited love and something Revere would deny til hell froze over.

"She's a…uh…friend of the mayor's and he set her straight not to go through with her threats." Revere slapped the pages into Jake's hand. "Anything else I can help you with?"

◇◇

"The mayor's friend?" Frank chuckled as they walked toward the lobby. "Maybe the mayor is doing a little blackmail. Miss CiCi sounds like a pole dancer's name."

"And you would know this how?" A smile tugged at the corners of Jake's lips as they passed the entrance to the restaurant. Jake stopped abruptly, then took two slow steps back.

"Why are you stopping?"

Jake scanned the entrance, took another step back then shook his head. "Could swear I saw Sam."

27

Sam wasn't sure if she was making any headway. She could be wrong about Donna but she doubted it. The word destiny had not been her imagination when she had touched her purse. It was as clear then as the day she saw it displayed on Marti's phone.

She watched as the Ford Taurus drove out of the parking lot. It would have been just her luck to run into the two, and Jake wouldn't have rested until he dragged every suspicion out of her. Until she had more proof, she wasn't ready to tie any of the deaths into one neat package.

Once she was sure Jake and Frank were out of sight, Sam made her way down the aisle to the executive offices. Connor Revere spared little expense in building the club house. Men with that kind of money usually had women draping themselves at their feet. Although she didn't think Marti would have cheated on Forrest, there still had to be some connection between Marti and Donna. If they didn't work together, maybe they were in the same yoga class, or met on a walking trail. Forrest claimed Marti wasn't the type to hang out in bars, especially with a baby. But perhaps Forrest wasn't aware of everything about his wife prior to their marriage.

Angry voices came from the last office. Sam slowed her approach in order to eavesdrop.

"I told you to take care of it. How the hell is that taking care of it?"

"Watch your tone with me, Connor. I have been around the block a time or two."

Sam thought the second voice sounded canned, maybe from a speaker phone. And it did sound familiar.

"Maybe in the business world but definitely not in your present position. It appears you need a little training on how things are done around this town."

Sam heard a loud pound, then silence. Connor must have hung up on someone. She waited several seconds then knocked on the open door. "Hope I'm not interrupting." She let her eyes dance around the room to give the impression she expected to see someone else in the office.

Connor's mask of anger quickly dropped and he smiled as his gaze drifted down her body. He rose from his desk. "Not at all. Can I help you?"

Sam introduced herself and reached across the desk to shake his hand. She pulled the photo of Marti from her purse. "Do you recognize this woman?"

Connor Revere gave the photo a passing glance and shook his head. "I don't think so. Who is she?"

"She might have known Donna Oberweiss."

His eyes took on a hardened glare as he sank back into his chair. Whatever playboy image he attempted to display quickly dissolved. "Sorry, I don't follow. I didn't know the woman whose body was found on the golf course so I don't see how I would know this woman. Who is she?"

"She died about a couple months ago."

"And this should concern me how?"

Sam pulled out a chair and sat down. "Sorry, I probably should have started with this." She handed him her business card.

He studied the business card with a sigh. "It's not enough I have Homicide turning my life upside down, now I have a private consultant. Mayor Schuler never told me he had an underground investigative unit."

"I'm very above ground but it was Marti Johnson's husband who hired me."

"And how did you come to connect the two deaths?"

This was where it usually got sticky. Abby preferred Sam not advertise her gift. In her younger days, Sam liked to broadcast it just to see everyone's reaction. But she was learning to play her cards closer to the vest.

"Let's just say I have a hunch."

"A hunch." Revere's gaze traveled to her chest and on up to the third earring of beads and feathers brushing against her shoulder, finally resting on her eyes. Sam's attention was drawn to the framed photograph on the back credenza. "Your wife?"

Revere jerked behind him with a look of a man caught doing something illicit. "Yes."

"She's beautiful. I often wonder why a man who appears to have everything would risk it all by continually having affairs."

If his face got any redder, Sam would have to douse him with a fire hose. Revere flung Sam's business card and Marti's photo back at her. "I think we are done here, Miss Casey. I don't know either of these ladies and anything you think you know about me is none of your damn business. I think you know your way out."

It was no secret in Sam's mind why she was summoned to the emperor's castle. She could hear the screaming even while riding the elevator to the second floor. It drowned out the easy listening music droning through the speakers. The mirrored walls glistened. Exactly how long would mirrored walls in the elevator last at the Sixth Precinct?

The doors opened and she stepped out onto glistening oak flooring. The last time she was here the floors were carpeted. Chief Dennis Murphy must have made sure he blew through his remaining budget before the new mayor took office.

Ruth, Murphy's secretary, pressed her lips together and gave a light shake of her head. The door to Murphy's office was open, something the mayor must have wanted so the entire staff could hear his rant. An assistant, who looked college-age, was busy cutting out newspaper articles, probably for Murphy's scrapbook. An intern was standing at the copier pretending to examine something that had spewed off the printer. Sam guessed she didn't want to actually use the printer and miss overhearing the argument.

"I don't give a damn what the City Council says. I want that bitch fired."

Sam guessed that wonderful voice belonged to Mayor Jefferson-not-Jeffrey Schuler, the same voice she had heard streaming from Connor Revere's speaker phone. And Sam was sure she was the subject of the conversation.

"How dare she intimidate close friends."

"Contributors," Sam mouthed for Ruth's benefit. Ruth tried to hide her smile. Since the day Schuler took office he had made few friends among the hired help. Rumor had it he had already lost two secretaries. He was demanding, egotistical, and already campaigning for re-election. His current term was only to fill the remaining term of the ailing Mayor Jenkins.

Ruth was a no-nonsense protector of her boss. Sam was surprised Murphy didn't have a cover girl for a secretary. Instead he chose brains over beauty and loyalty over a fashion plate. Ruth wore sensible shoes, comfortable clothes, and very little makeup. Because Murphy and Sam had always displayed a volatile relationship, Ruth had never been too friendly toward Sam, until Sam saved his life.

"Do it now. Have I made myself clear?" Schuler straightened and pulled back, the haughty look having been a practiced move since winning the election. Murphy invaded Schuler's personal space, blinking slowly. Schuler was boring him. The mayor took the hint and stormed out of Murphy's office.

Sam smiled like a cat who had just cornered its prey. The comb-over Schuler had eliminated during the campaign was slowly growing back. And although he had trimmed down for campaign photos, he was eating at the best restaurants lately and developing a paunch. Schuler stopped abruptly and jabbed a thick finger in the air. "Your days are numbered, little lady. You obviously don't know how things work around here."

"SAM!" Murphy bellowed from his doorway. "Get in here. What the hell possessed you to badger Collin Revere?" Murphy closed the door behind her but kept up his tirade.

Sam sighed and took a seat in front of the desk while Murphy continued his rant. "I heard the elevator doors close," Sam said.

"Good. I was beginning to get a scratchy throat," Murphy said in a normal tone. "What an ass."

"Another election year is coming up."

"No thanks. Been there, done that." He poured two cups of coffee from the carafe on his desk and slid one across the desk toward Sam."

Sam and Murphy had a love-hate relationship, fueled by the unfortunate close association Sam had with Murphy's predecessor. Connelley had better connections to snag the police chief job first and had used his goddaughter to dig up dirt on his competition. But mummified remains found in an aging hotel turned out to be Gina Barlucci, a former girlfriend of Murphy's from over thirty years ago. He had been a suspect in her murder until Sam found the real killer.

The case exposed a different side of Dennis Murphy. Although his animosity toward Chief Connelley had been real, as well as his distrust of Sam who had been her godfather's main "spy," they had come to a mutual understanding and admiration when Murphy realized Sam was the only one who could clear him of murder charges.

Murphy and Sam also had a mutual disdain for Jefferson Schuler. He was clever, managing to hide all of his suspected illegal transactions. No one was better than Murphy in playing the game. For now, Schuler was careful but it was just a matter of time.

"So you don't think the two cases are connected?"

"Oh no, I do think they are," Sam replied. "I'm just not sure yet how Connor Revere is connected. What I would like to do is look into some of our past suicide cases, to see if they are connected to Marti's."

"Is this one of your hunches?"

"You could say that."

They sipped their coffee for a few minutes until Murphy caught Sam looking at a picture of Murphy with his wife and daughter. "Things are getting better. Donna and our daughter actually went to Florida to visit Rafe and his Aunt Sonya."

"How is Rafe doing?" During the previous case, Murphy had learned that he had a son. Rafe was a former cop himself but now ran a successful business locating missing people. One of the missing cases had been his mother. The search brought him to Chasen Heights and involved him in the case of the body found at the Embers Hotel. Posing as a reporter, Rafe had investigated Murphy as a possible suspect. Murphy hadn't known that Rafe was his son.

"Really good. Actually Rafe and Deanna clicked. She is a whiz at computers and Rafe would rather be on the road chasing down leads so he is hiring her to handle his web site. She's going to move down there next month. She'll be living with him and his aunt. I understand they have a fabulous mansion."

"He hasn't asked to see you?"

"We're taking it slow. I'm sure it was difficult for him to hire Deanna. Although he appreciated her talents, he also wanted to make sure she wasn't some spy I was sending down there to keep tabs on him. I was thinking of helping Deanna with her move."

"You should. I think he realizes now that you were as much kept in the dark about him as he was of you. Take a list of missing persons from our database."

He looked around the office as if there were stacks of work to be done. Actually, Murphy was even neater than Jake. Whatever working files he had must be hidden in his credenza. "It would be hard to get away. Meetings, press conferences." He let his voice drop, aware he wasn't even doing a good job of convincing himself.

"All those can be rescheduled. When's the last time you took off?"

"When I was in the hospital. I doubt you could have forgotten since you were there, too."

"Perfect excuse. You had a relapse and need more time off, something the Florida sun could cure."

He flicked a hand through the air, cutting off further discussion of the topic. "I would have Ruth set you up in an empty office to go through cases in the computer but someone would snitch to Schuler. I think your best bet is to go down to Archives. It's quieter there and people won't be looking over your shoulder like they would at the Sixth."

"Schuler has spies at the Sixth?"

"There are ass-kissers everywhere." A whisper of a smile played at the corners of his mouth. "Course, I have my spies watching his spies."

Sam's coffee cup hovered inches from her mouth. "You have spies at the Sixth?" Then she gave that thought a couple seconds. "Of course you do. Who are they?"

Few played the political game better than Murphy. He was even better than former Police Chief Don Connelley had ever been on his best day. Murphy pulled on the sleeves of his four figure suit. His eyes were cold and all business. He could turn off the charm faster than a debutante on a disastrous blind date. "Now why would I want to reveal their names?"

"More than one," Sam deduced. "Or do you have the entire floor wired for sound and video?"

Murphy stood, ending their friendly repartee. "Go to work." He walked to the door, opened it while yelling, "This is your last warning."

Sam rolled her eyes and whispered, "You only wish."

"Shall I call Security, Chief?" Ruth asked.

"No need. I'm personally escorting her out of the building." As though on command, the elevator doors opened. Once the doors closed Murphy hammered the button for the basement, the bowels of the building where the archived files were kept.

"Don't you get tired of all the acting?" Sam asked.

"Who says I'm acting?"

28

"This is it?" Sam stared at a small cubicle in the corner of the reception area. Privacy rooms at banks where people haul their safe deposit boxes for inspection were larger than this cubicle. She felt the walls closing in on her.

"Sorry, your majesty. But the west wing of the palace is being renovated," Murphy said.

"It's about the size of my bathroom."

"I have seen the bathrooms in your house, missy. Quit complaining. You've got access to the files and a computer. What more could you want?"

"Cookies?"

"Sure. I'll go down to the kitchen and whip up a batch." Murphy walked over to the counter and spoke with a relic of a man dressed in a shirt and tie. Sam already sized him up as divorced or a widower. His shirt could use a good pressing and the tie had remnants of a previous meal.

"Charlie will take care of you. Do you know Charlie Buckmeister?" Murphy made a quick introduction. "You have two hours before his break when one of Schuler's minions fills in. There is a vending machine down the hall if you need munchies."

"Wow, Mister Chef with the words."

Murphy wasn't smiling. "I can save you a little time. On average there have been less than ten suicides in any given year. You can eliminate the two police officers and one Desert Storm veteran." Sam opened her mouth to remind him of his own edict not to "assume" anything, but he held up one hand and said, "Two hours." He turned and marched down the hall as she yelled "thanks" at his back.

Sam tossed her sweater coat on a chair, pulled her hair up in a banana clip and strolled over to the marred and chipped counter. Charlie shuffled over to the counter and plopped down a short stack of folders.

"Okay, little lady. You heard the man." He returned to his desk and snapped open the latest issue of *Law Enforcement* magazine. That was when Sam remembered Charlie was a retired police officer who didn't know what to do with himself after retiring.

She thanked Charlie and carried the folders to the desk in the cubicle. Once settled, she quickly separated by gender. Women didn't normally commit suicide, unless it was an accidental drug overdose or carbon monoxide poisoning. Women usually avoided using any form of suicide that would mar their appearance. Knives, guns, even jumping off of an overpass, are not normal. Granted, some have slit their wrists but few people knew exactly where to slice or how. For the city to have two suicides by women within three months is unheard of. Even hanging wasn't a suicide choice by women unless it was accidental, like autoerotic asphyxia. Teens were different. Luke's sister felt bullied and despondent. Hanging was an easier choice than trying to get her hands on a gun or keep her hands from shaking long enough to slice her wrists. Carrie's sister might have been despondent and gone the drowning route, but Carrie hadn't seen anything but excitement from her twin on her impending marriage. Something unusual was definitely going on.

She scoured the files closely. It was a quick process of elimination. Some elderly, frail and sickly, had taken an overdose of pills. She found the three cases Murphy had mentioned. One case of murder suicide did involve a woman. Sam scanned through the police and M.E. reports on the mother who had driven her car into Lake Michigan with two young children in the back strapped to their car seats.

Sam checked the clock on the wall. Thirty minutes left. She opened another folder. A thirty-year-old mother from Michigan City had checked into the Ritz. Another case of an overdose but this one didn't have anything to do with a failed marriage. She had a debilitating, incurable illness. The suicide note was in her handwriting and explained how she didn't want to be a burden anymore to her family. Suicide notes. Not everyone left one but when police couldn't find one that usually raised alarm bells. Neither Marti nor Carly had left one.

Sam grabbed the next folder and opened it. A stack of photos were in an envelope. Sam poured them out and studied the picture of a forest preserve. A dried creek was in the background, trees were skeletal, dried leaves scattered in mounds. A column of icy fingers crawled up Sam's spine. The image from her dream suddenly came into focus. An officer stood near an object hanging from a limb. The object looked like a piece of dark taffy that had been stretched to within a few feet of the ground. The officer obviously stood there to give some gauge of measurement. She looked closer at the dark taffy, then pulled back. Sam read the police report. The seven-foot object was a five-and-a-half foot tall female who had been dead at least six months. The dense foliage had hidden the body, and the remote location prevented any detection of a decomposing body. Upon death the skin develops blisters and accumulates liquid. Eventually the skin begins to slip from the body and gravity does the rest.

Nina Logesta had been a casino dealer at the River Queen Casino. According to the investigator's report from a year ago, co-workers thought she had moved to Las Vegas. Nina's gambling problem had plunged her into debt and jeopardized her friendships and family relationships.

There hadn't been any witnesses that day, not one person saw her walking into the preserves. Her car had not been found nor a purse. A driver's license was found in one pocket and twenty six dollars in the other. By all indications, it certainly appeared to be a suicide. That section of the forest was not a common walking trail. Although the deceased was dressed casual, she didn't wear comfortable walking shoes. Police could only assume she had parked her car off the shoulder of the road, an isolated place just ripe for thieves.

Sam checked the clock again. Five more minutes. As she gathered the folders, one of Nina's photos skirted onto the table. Sam picked it up, then paused. If Nina had known what she was going to look like in her coffin, would she have picked this method? Maybe she probably had counted on being found quickly. Why wasn't there a suicide note?

Sam scanned the medical examiner's report. He estimated that Nina had been dead for close to six months. Sam checked the date that the body had been found. Memorial Day. There wasn't any need for her to search newspapers, as Doctor Collier suggested. Sam didn't start having the transformer dreams in July. They started in May. Alex had brought in the flag after Memorial Day.

Sam flipped through the file to see the name of the detective who had worked the case. Sal Marino at Precinct Three. She vaguely remembered Sal from Murphy's congratulatory dinner during the time of her suspension. He thought of himself as Serpico, but she remembered him as arrogant. He prided himself in having the highest closing record at the Third. Frank had once commented that Sal was known as *grab and slap*. Grab only the easy cases and slap the file closed on them as quickly as possible. Cops like that usually missed something. What had he missed in this case?

29

"To what do I owe the honor of your presence?" His smile was more than warm. When the smile widened she could swear several of the pearly whites twinkled like a toothpaste commercial. William Borden Junior was one of the owners of the River Queen Casino and resembled a young Robert Redford. Sam had met him during a previous case involving a homicide in the casino. He sandwiched her hand between his two, then kissed the top.

Sam slowly slid her hand from his. "Always the charmer." Although Sam conveyed a bit of standoffishness, she had taken great care in dressing this morning. Her black boots hit above the knee. Cable-stitch black tights showed off the curve of her legs under a blue and black tunic top that hit mid-thigh. No banana clip today. Her hair was wild and carefree in a controlled way. It took time to get her natural curly hair tamed.

"I wanted to ask you about a former employee, Nina Logesta."

William winced. "Sad. What kind of information do you need?" He sat behind his desk and pressed the intercom. A sexy voice oozed through the phone. "Maxie, can you bring me the personnel file on Nina Logesta. She'll be in the archives." William punched the phone off.

Sam imagined his secretary to be a leggy model, probably blonde, wearing something that showed off a lot of cleavage.

"I also ordered some snacks for us." He stood and motioned toward the conference table where two covered silver trays had been placed.

Sam had to admit she was getting tired of eating. "I trust you aren't on a yogurt kick."

"I remember you have a sweet tooth, Sam." He joined her at the table as there was a knock on the door. Maxie entered and Sam gave herself a mental pat on the back. Maxie was everything she imagined.

"Thanks, Maxie." Once she left, Junior lifted the lids on the trays to reveal melons and strawberries on one and croissants and pastries on another.

Sam thought it was only polite to eat since he went through all the trouble. She wasn't sure what to eat first. She stabbed at the melon, grapes and strawberries. Then selected small cream puffs in the shape of swans, a brownie, and an éclair. Across the table Junior was grinning. "Sorry. Guess I'm being a bit of a pig." *Diet be damned.* The babies are hungry.

"I love a woman with a healthy appetite."

Sam opened the personnel file and read while they ate in silence. Nina had been hired as a change girl. When the casino went the way of slot machines spitting out paper vouchers vs money, Nina took dealer classes the casino offered and became one of their best poker dealers.

"What does debt risk mean?" Sam noticed all Junior did was drink coffee while she was shoving down cream puffs like they were M & Ms. She wiped her mouth with a napkin and willed her hands not to reach for another bite of food.

"Nina was one of our whales. She was a high-roller here for a couple years. Played only high stakes baccarat. When she was on a winning streak she could hit us big. But when she got on a losing streak, she just kept going down until she was into us for a considerable amount of money. She lost her house, her marriage and her job at a law firm."

"And you allowed her to work here?"

"Her way of paying us back. We have done it a number of times. Gives the person an income and we withhold a portion each week as her repayment of debt. She turned out to be one of our best dealers."

"How long ago was she divorced?" Sam studied Nina's picture. She had been attractive in a Meg Ryan sort of way, more girl next door. Blonde with brown eyes and a small scar above her eyebrow.

"Not long after she started gambling here. I usually don't involve myself with the hiring part of the business but the debt risks I do. I need to find out exactly what kind of person I'm putting behind the bankrolls. As long as they make it to work every day, show an effort to do the best job possible, and adhere to the requirement to attend gamblers anonymous, then they are fine in my book."

"She was going to gamblers anonymous?" This surprised Sam. She thought the police report said her money problem was the reason for her suicide.

"Yes. And she had been clean for two years. Hadn't set foot in any of the casinos."

"How can you be sure?"

"Her sponsor gave us monthly reports." Junior flipped through the pages, then unclipped a business card and handed it to Sam. "That's his name. Jason Biersman."

"Did Nina get along with everyone here?" Sam wrote down Jason's name and phone number, then handed the card back to Junior.

"That I don't know. Unless I see a complaint or a write up of incidences, I would have no way of knowing. And as you can see from her file, she hasn't had any such write-ups."

Sam thanked him for the information and the food and left. Ten minutes later she was seated in her car in the casino parking lot re-reading the investigator's report. Nina had shared an apartment with Fiona Vasquez, another employee of Jasper and Kinard law firm. When she called the firm she was told Fiona had called in sick. Good. Sam would rather talk to her at home.

Fiona's apartment was in the large party complex on the west side of town. The Meadows boasted five buildings with four hundred apartments and a large recreation center available for rent by tenants. The police log was filled with reports of rowdiness, gun shots, suspected drug sales, fights, and domestic abuse. It was party central on weekends.

When interviewed, Fiona claimed that Nina had stolen money from her to support her gambling addiction. They had fought and Fiona had kicked her out. Yet Nina had never cleaned out her clothes or other belongings. All of the furniture belonged to Fiona so Nina only had clothes and a few personal items.

Sam checked the address on the side of the building. From the outside the Meadows looked like a nice place to live. Considerable money had been spent on landscaping. Several workers were busy planting yellow and purple mums around the entrances and what looked to be the rec building. She had expected to see screens hanging from the windows but they weren't. Doors weren't hanging by their hinges nor were there overflowing garbage bins or bicycles left lying on the lawn. Graffiti was non-existent.

Sam had no reason not to believe Junior about his employee. After all, she spent more time at the casino than she did in her apartment, so why did Fiona give the investigator a different story? Could Nina have hidden her addiction that well, especially when she worked in a business where all kinds of money could be hers for the taking?

Apartment 401B was on the fourth floor. Sam found an elevator but decided to take the stairs and work off all of the cream puffs. By the third floor she was kicking herself for not taking the elevator. By taking the stairs Sam was able to see that the interior of the building wasn't as pristine as the exterior. Carpeting was worn and the walls marred as though movers weren't careful when carrying furniture. Rather than painting entire walls, it appeared that only patchwork was done. Baseboards were chipped and hallways didn't appear to be vacuumed on a daily basis.

Sam found the apartment and put her ear to the door. Silence. She rapped several times. A door creaked behind her and Sam turned to find a gray-haired woman peering out, her hair up in rollers. The door quickly closed. Sam knocked again, a little louder and a little longer this time.

"Who the hell are you?"

Sam turned to see a dark-haired woman in skin tight running slacks and a halter top charging off the elevator. She was sweating as though she had just biked a five-mile marathon. "Fiona Vasquez?"

"Who wants to know?"

So this is how it's going to be, Sam thought. *Wonderful.* Sam held out her business card. Fiona glanced at it and flicked her gaze back to Sam.

"What's this about?"

"Can we talk inside?"

"No. Here is fine. I don't plan on you being here long."

"Nina Logesta. What can you tell me about her?"

"She was a lying bitch and she's dead. What else do you want to know?"

Sam wondered how Nina lived with her as long as she did. "You told the police Nina still had a gambling problem but that isn't what my contact at the casino tells me nor does her sponsor concur." Sam hadn't called the sponsor yet but doubted he would counter what he had already reported to Junior.

Fiona narrowed her eyes so much Sam thought she had fallen asleep. "What is this about? Nina's been gone for a year already. I don't have anything more to say." She pulled her keys from a small pocket on the front of her pants and aimed it for the lock.

The outfit Fiona wore would make even Jackie drool. It was high end as were the running shoes. There was a diamond tennis bracelet on her wrist and three gold rings on her fingers. Sam was beginning to draw a pretty good picture. "So if I talk to your landlord he will confirm that Nina was the one in arrears for rent?"

"What the hell are you accusing me of?"

"Where are all of Nina's belongings? Did you keep her cell phone?"

"Goodwill got the clothes and the cell phone was out of contract. I have nothing more to say so get lost." The key was in the lock and the door slammed before Sam could even utter another word. She stood staring at the door when she heard the apartment door behind her squeak open and a "pssst" sound. Sam turned to see the head of rollers. The woman motioned for Sam to come in.

Nothing like nosy neighbors to give you the full scoop. "Nina was a very nice young lady," Flo said as she poured two cups of coffee. Sam didn't think she could fit another ounce of anything in her stomach but to be polite she had said yes to the coffee. The rollers in Flo's head were a hard green plastic and looked painful to sleep in. The room was doilies and afghans, everything you might expect in an elderly woman's apartment. The only thing missing...Sam no sooner thought it then a burly tabby cat came prancing around the corner, took one look at Sam, lifted its nose as though catching a scent of Poco, then scurried out of the room. "I sprained my ankle one year and Nina would call me from work and ask if I needed anything from the store. She'd do my shopping. Never made me feel like I was imposing."

"You wouldn't happen to still have her phone number, would you?" Sam was hoping Beast could do some magic with just the phone number and not need the SIM card.

"Why yes." Flo rummaged around in the top drawer of an antique secretary and pulled out an address book. "Here we go." Flo read off the number and Sam wrote it on a notepad.

"Why would Nina room with Fiona if they didn't get along?"

"Oh, they were the best of friends. Both were receptionists at that law firm. Nina had already been divorced. She told me all about her addiction, was pretty open with her past. But their problems started when Fiona's boyfriend dumped her for Nina. Being the considerate friend that she was, Nina didn't want anything to do with him because it hurt Fiona. But Fiona still blamed Nina for the breakup." Flo set a cloth bag on her lap and proceeded to take the green rollers out of her hair. Sam winced as she saw the Velcro pulling on strands of gray hair.

"Would Nina have told you if she had started gambling again?"

"Absolutely. She was so proud of herself that she was clean for two whole years. Did you see how Fiona dresses? She tries to live like a princess on a pauper's salary. Nina paid her share of rent like clockwork. I told her she should give her share directly to the managing office but the lease was in Fiona's name so the check had to come from Fiona. Nina of course had given Fiona cash but Fiona spent the rent money on god knows what."

"How does Fiona afford the rent by herself?"

Flo stopped torturing her hair and glared at Sam with a knowing smile creasing her lips. "Let's just say there are a selection of men coming and going through that apartment at all hours of the night and day. If you found her home today it's not because she's sick. She told me before she is just one sugar daddy away from moving into a dream condo on Chicago's lakefront. Right, and I'm one curtsy away from Buckingham Palace."

30

"Got some action on Donna's credit card at the ATM on Caulfield." Jake shoved the tape into the player. "We got the tape from the bank so we should have a pretty good picture of the person using it."

The conference room used to be Jake's and Frank's offices and was now equipped with state of the art equipment. Captain Robinson stood in front of the monitor as though threatening it not to give them a suspect.

Frank pressed the stop button and froze the image of a skinny guy, hair hanging down past his eyebrows. He jerked as though wired up on something. The man punched a few buttons, then his eyes lit up as the machine spit out money. "He took three hundred dollars, according to the bank. He then tried for a couple hundred more and got that, but Donna had a five hundred dollar limit on her withdrawals."

Jake used the second monitor and shoved in the tape while Frank printed out a photo of the thief. The second tape from the camera off the building showed the parking lot. "We might be able to catch his license plate." The camera showed a rail thin man hurrying to a rusted pickup truck. Jake zoomed in on the plate number. It was a clear image. Robinson jotted down the number and lumbered out of the room.

"Why the hell wouldn't he have used the ATM card immediately before Donna's body was found?" Frank popped the tape out of the machine.

Jake shrugged. "Maybe he was passed out in a gutter somewhere and forgot he had it."

Within ten minutes the police had located the pickup truck parked outside of the Honeydew Drop Inn. Frank parked in a side street in clear view of the truck. The bar was only a couple blocks from the remnants of the original downtown district and around the corner from the unemployment office.

Two brown-skinned men with distrusting eyes glared at them from the listing stoop of a halfway house. Two more were seated on a bench under the overhang of a wrap-around porch. Although their jackets hid their guns, the detectives weren't fooling anyone.

They entered the bar and walked in as though they belonged there. Daylight streamed in through the window haze as six heads swiveled from bar stools. Two patrons quickly stabbed out their cigarettes since smoking was illegal in bars and restaurants. The bartender was a sack of sagging skin and white hair and appeared to size them up before they stepped less than four feet into the establishment. He straightened and kept his hands flat on the bar.

Once his eyes adjusted to the dim light, Jake quickly scanned the faces at the bar but didn't see their guy. Davey Karston was twenty-three years old but you wouldn't know it by his photograph. He looked more on the forty-year-old side. According to the records, he still lived with his parents, had been unemployed for three years, failed a drug test at his last place of employment, and spent five days in jail last year on a drunk and disorderly charge.

One patron was slouched in a back booth nursing a beer in one hand with two empties sitting next to him. Frank looked at Jake and grinned. By the looks of all the beer bottles on the bar, it appeared Davey had been buying a round or two for the house.

As soon as Davey caught sight of them strolling up to the booth, he started scrambling out like a puppy on a slick floor. He couldn't quite get his hands and feet to grab hold.

"Where you going, Davey?" Frank asked. "Looks like you been spending a little money."

Up close, Davey was a scared kid but worse for wear. Drugs and alcohol had ravaged his body. His clothes hung on his frame and were in need of a washing.

Jake grabbed fistfuls of fabric and hauled him out of the booth. He didn't feel much heavier than Dillon. "We need to have a little talk downtown, Davey."

"I didn't do nothin'," Davey stammered.

"Thanks for the beers, Davey," one patron yelled.

Davey looked up as they walked in. Jake wasn't sure how Davey fit into the scenario but he was certain he didn't have the strength to kill someone. He barely weighed over one hundred twenty soaking wet.

"Thought you could use something to drink." Frank set a bottle of water on the table. "Maybe it can help dilute that beer so you can think clearly." They had already let him sit and stew for an hour to help him sober up.

"Tha-thanks." Davey grabbed the bottle and twisted off the cap.

Frank took a seat across from the kid while Jake hefted one cheek on the table next to Davey and glared at him. "Pretty nice of you to buy those boys a few drinks," Frank said. "Where did you come up with the money? We know you don't have a job."

"Uhhh, unemployment checks."

Frank smiled and shook his head. "Those ran out last year."

"I do odd jobs for cash."

"Like what?"

Davey's eyes drifted from Frank to Jake. Jake had shoved the sleeves up on his Henley shirt revealing forearms larger than Davey's neck. Jake flexed his hands as though they were itching to wrap around something. Davey swallowed hard.

"I clean up around the bar. Duke pays me, uhh, off the books. Just a few bucks here and there."

"Want to empty your pockets for me, Davey?" Frank smiled all friendly like. "Just put everything out here on the table."

"Uhhh, do I have to?" Davey's eyes drifted to Jake's hands, the fingers still doing their flex dance.

"Right here." Frank rapped his knuckles on a space in the middle of the table. "Lighten your load a little."

Davey reached into his left pocket and pulled out a comb, driver's license and some change. "Don't I get a lawyer or somethin'?"

"You're not under arrest, Davey. Now the other pocket." Frank flashed him another friendly smile. "Don't be shy about all that extra money you were paid under the table."

Davey slowly reached into his right pocket. "You aren't gonna take it from me, are you?"

"You'll get it all back."

Out came a wad of bills, a receipt, and a card. Davey tried to pull the card back but Jake's hand whipped out and slammed on top of Davey's so fast that the man yelped.

"Not so fast." Jake plied Davey's fingers from the pile.

Frank pulled the contents from the table and counted the money, separating it by denomination. "You've got around four hundred dollars here, Davey. That's a lot of sweeping. And what's this?" Frank turned the ATM receipt around and read it. Then he picked up the ATM card and read it, flicked his gaze to Davey, then back to the card. "You sure don't look like a Donna. Where'd you get the card, Davey?"

Beads of sweat started forming on Davey's forehead, making a lazy trickle down the sides of his face. He swiped at the beads with shaking hands.

"How about we let you meet Donna, Davey?" Jake clamped a hand on Davey's shoulder. The man moaned and slouched as though the weight of Jake's grasp was crushing.

"What do you mean?"

Frank scooped the contents of Davey's pockets away from the man. "Donna's down in the morgue, Davey. She's been dead for about a couple weeks so why don't you tell us where you found the ATM card."

Jake released his grip and Davey sat up a little straighter. "I found it on a sidewalk...uh...outside the Jewel store." Davey's hair started to cling to his forehead.

Jake grabbed a chair and slammed it next to Davey's. He sat down and leaned in close. "I don't think so, Davey. See, I don't like it when I'm being lied to and I HATE to waste my time running around chasing false leads. I bet if we compare the footprints found near the body with the imprint of your shoes, we can prove you were there. How did you kill her, Davey?"

"WHAT?!" Davey tried to jump up but Jake jerked on his arm. "I... she was dead when I found her. The card was in her pocket."

"And you didn't think to call the police?" Frank feigned shock. "A young woman dumped in the woods. She could have still been alive."

"How would I know? She wasn't breathing and her eyes were open."

"So you waited til things cooled off before you used the card." Frank started stacking the bills into one pile. "Pretty smart on your part."

Davey beamed and nodded his head in agreement. "I learned that from a buddy." He stopped when Jake leaned in closer.

"If you didn't dump the body, who did?" Jake checked his watch. "Did I tell you I hate to be late for dinner? Talk quick." He clasped his hands and squeezed. The sound of his knuckles cracking made Davey wince.

"What do you want to hear? I was walking at the first crack of daylight."

"Be more specific." Jake checked his watch again.

"Uhh, a Sunday, cause I heard church bells ringing. But don't ask me the exact date. Wait." He closed his eyes and tapped his fingers as though counting. "Last Sunday I was home carving a pumpkin for my mom, so it had to be the Sunday before that."

"Up early or getting in late?" Frank asked.

"Well," he grinned and then stopped himself. "Guess I was trying to walk it off before going home."

Frank checked the file folder in front of him. "According to our records, you live on the other side of town. What were you doing by the golf course?"

Davey's eyes shifted along the length of the table, then the walls, as though looking for answers. He ran a hand through greasy hair and slouched further in the chair.

Frank lifted his eyebrows as if to ask, "what do you want to do?"

Davey may not have had the strength to kill the victim but he was at the scene of the crime. Jake stood and walked over to the mirror behind Frank where he could stare into Davey's eyes but the man kept staring at the table. "What we do know is Davey was at the crime scene. What we don't know is if he stumbled on the body or helped the killer unload it from the car."

"No, no. It was like I said. I stumbled onto the body. All I did was steal the card but you got all the money back, as well as the lady's card there."

Frank grabbed the bills and fanned them near his ear. "Feels a little short. Not all the money is here, Davey."

"I can make it up. Just give me a little time but I can't go back to prison." His beady eyes pleaded as he started to rock in his chair.

Jake pushed away from the wall. "I don't have time for this. Either he knows something or he doesn't. Let him think about it overnight." Jake reached for the door handle.

Davey jumped up. "Wait, wait."

They waited.

"I can show you where I was when he dumped her."

Jake stepped away from the door. "You were there when he dumped the body?"

Davey bobbed his head. "Yeah."

31

Sam sat in her Jeep in the parking lot of Precinct Three. Since leaving Flo's apartment she had re-read the police report on Nina Logesta and couldn't believe the investigating officers had never questioned Flo much less knocked on her door. Even when she offered them information, according to Flo, Detective Sal Marino had dismissed her. Marino's partner at the time was Reese Banks. Although she didn't know Marino, she could recognize Banks. He played racquetball with Andy Brainard, or at least he used to when she had worked at the Sixth. He was the only guy with a full head of white hair at the age of thirty. He also drove a yellow Charger, the vehicle that was parked next to her Jeep. A quick phone call to Andy confirmed that Reese was no longer partnered with Marino. He was now with the swat team.

At fifteen minutes after, a cluster of cops erupted from the side door. Sam could spot the full head of white hair. Reese was walking with two uniformed police. He had a gym bag in one hand. As he approached his car, Sam pressed the button for the passenger window to roll down. Reese caught the action and peered in.

"Hey, Reese. Gotta minute?"

Reese looked puzzled for a few moments, his eyes glancing at her legs, then her face. "Must be my lucky day."

Sam leaned over and pushed the door open. "Sam Casey. I used to work at the Sixth with Andy. Climb in."

Reese looked around the lot for some reason, then climbed in.

"I need to ask you a few questions about the Nina Logesta case." The file folder was propped up on the center console.

"I'm not in that department anymore."

"I know, but you worked the case. Or I should say Marino worked the case and you tagged along."

Not quite the way Sam meant for it to sound. Whatever trust she had hoped to cobble together was starting to spring leaks. "I know Marino's type. *Grab and Slap*. Isn't that what they call him?" Reese still didn't seem convinced. He was sticking to the code of not speaking ill of a partner. "I'm working another suicide case to see if there are any similarities."

"How did you get involved?"

Sam handed him her business card. "Captain Robinson asked me to look into one of the cases which led me to others." She opened the file folder with copies of the Logesta investigation. "Can you tell me why Florence Dempsey, the neighbor across the hall, wasn't interviewed?"

"Marino didn't think it was necessary. Miss Logesta's roommate confirmed the deceased's state of mind. She was working at the casino as a way to pay back money she owed them. She did have a gambling problem."

"DID is the operative word. I have it from the casino owner that Nina had been attending her GA program and doing great. Fiona claimed Nina owed her three months rent. Nina had paid in cash so couldn't prove it but, according to a neighbor, Fiona had expensive taste in clothing and jewelry."

Reese remained quiet. Either he was digesting everything or was waiting to hear more. "Fiona is a very beautiful woman. Did Sal have a reputation for getting overly friendly with witnesses? Is that why you transferred to another department?"

Reese pressed his lips together. He didn't have to say anything. Sam could read it all on his face. "Maybe you can just nod."

"I don't think I should be talking to you." Reese opened the door and climbed out. He didn't slam the door and didn't tell her to go to hell. Sam wondered how long until word made it back to Sal Marino.

"Here." Davey walked off of the shoulder of the road and into a wooded area running along the side of the golf course. "I was a little, uh, tired."

"You mean buzzed?" Frank asked.

"Well." Davey's head did a little bob back and forth. "Kinda. Anyway, my truck wouldn't start so some guy gave me a ride but he had to make a stop first to pick up some money."

"What time was this?" Jake knew bars had two o'clock liquor licenses but what time the bar closed and what time the patrons staggered out were two different things.

"Right at closing because the guy offering the ride had to leave. He was headed to Chicago to make a score." He gulped, aware he might have just blurted out a possible drug deal. "I didn't want to go to Chicago, I wanted to go home. So when he stopped at a light, I climbed out."

"You were going to walk home." Jake looked skeptical. "That would have been about a three mile walk for you."

"That's why I had to sit down for a few minutes to sleep it off." He slogged through the underbrush to an oak tree and plopped down. "See here? These are my cigarette butts. I had a couple cigarettes while I thought about what to do next. That's when I heard a car coming down this back road."

The two detectives ambled over to where Davey sat. Frank bent down to inspect the brand of cigarette. He held it up, pulled out a zip lock bag from his pocket and dropped it in. "Same brand we found by the body," he told Jake. And the same brand Revere smoked.

"What kind of car?" Jake asked.

"How the hell should I know? It was dark out, he didn't have his headlights on. The car crept up, like it didn't want to make any noise. I watched as it kept crawling on the side of the road for another fifty or so feet. It stopped by that big tree up there, the bent one that leans over the road. I could see it from here."

"Did the interior lights come on when he opened the door?" Jake imagined what visibility would be like at two or three in the morning in a moonlit sky.

"No lights. Couldn't see him. He opened the back door and dragged something out. I could see him lift something, walk further into the woods. Then I couldn't see a damn thing other than a figure walking back to the car empty handed. He shut the back door, climbed into the car and took off."

"Did he turn his headlights on after that?" Frank asked.

"A couple blocks away."

"How long did you wait until you checked out what he dumped?" Jake took a step back and gauged how far away they were from the dump site.

"I waited til I couldn't see the taillights anymore. Then I kinda crawled over there on my hands and knees. Wasn't sure what I was going to find. Practically fell over her."

"So you checked the pockets for money and didn't think to call the police." Jake moved toward the dump site while Davey scrambled to his feet. "Show me."

Davey wrapped bony arms around himself as though attempting to hold everything in. His eyes jerked left and right, and if Jake didn't know better he'd guess Davey was wondering how far he could get if he made a run for it. Jake lifted his jacket and placed a hand on his gun, a movement not missed by the skinny suspect.

Davey looked toward the road where the bent tree was. "Right about here."

"Close enough." Although the crime scene tape was gone, there was no mistaking the trampled ground where all of the investigators and police had worked. "Then what," Jake barked.

"I, uh, checked her pockets."

"Before or after you rolled her over?" Frank asked. "Was she laying face up or down when you found her?"

"Face up. I found the ATM card in her back pocket, but that was all. You can't pin me for anything else taken from her."

"How did you get home in your condition?" With all the talk of cigarettes, Jake was having a weak moment. He pulled one from his shirt pocket and lit up.

"Well, I uh…" Davey's face couldn't get any redder if he had been left in the sun for three days. "I was really tired."

"Ewwwww, gad. You slept next to a dead body?" Frank took a step back from Davey. "Were you out of your fuckin' mind?"

"It was cold out and she was still, you know, warm."

"Christ. Let's get him back to the precinct." Jake placed a hand on the bony shoulder and gave it a shove.

32

The next morning Sam called Beast on the ride over to meet Jackie. She gave him Nina's cell phone number. Without the SIM card he would have to contact the phone company and wait for their report on the last calls made and received from Nina's phone. He promised to get something to her by the end of the day, if not sooner.

It wasn't difficult to miss Jackie. She was an abstract watercolor in a lime green cape and multi-colored scarf dress layered over black leggings. Jackie paced on five-inch lime green heels Sam would have never attempted. A scarlet-colored bag that looked like it weighed more than Jackie was slung over one shoulder.

"It's about time, girlfriend. I have been out here for two long minutes. Three men have already tried picking me up."

"Did you get their phone numbers?"

Jackie pointed at the sign. "They came out of this place. Who knows what kind of phobias and itises they have."

"And you want me to go in there?"

"Well, guess they cure more than addicts and sociopaths with serial killer thoughts."

They pushed through the front door of the Morning Glory Clinic and were greeted with soft tinkling music piped in the background. To their right was a waterfall seeping down a marble wall and into a pond. Oriental was the theme of the clinic. Bonsai trees in colorful planters were on each of the tables. The marble floor glistened and overhead lights were muted. Either they were saving on electricity or they wanted to keep the mood calm and serene. A marble staircase swept up to the second floor.

"May I help you?" The receptionist was as clinical and refined as their surroundings. She would fit comfortably behind a cosmetics counter with her peaches and cream complexion and blonde hair that gleamed under the lights. She and her assistant were dressed more for a business office. Starched white uniforms were not to be seen anywhere, at least not in the front office. The name plate for *Miss Blonde and Gleaming* said Olivia.

Jackie stepped up before Sam could open her mouth. "We wanted to find out more about that HypnoBirthing that's all the rage." Jackie appeared so excited it was hard to tell who was the expectant mother.

"Is this for both of you?"

"Oh, no, no." Jackie dragged Sam to the counter. "My friend, Sam, is pregnant with twins. Over three months now."

Sam was hoping for a hole to open in the floor so she could drop through. She already had a struggle with her closet this morning to find a pair of slacks without an elastic waistband that would button. Just to feel comfortable she had to surrender and grab a pair of gray leggings and layer a plaid painter's smock over a turtleneck. The ankle boots were gray suede with a comfortable two-inch heel.

"Congratulations. Why don't you have a seat and I'll see if one of our consultants can spend a few moments with you." Olivia picked up the phone as Sam and Jackie turned from the counter and picked seats by the waterfall. One woman in a rhinestone jogging suit sat across from them thumbing through a *Self* magazine. A young woman with blue streaks in her hair tapped her nails on the chair arms while her right leg bounced nervously. The blue polish on her nails was chipped and in need of a do-over.

"This place looks more like a spa," Sam whispered.

"Nuh uh," Jackie mumbled. She leaned in and whispered, "The jogger is hooked on sleeping pills. Don't you see the bags under her eyes? And the teen is going through major withdrawal, probably meth or those bath salts. A stupid waste of the most important years of her life."

"How did I miss that?"

"Ladies?" Olivia motioned them to the counter as a woman in a Wall Street business suit walked through a back doorway. "Doctor Stone can see you now."

Sam and Jackie followed a statuesque blonde down a hallway to an office on the right. Certificates and photos lined the walls while a bulletin board of a variety of pictures was on the wall by the door. It contained individual snapshots of women. The furniture was plush and reeked of money. The office should have been in Chicago's Merchandise Mart, not a doctor's office, and the statuesque blonde looked more like a Parisian model than a therapist.

"Which one of you is the lucky mother-to-be?"

"I am." Sam took a seat in a plush cream-colored chair. Jackie took a seat next to her. "I'm not familiar with HypnoBirthing. Can you tell me what it involves, how long it takes, and most importantly, is it effective?"

"Most definitely." Doctor Stone handed Sam several pamphlets. "It was developed by hypnotherapist Marie Mongan and uses the natural birth philosophy developed in the nineteen twenties."

"Am I actually hypnotized?"

"Oh no. It's more like daydreaming. You'll be able to converse but you'll be totally relaxed and in total control. The pain actually comes from fear. Believe me, I've had three children, two children using this technique. I know the difference between the pain I felt with my first and the total pain-free of childbirth with my next two. Most women aren't aware of what to expect, so their muscles contract and resist the natural function of the body. That is what causes the pain. HypnoBirthing puts your mind in a natural calm relaxed state which releases endorphins and suppresses the pain."

Sam doubted this woman ever had a baby. Her body was too well toned. She opened one of the brochures with the smiling babies and wondered if they kept the mothers' screaming faces away from the camera.

Jackie asked, "How long does this training take?"

"There are five two-and-a-half hour sessions. We provide you with two CDs to watch at home, plus provide suggestions for good pregnancy nutrition, relaxation techniques, body toning exercises, all of this for the home besides the classes here."

"So how does it work if you aren't hypnotized?" Sam still wasn't sold on the procedure.

"I would think it's the same as yoga," Jackie offered. "You know, all that mantra stuff and putting yourself into a Zen state. After all, I've seen those live hypnotist shows where they have people barking like a dog and pretending they're all naked and stuff."

"Please, don't compare us to carnival acts."

"But aren't there some people who can't be hypnotized?" Sam asked.

"Of course, but hypnosis isn't all dangling medallions and looking into a light. It's all in getting the patient into a relaxed state."

Doctor Stone's phone rang. Sam pushed away from the desk and walked over to the window. There was a great view of the nature center with its walking trail. The clinic and its property sprawled across ten square blocks. It stood two stories high and boasted two sleep research labs. Sam strolled past the wall of certificates and stopped in front of the bulletin board. She heard the doctor end her call and was just ready to return to her seat when a photo of someone familiar caught her eye— Marti Johnson. Why was Marti's picture here?

"Are these patients?" Sam asked.

"We refer to them as clients. Some have agreed to the use of their name and testimonials in marketing pieces."

Leave it up to Jackie to think of money. "This all sounds pretty expensive. After all, you gotta pay for all this marble and that waterfall in the lobby." Jackie's nails reached for the ceiling. "Lordy, that had to cost a fortune."

"Our prices are in the brochure but everything is piecemeal. Not everyone wants the CDs and binder with nutritional and exercise diets. Now, I do have another appointment."

As Sam thanked her for her time she caught sight of another face she recognized. Had she finally found the missing piece that linked all the victims together? Several photos away from Marti Johnson's was one of Carly Farnswood.

33

"Oh my, oh my." Jackie's head was close to snapping off if she bent it back any farther. She was staring at the ceiling of the Café Fleurs Grotte. "They have a replica of Michelangelo's Libyan Sibyl. Her name if Phemonoe."

Sam stared at her friend. "How do you know all that?"

"Qui ne sait pas du français?"

"What?" For all the years she had known Jackie, she was unaware she spoke French.

"She said 'who doesn't know French?'" The man in the beret grabbed Jackie's hand and kissed it. *"Comment vous faire fait, madame?"*

"Très bien, merci."

Sam rolled her eyes. "Christian, this is my friend, Jackie."

Jackie fanned her face with one hand. "My, my. You are one fine French pastry."

"Please, your table is ready and Evan is already here." Christian walked quickly to the corner table while Sam pulled on Jackie's arm.

"He's gay," Sam whispered.

"Of course, sweetie. The gorgeous ones are always gay. Now, who is Evan?"

Christian pulled out their seats and placed menus on the table. "I took the liberty of preparing Li Zhi Hong iced tea for you."

"That sounds great." Christian left and Sam introduced Jackie to Doctor Evan Collier. "Doctor Collier is my shrink."

"Poor boy." Jackie snapped open the menu with a smile. "I've been wanting to sit in on one of Sam's sessions. I can have it up on YouTube in ten seconds."

"Fat chance," Sam said. "I hope I didn't pull you away from an appointment."

"My next appointment isn't until three. I'm all yours."

Christian brought a tray and set out three glasses of iced tea."

"Merci, magnifique." Jackie flashed her Whitney Houston smile.

"Even I understood that." Sam slipped the paper off of a straw and jammed the straw in the glass. They each selected the mini crab quiche and tartes aux fruits. Once Christian left with their order, Sam turned to Evan. "Tell me about hypnosis."

"What do you want to know?"

"Do all psychologists use it?"

"It's post graduate work so no, not all psychologists use it. I don't, if that is what you are looking for."

Christian returned with a tray containing a basket of muffins and bread. He set a small bowl of honey butter in front of each of them.

"What do you know about the Morning Glory Clinic?" Sam asked.

Jackie studied the flower floating in her iced tea. "It's certainly a stupid name."

Christian folded the tray under one arm. "Actually, the morning glory flower is the symbol for rebirth so the name is quite appropriate."

"Well, sugar, I stand corrected." Jackie fished the impatiens flower from her glass and set it on her napkin, tapping it with one long talon as though it were a specimen under a microscope.

"It is edible," Christian said. "Do let me know if you'd like to graze on more. I'll go check on your food."

"I've only heard good things about them," Evan commented. "I have sent several patients once I determined they needed certain help that I was unable to provide."

"Like hypnosis."

"Look at it this way. I'm like your primary care physician. Morning Glory is more of a specialist. Think of hypnotherapy as power of suggestion."

Christian returned with a young waitress who unfolded a stand. Once he placed the tray on the stand, she assisted in distributing their meals. "Just let me know if I can get you anything else," Christian said.

Jackie tackled her food while Sam continued to pick Evan's brain. "Power of suggestion is just that, though, isn't it? It can't really make you do anything."

"I'm sure you've heard of subliminal messages. Anyone who sits in front of a television screen and watches commercials hardly realizes they are being assaulted with a hypnotic-like suggestion."

"But they still have the power to purchase or not to purchase. Hypnosis can't force someone to do something they don't want to do, right?"

Evan set his fork down and studied Sam's face. "This is about the suicide, isn't it? And before you ask, no. I haven't heard of any cases of anyone being hypnotized to kill themselves much less kill someone else or rob a bank."

"But isn't hypnosis a sort of mind control? Look at Patty Hearst."

"And don't forget Jim Jones," Jackie offered. "Anyone who can get a crowd of people to drink poison, that is one mean mind control act."

Evan caught the eye of a waitress and held up his glass gesturing for a refill. "Now you are talking fear and desire. Fear can influence thoughts and actions. If someone is stripped of all self-control they are easy to manipulate. With desire and love, the ability to persuade people to do something they would never consider doing takes a very strong personality and a roomful of very weak people. Opposites attract, as they say."

"So if Jim Jones can get people to commit suicide and he didn't even use hypnosis, why couldn't hypnosis make people do something they would never dream of doing?"

"There's a big difference between convincing someone through hypnosis that they are holding a real gun when it is actually plastic and getting a young mother whose life centers around her beautiful nine-month-old baby to jump from an overpass and kill herself."

Jackie dropped her fork. "Oh my gawd! You think that young woman was hypnotized to kill herself?"

Sam realized she hadn't touched her food. Truth was she couldn't get the thought of the victims from her mind. "I saw Marti Johnson's picture on the wall. She was one of their patients as was Carly Farnswood, another young woman who stripped naked and walked into Lake Michigan one week before her wedding. Both women had everything to live for yet calmly took their own life. Marti left a warm jar of baby food on the counter and a beautiful baby in a high chair." Sam took a deep breath and fought back the hormonal tears.

"Okay, sugar." Jackie patted her left arm while Evan grabbed her right hand.

"Sam." Evan's voice was soft and low. "Look at me. You are making some bizarre assumptions. I can tell you without a doubt that what you are suggesting is completely impossible."

"You wouldn't be hypnotizing me, would you, Doc. Because it doesn't work on me." She forced out a laugh and Evan smiled. She shook both of their hands off. "I'm fine."

"Is there anything wrong with your food, Sam?" Christian asked. "Can I get you something else?"

"No. I guess I'm not as hungry as I thought. Can you wrap it all to go?"

"Sure thing." Christian motioned for a waitress to clear their table while he grabbed Sam's plate and carted it off.

"Who owns the Morning Glory Clinic?" Sam asked.

"There are two owners. They have done quite well for themselves having sold at least thirty franchises last year and more scheduled for this year. Young guys in their mid-thirties, but from what I hear the spoons in their mouths growing up weren't silver but more like platinum. Matthew Bordeau is one of the owners. He and Austin went to high school and college together. There was a huge write up last year on both of them in *Shore* magazine, the one that highlights all the happenings in this area."

Sam scribbled both of their names on a napkin. "What is Austin's last name?"

"Revere. Austin Revere. His father owns the Lake Bluff Country Club."

34

Sam gave her carryout box to Jackie and drove back to the Morning Glory Clinic. She had to keep taking deep breaths to slow herself down. It could all be one big coincidence. Why would Marti and Carly both have been patients at the clinic? Carrie did say her sister was thrilled to have lost some weight before her final fitting. But what about Marti? Should she wait and talk to Forrest and Carly first? And then there was Donna Oberweiss. Although Sam had heard the word *destiny* when she touched the purse, Donna hadn't committed suicide. Had she been a patient at Morning Glory? Or perhaps she dated one of the doctors.

Sam weighed her options of showing her hand now or playing it close to the vest. Chess was never her strong suit. She would just as soon upend the board and let the pieces fall where they may.

Sam walked up to the counter and presented her card. "I'd like to see Doctor Bordeau and Doctor Revere."

Miss Blonde and Gleaming was still manning the front desk. She looked at Sam's card and appeared puzzled. "Weren't you just in here about HypnoBirthing, or was that a ruse?"

"Oh, I am interested in it but right now I know of two former patients…"

"Clients."

Sam gritted her teeth. "…clients who have committed suicide. I need to discuss that with them today."

Olivia picked up the phone and turned her back, her voice low. After a short conversation, she hung up the phone and held Sam's card as though she had just found it in a dumpster. "They won't be back until tomorrow but I'll give them your card and have them call you."

Right. Like that's going to happen. If they wanted to play it that way, Sam was more than willing to wait them out.

Sam thanked her and left, but she felt eyes on her back as she returned to her Jeep. She soaked in the warmth of the vehicle as she gathered her thoughts. What could the good doctors gain by forcing women to commit suicide? Were they having affairs and the women threatened to expose them? Sam dismissed that reason immediately. Carly had planned to marry the love of her life and Marti was devoted to Forrest and their baby. Maybe they were two patients who said no to their doctors' advances and threatened to expose them. There goes the multi-million dollar business. She could ask Jackie to sign on as a patient and see if either of the doctors would hit on her. But what if they made her their next victim?

She studied the two-story building of marble and glass set back one hundred yards from the street. Must have cost a fortune to build. The property alone in this part of town was expensive. From this view it resembled an elaborate courthouse. Trees and shrubs hugged the building while fall mums added color to the landscape.

Through the expansive glass Sam could see the marble staircase leading to the second floor. According to the brochure, the sleep lab was housed on the second floor, as were the executive offices. Morning Glory wasn't a rehab center, though. People weren't admitted for months on end, only overnight for the sleep lab. Sam shoved the key in the ignition and watched a young woman exit the building. She had an attractive face but hid her body in a jogging suit. Her long hair was pulled back in a ponytail. Sam watched in the rearview mirror as the woman crossed the street and entered a shop.

Sam pulled the key from the ignition, exited the Jeep and crossed the street. The woman entered a coffee shop named Java the Hut. Sam hoped she planned to sit down and relax for a while. There were two people seated at a table against one wall pounding on their laptops. An older woman was shoving a pastry in her mouth and was none too dainty about it. The pastry was crumbling in her hand. A man in a baseball cap and sunglasses sat at a table near the counter reading a newspaper. The young woman from the clinic left the counter and carried her coffee to a table by the window. Sam ordered a caramel latte. She turned to see if the woman was still by the window but then her spidey senses went off. The man in the baseball cap was peering over his sunglasses at the woman from the clinic. Sam heard a sound. *Click... Click.* As he held the newspaper in his left hand, his right hand was playing with his car keys. The remote key was the type Abby had for her van. You had to press a button to get the key to pop out. Then you folded the key back in. The man was flicking the key out and snapping it back in. *Click... Click.* A nervous habit, obviously. It shouldn't have set off alarm bells, but Sam never questioned her instincts.

She paid for her latte and slowly approached the woman. "Hi. I'm Sam. I don't mean to pry. I saw you exit the clinic across the street and thought maybe you could calm my fears. Hope you don't mind."

"No. Please sit. I'm Tamara." The woman closed her book and set it aside. She had dark features, exotic in the way her eyes were shaped.

"I was apprehensive about going into the clinic because I don't know much about it. I have their literature but I really would like to get some feedback."

"I have been going to the clinic for six weeks now. I've always had a problem with food." She raised her hands in a *what are you gonna do* motion. "I love food."

Sam leaned across the table and whispered, "They don't hypnotize you, do they?"

"Oh, no. At least I haven't been hypnotized. What are you going for?"

Sam patted her stomach. "HypnoBirthing. My friend says it's all the rage."

"Is that like the Scientology quiet child birth?"

"I'm not sure. I thought they just slapped a piece of duct tape on their mouths."

Tamara laughed. She had beautiful teeth and a beautiful smile. Wide hips were probably genetic but Sam didn't want to tell her to live with it.

"Did you know Carly Farnswood? I believe she went to Morning

Glory when she wanted to lose weight before her wedding." Sam wasn't sure if Carly had died before Tamara started going to the clinic but she had to keep her talking somehow.

"I don't think so. The name doesn't sound familiar, but we really don't interact with the other clients. There's at least fifteen minutes from the end of my session until the beginning of another."

"But you talk in the waiting room, don't you?"

Tamara shook her head. "Once you check in you are taken to another waiting area for your specific therapist. Even the sleep clinic patients have a different entrance. Guess they must think people would be embarrassed if they ran into someone they knew."

"Interesting," Sam murmured. "How about the owners? I mean Doctors Revere and Bordeau. Are they the ones treating you?"

"Unfortunately, no. They are really hot." Color flushed Tamara's cheeks. "I have a female therapist and she's actually a nutritionist. I'm learning more about controlling my metabolism by the foods I eat." She lifted her latte. "I don't think this is on the menu."

"Well, a good nutritionist would allow you a treat every now and then. Depriving the body of those little pleasures kills the metabolism."

"Wow, wish you were my nutritionist." Tamara checked her watch. "Oops, I've got to run. It was a pleasure meeting you."

"Thank you for the information. I think I feel a little better about the place." Sam watched her leave, then checked her phone. If she had expected a frantic call from the doctors, she was sorely mistaken. They were probably having her checked out, perhaps making a call to Daddy Revere who would then make a call to the mayor. She decided to talk to Forrest and Carly first, maybe catch them both at their next support meeting. As she finished her coffee she noticed the man in the baseball cap was standing on the curb watching as Tamara crossed the street.

35

"Jacob didn't have breakfast this morning." Abby set an ivy planter in the sink, its long tendrils hanging over the side. She gently lifted the tendrils and placed them in the sink.

"He mumbled something to me at five this morning about a possible hostage situation. He was picking Frank up."

"Jacob doesn't have anything to do with hostages." Abby used the sprayer on the sink to water the plant and rinse the dust off of the heart-shaped leaves. Her green thumb was evident in all of the plants. Sam only had to look at a plant to kill it.

"This one involved a cop and his wife. I'm not sure who, but it appeared to be all hands on deck." Sam opened the pamphlet she had received at the Morning Glory Clinic while Abby turned on the radio. The pamphlet did give some background information on the two doctors. Matt and Austin had attended Reed University. Both were board certified hypnotherapists and members of the American Board of Hypnotherapy. The back pamphlet showed them in business suits that looked tailor-made. Matt's dark hair and dark eyes were a stark contrast to Austin's beach boy tan, sun-streaked hair and blue eyes. Hair and teeth were GQ perfect. Sam could imagine most female patients having a crush on either one. Another photo showed the doctors with their support staff, more pretty people. Not one average-looking person in the bunch.

"Is that the clinic you and Jackie went to?" Abby wiped the water spray from the sink and counter then laid the damp towel on the edge of the counter.

"Yes. This HypnoBirthing sounds interesting." Sam handed the pamphlet to Abby, then opened her laptop and did a search on both of the names. There were a number of sites with extensive biographies. Both Matthew Bordeau and Austin Revere came from family wealth.

The Revere name was big in land development, mainly resorts and golf courses. Bordeau was equivalent to Eli Lilly and Pfizer. Grandpa Bordeau was on the cutting edge of psychotropic drugs. There wasn't any mention of wives or children.

"They have very attractive people working for them."

That was one thing Sam had also noticed. "You'd think at least one woman would have hair with a mind of its own." She absentmindedly touched the top of her head to see if her natural-curly hair was spiking.

The announcer on the radio caught Abby's attention. They listened as he reported a murder-suicide by a Chasen Heights police officer.

Charlie Stanhope, a twenty-five-year veteran with the police force, shot his wife, then calmly poured himself a cup of coffee and waited for the police to show up. Neighbors reported hearing loud voices and screams around four-thirty this morning when Charlie returned home. One neighbor claims Charlie had driven his truck across several lawns before crashing into a tree. He then fell out of the truck and staggered to the front door yelling his wife's name. Betty Stanhope was seen at the front door holding a baseball bat. It is alleged that Charlie forced his way in and closed the door. Sergeant Stanhope engaged in a two-hour standoff with police before shooting himself. Unconfirmed reports claim the couple had been having marital problems. We will report additional details as they unfold.

"Did you know him, Samantha?"

Sam shook her head no. "Never met him." But Stanhope was from the Third Precinct. Another open and shut case for *grab and slap*.

The precinct was the last place Sam wanted to be. Although Stanhope hadn't worked at the Sixth, there would still be I.A.'s, press, and all kinds of commotion at every precinct. She opened her laptop and did a search on Matt Bordeau. A Facebook page showed pictures of his wife.

From there she was directed to Crystal Creations, a web site showing the jewelry Crystal made and pieces that were available exclusively in upscale boutiques. One such boutique was the shop at the Center for Performing Arts. With one quick phone call Sam learned that Crystal Bordeau would be dropping off an order within the next few minutes.

On the way over to the Center, Sam called Forrest and verified that there was another support group meeting tonight. She said she would stop by to ask him and Carly a couple questions. She still had to figure out how Donna fit into the scenario. Had she been a patient and witnessed something at the clinic? And then there was Nina. Of course! Sam pounded the steering wheel. According to Junior, Nina had gone to Gamblers Anonymous, but what were the chances she might also have been a patient at Morning Glory?

She pushed the Blue Tooth button on the dashboard. "Hey, Junior. You mentioned that as part of Nina's employment agreement she had to attend Gamblers Anonymous. Do you know if she also went through therapy?"

"I never did send that file back to Human Resources. Let me check." The sound of papers being shuffled could be heard. "Here it is. She had six weeks of sessions at the Morning Glory Clinic."

Sam's head was spinning. There was a link to three of the victims to the clinic. All she needed was to find out how Donna fit in and what all four of them had in common. She entered the Center for Performing Arts and walked past a promotional display of *The Adams Family* play currently running on weekends until after Halloween. Beyond the large foyer was a restaurant, doors to the theatre, a ticket office, and the gift shop. She walked into the shop and was amazed at how such a small shop could hold so much. There were paintings, sculptures, clothes and jewelry created by local artists. Every inch of floor and wall space had been utilized leaving very little room to walk. Sam hoped she didn't bump into a display and have to pay for some four-figure art piece.

"Welcome. I'm Maureen. Can I help you with anything?" The woman behind the counter looked made of bone china. When she spoke

Sam could swear her face never moved. Her silk blouse, broach, scarf, jewelry, everything appeared to be a walking advertisement for the gift shop.

Sam felt like a street urchin next to Maureen, even though her sweater coat was pure alpaca, not a cheap purchase, and it was made by a woman on the Eagle Ridge Reservation, so she knew her money was going to help someone in need.

"I called earlier and was told Crystal Bordeau was here. I was hoping to have a moment of her time." Sam handed her a business card.

"Of course. She's finishing up some business in the back room." Maureen disappeared behind a beaded curtain. Sam took the opportunity to check out the stained glass, framed paintings, and miscellaneous artwork. The glass cases displayed a number of jewelry pieces with small cards on stands identifying the artist. She wondered why Alex didn't sell some of his jewelry in this shop. He was, after all, a local artist.

"Miss Casey?" Maureen stood next to a striking blonde who could have just come from a Vogue magazine photo shoot. Even her perfume smelled expensive. If the silver and opal necklace was any example of her artwork, she did extremely good work. Maureen introduced the two women, then excused herself and departed to the back room.

Crystal held up Sam's business card and cocked her head like a cocker spaniel puppy. "This says you are an investigative consultant for the police department. Are my licenses not up to date?" She added a light laugh that sounded forced.

"Is there some place we can talk?"

"Of course. We can go to the restaurant."

Sam found a table by the window overlooking the parking lot. A salad bar filled the center of the room, its cooling plates waiting to be filled. Lunch wouldn't be served until eleven o'clock so before then patrons could use the self-serve coffee and pastry bar. Crystal must have been well-known or a heavy contributor because the staff immediately brought over coffee and a tray of pastries.

"You have stunning jewelry. May I ask where you purchased it?"

Crystal fingered Sam's inlaid wedding ring and the turquoise and coral necklace she wore.

"A family friend makes wonderful jewelry. Alex Red Cloud is from the Eagle Ridge Reservation, as is my mother."

"Really." Crystal scrutinized Sam's hair and eyes, trying to find some Native American features.

"He lives with us and has made jewelry for quite a few people."

"He should bring some samples here to the Center. I'll put in a good word for him."

"Thanks. I'll let him know."

Once the wait staff left and Crystal had doctored her coffee with sufficient amounts of sugar free substances, she said, "If I'm not in arrears with my licenses then what is this about?" Crystal picked at the pastry with a fork, placing a small bite in her mouth that would barely fill a thimble. The woman was model thin. Sam was too wired to eat.

"What can you tell me about Collin Revere?"

"Austin's father?" Crystal made slow, crazy eight stirrings with her spoon. Sam assumed she'd need to do a lot of stirring to melt all the sugar she had dumped into the cup. "Is this about the body found at the golf course?"

"In a way. By telling me about the father, I might learn more about the son." Sam couldn't tell if the tight smile Crystal was attempting was a positive or negative impression of the Reveres.

"I thought the police were through interrogating Collin."

"They are, but I'm more interested in Austin."

Crystal finally stopped tormenting the cup and placed her spoon down. "I'm not sure I understand what you are getting at."

Sam ran a cop's eye over the stunning platinum blonde. Her teeth were far too perfect, probably veneers. The makeup was flawless, nails sculptured, jewelry not too flashy but still screamed wealthy. She remembered the corporate picture in the pamphlet of all the employees at the clinic. They were also too perfect.

"There are possibly three patients of the Morning Glory Clinic…"

"Clients," Crystal corrected her. "Matt and Austin hate the word patient."

Sam smiled, a tight cunning smile of curiosity at how the good doctors had trained family and employees when it came to speaking about the business, even in the choice of a simple word for patient. "Sorry. Clients who have died of an apparent suicide." Sam could see the woman's chest slowly rising in a controlled deep breath.

"What are you saying?" Crystal held up one dainty hand to stop Sam. "Are you implying that Matthew and Austin had anything to do with a client's death? Have you spoken to my husband about this?"

"He's not returning my phone call, unfortunately."

"Whatever you are accusing them of, you are wrong." Crystal stopped and scanned the room. Several waitresses quickly turned their backs and moved away. Crystal leaned closer. "Matt is a wonderful doctor and a wonderful husband."

"Funny you should list them in that order." If Sam had hoped to get Crystal to open up, she was going to have to work harder. A tinge of fury was staining Crystal's cheeks and her dainty hands were clenched as far as the sculptured nails would allow. "And Austin? What would his wife say about him?" Sam hadn't been able to find information on Austin Revere's personal life other than he liked sailing and golf.

"Divorced. His wife didn't care too much for the business or Matthew for that matter. Matt…"

"Let me guess. Matt had a certain image in mind for everyone surrounding him. I saw the women who work at the clinic. Just about every one of them could be a runway model. Even the older women, and there weren't that many, looked like Hollywood starlets."

"The marriage only lasted a couple years, no children. Emma let herself go, according to Matt. She was Italian and loved food. And Austin liked to play the field."

"Do you know any of Austin's playmates?" Sam turned a page and read off the names of the victims.

Crystal shook her head. "I've never heard of any of those names.

One nice quality about Austin is that he doesn't kiss and tell." She used her napkin to wipe lipstick off of her cup. Then she folded the napkin prim and proper before setting it next to the cup.

"How did you get along with Austin? Did he ever hit on you?" Sam couldn't see a player like Austin passing up such a beautiful woman, even if she was married to his partner.

"He tried, well, not in so many words, but I got the meaning. I shut him down. Told him I would let it slide but if he ever so much as undressed me with his eyes I would let Matt know. It worked." Crystal checked her watch, then shoved her chair away from the table. "If you will excuse me, I have another appointment."

"If you think of anything else, you have my card." Sam watched her leave and wondered how long it would take for Crystal to call her husband.

36

Sam checked her phone to make sure it wasn't on vibrate. Why hadn't Matthew or Austin taken the bait? They should have called by now, or at least had their lawyer call charging her with harassment.

"My grandson is going to be shriveled like a prune by the time you finish, Samantha." Abby held up a towel and waited for Sam to lift Dillon out of the tub.

"Sorry, Mom. My mind is several miles away."

"Is it about that police officer who killed himself?"

"No. It's the other suicides, the women I told you about." Sam pulled up the drain plug to drain the water, then tipped the baby bath seat over to let it dry. "I'm meeting Forrest and Carrie tonight at the support center to ask them a couple questions." Sam ran her hand down Dillon's head to flatten the strands that were standing on end. She followed Abby down the hall to the nursery. "I spoke only for a couple minutes to Jake. He didn't have time to talk other than to say the cops who worked with Stanhope knew he had a drinking problem, but he was a nice guy, never late for work, never called off."

Abby placed Dillon on the dressing table and between the two of them got him diapered and dressed for bed before he had time to scream his disapproval at being tossed and tumbled. "What time are you leaving?"

"Around seven." Sam lifted her whimpering son in her arms and trailed Abby to the kitchen. "It's okay, sweetie. Grandma's heating your bottle now." Dillon whimpered again as he watched Abby place a bottle in the microwave to warm up. His attention was averted to Sam's ringing cell phone which sounded like birds chirping. It was Beast. "Hey, got news for me?"

"Yep. Phone company gave me the message log of calls to and from that phone number. The last call she received was from another disposable phone and the call lasted four seconds."

Sam drove trance-like to the Christian Family Center. Now there were four victims, or at least three with links to Morning Glory and Donna who was linked in a way not yet clear, but linked nonetheless. Traffic thinned out as she made her way to the older section of Chasen Heights. Shadows pulled back as though the beam from the Jeep's headlamps would burn them. She swerved as she almost hit a rider on a bike. No lights, all dark clothing. Real smart.

It had been more than eight hours since she spoke to Crystal Bordeau and still not one peep from either her husband or his partner. Maybe Matthew Bordeau had a violent temper and Crystal knew better than to tell him anything that might anger him.

Sam switched on the bright lights. Street lights in this part of town were few and far between. It was suspected Chasen Heights' law abiding citizens practiced their aim on the street lamps every time the city replaced the bulbs. Now it was getting too costly to replace them every time some idiot shot one out.

The parking lot at the Christian Family Center was small and L-shaped and Sam had to pull around to the side of the building to find an open space. The clock on the dashboard showed she was twenty minutes early. That should give her a little time to speak with Forrest and Carrie before the session started.

Sam weaved between cars and hurried down the steps to the basement entrance. She found Forrest and Carrie by the coffee pot. Grace gave her a quick wave, then turned back to a new member Sam hadn't seen the last time she had visited.

"Hey, Sam." Forrest gave her a hug.

"Coffee, Sam?" Carrie asked.

Sam declined as she led them several feet from the refreshment table. "Does the name Nina Logesta sound familiar to either of you?"

"No." Forrest looked to Carrie, who shook her head.

"Who is she?" Carrie looked thinner than the last time Sam had seen her and Forrest looked as though he hadn't slept in several days. Sam was hesitant to say too much to Forrest for fear he would charge into the Morning Glory Clinic demanding answers.

"Let me ask another question. Carrie, you said Carly had lost some weight before her final fitting. How was she able to accomplish that?"

Carrie shrugged. Sam forgot Carrie didn't live at home any more, but she and Carly were close so hopefully she would be able to confirm what Sam already knew. "She dieted, I think." Carrie took a sip of coffee, then paused. "Wait. She went to that clinic. It's the name of a flower."

"Morning Glory?" Sam prompted.

"Yes."

"Wait." Forrest rested a hand on Sam's arm. "Marti went there to quit smoking when she first learned she was pregnant. But she only went for a few months. It ended months before Savannah was born. Do you think someone there had something to do with Marti's death?"

"Okay, everyone." Grace clapped her hands. "Let's get started." Attendees started moving toward the front of the room. The pink and blue streamers that had hung from the walls previously had been replaced with streamers and paper leaves in fall colors.

"Can you stay?" Carrie asked. "I want to find out more."

"There isn't anything more…yet. But I want you, Carrie, to talk to your mom. Find out if Carly ever spoke about anyone in particular she befriended. And Forrest." She clasped his hand between hers, hoping not to agitate him into some action he would regret. "I need you to go through Marti's files and notes. Maybe talk to any close friends and see if they know if she was having problems with someone. Maybe they both witnessed something. I'm grabbing at straws right now but it's all I have to go on."

"What about that other woman you mentioned?" Carrie walked back to the coffee pot and refilled her cup.

"She's another name that popped up in my investigation. When I find out how and if she fits into the puzzle, believe me, you two will be the first to know."

◇◇

Sam walked into the dark parking lot, confident she was vague enough to be assured Forrest would not act on his own. She clasped her keys in her hand. There was a small LED flashlight hanging from it. She pressed the button and the halogen beam lit up a path to the Jeep. The air was thick with the odor of wood burning in a nearby fireplace and she couldn't wait to curl up in front of her fireplace with a cup of hot tea.

Forrest had made a good point. Savannah was nine months old. If Marti had stopped her therapy at three or four months into the pregnancy, then it had been over a year since Marti was at Morning Glory. Had she been continuing her therapy after Savannah was born without Forrest's knowledge? How could Morning Glory be involved after so long of a time?

Sam was too engrossed in the case and focused too much on the pavement in front of her to notice that it was unusually quiet. The normal chattering of squirrels, chirping of crickets and other multi-legged creatures were missing. If she had been more observant she would have heard the warning from an owl in a nearby tree. She even ignored the tingling creeping up her spine, dismissing it as the crisp chill in the air. Muffled footsteps rushed from behind and suddenly someone grabbed a handful of her hair and slammed her against the brick building. She felt grit and sharp edges bite into her forehead. Sparks flashed before her eyes as she felt herself falling. The car keys and flashlight skidded across the pavement as she reached out an arm to break her fall. But her attacker wasn't done. He grabbed her hair again. Sam struggled to get up but he was too strong. She saw a slice of the LED beam shining on her attacker's brown deck shoes, no socks. He leaned down and growled, "Keep your damn nose out of other people's business or the next time I won't be so gentle." He slammed her head down again. Sam ignored the pain as she reached out and dug her nails into his bare ankle, feeling the skin scrape.

"You bitch!" He scrambled up and just as Sam thought he was

leaving, she caught a glimpse of his foot rushing toward her, connecting with the right side of her body, just below the rib cage. She tried not to cry out, and instead remained still so she could listen to the footsteps. There was only one set, only one attacker. She heard a car door slam in the distance, probably parked on the street. An engine from some type of sports car grumbled and roared to life. Soon after she could hear it race down the street.

Then the tears started. Sam lay on the pavement smelling dirt and grease and not caring. She was trying to assess her body parts, sense if any ribs were broken. She reached out to grab the flashlight but it was out of her grasp. After several minutes she slowly pushed herself to a sitting position and stifled a sob. She felt something running down her face and dripping onto her sweater coat. Her forehead started stinging and her side throbbed where she had been kicked. Sam dragged herself to the nearest car and held onto the bumper. Her keys and the flashlight were within reach. She grabbed them with a shaking hand, careful to only use her left hand. Through the throbbing pain, tears, and anger she smiled. She had her attacker's skin and blood under her nails and she wasn't about ready to ruin the evidence. After several seconds she pulled herself up and leaned against the front of the vehicle until the shadows stopped spinning.

With her left hand Sam pressed the remote to her Jeep, turning on the headlights. The Jeep was two vehicles away. Sam staggered like a street bum, stopping once to wipe the blood out of her eyes and wait until the nausea passed. It was then she thought of the baby...babies. She took deep breaths and concentrated, as though somehow she could tell if there was any damage to the fetuses. Her attacker messed with the wrong woman.

With anger morphing into fury, Sam found the strength to reach the Jeep. She climbed in and sat still for several minutes. She didn't have the energy to walk back into the center. She could lay on the horn and hope someone inside heard it. Jake was the last person she could call. He was still neck deep in the murder/suicide. And until Sam got her evidence to

Benny, she couldn't handle Jake's rage. Not yet.

Sam touched the Blue Tooth button and called Alex. She tried to keep her voice calm but hearing his deep, soothing cadence, she lost it. "Alex...I need help." After telling him where she was, Sam leaned against the headrest and wept tears of pain, anger, and fear. She had shaken someone up and if he had already killed four women, he wasn't afraid to add a fifth.

37

"Are you sure you didn't recognize the man?" Benny scraped the skin samples from under Sam's nails then placed the samples in a tube. "What about the voice?"

"The parking lot was dark and he hit me from behind. And his voice was muffled. I think he was wearing a mask of some type." The cold from the metal table chilled her, even though Anya had placed several towels on the table first.

"O'hitike Sni."

"What did he say?"

"He called the guy a coward."

Alex threaded his hat through his fingers. "This is creepy, Sam, seeing you lying on this table."

"He's right, Sam. You should be in an emergency room, not on my morgue table."

"I knew once I called an ambulance, word would get back to Jake. I don't think we are ready to have this city shot up as Jake looks for the culprit."

"Good point." Benny waited for Anya to move Sam's hair away from her face. "I had never wanted to see you on my table, Sam. But you didn't want the hospital so this is the best I could do."

"It's perfect for washing the blood out of your hair." Anya pulled the nozzle over and gently sprayed Sam's hair. The excess water ran into a tub just below Sam's head. "Your sweater coat and top are ruined."

"I kinda like Benny's shirt." Sam had slipped into one of Benny's Hawaiian shirts after stripping off the stained coat and tunic top. Anya had insisted on taking photos of her injuries.

"This is going to hurt a bit." Benny started scrubbing the dirt and debris from the cuts and scrapes on Sam's forehead.

"Owww. What are you using, a Brillo pad?" Sam clenched the sides of the table. "Can't you freeze it first?"

"I could, but this is quicker."

"Tell me about the man," Alex said in an attempt to get Sam's mind off the pain.

Sam thought back to the parking lot. "The parking lot was so dark that I was focusing on where I was going. I used that small flashlight on my key ring. He had soft-soled shoes because his footsteps weren't loud."

"Maybe he was waiting behind a car?" Alex suggested.

"Not sure. He didn't just jump out at me. He moved fast and took me by surprise. Next thing I knew I was kissing the bricks on the building. Then I lost my balance, lost my key ring."

"What about your purse?" Anya asked.

"I locked it in the Jeep or I would have grabbed my gun and shot the sonofabitch."

"That and several car windows. Your aim was never that good, Sam."

Benny laughed at Alex's comment. "How were you able to scratch him?"

"When I fell to the ground he grabbed my hair again and did an encore, letting me get a taste of every conceivable germ on the pavement. My flashlight had rolled several yards away but the beam was close enough that I could see his shoes. He didn't wear socks so I reached out and dug my nails in, scraped him pretty good."

"I'd say. I got some pretty good samples. Now we just have to hope he's in the database."

"So he didn't want your money?" Anya turned off the water, then patted Sam's hair with a towel.

"No. He wanted to give me a warning." Sam kneaded her temples slowly. Any more vigorous motion made her head hurt more. "He said something about staying out of other people's business. I don't remember the exact words."

"Your memory will come back," Benny said.

"Who have you angered lately?" Alex set his hat down and grabbed a jar.

"Who hasn't she angered." Benny glanced at the small jar in Alex's hand. "What the hell is that?"

"Berry root paste," Sam replied.

"And what does he plan to do with it?"

"It has a numbing effect and helps to prevent infection." Sam's eyes pleaded with Benny not to reject Alex's help.

"Okay." Benny walked over to a wall of cabinets and opened one of the doors. "What's your choice, Sam? I can use sutures, adhesive strips or an adhesive glue."

"Strips definitely. I don't want stitches."

Benny set several items on a tray and carried them to the examining table. While Benny worked on her head, Anya used a warm, soapy rag to wash the blood from her neck and hand.

"Okay, Alex. Do your berry thing." Benny carried the tray back to the counter.

Sam winced as the root paste stung. "Blow on it, Alex." Alex complied and soon the numbing took effect.

Alex was studying Benny's work as though wondering if he could use the adhesive strips on the animals he tended to. "Shouldn't she have an MRI or X-Ray?"

"I suggested the same thing but she's stubborn." Benny helped Sam to sit up. "Do you have any nausea?"

"I did at first, but no longer."

"Are you drowsy, dizzy?" Benny checked her eyes again. "Pupils still look fine. Do you want some pain killers?"

"No, not with the babies."

"And how are the babies?"

"Fine, I guess. I don't have any cramping."

"You should see your doctor first thing tomorrow." Benny and Alex helped Sam off of the table. "Hope you didn't drive over here."

"I drove," Alex replied. "Left my truck in that church parking lot. I just hope it's still there in the morning."

"Well, take it easy for a few days and if you have any balance problems, loss of memory, sensitivity to light or noise, get yourself to an emergency room."

"I feel fine from the neck on down." Sam winced and added, "I take that back." She lifted the right side of the floral shirt revealing a bruise that was starting to form. "I forgot. He kicked me."

Benny pressed his fingers on her ribs. "Does that hurt?"

"Owww. You are lucky your normal patients don't feel anything. I think it's just a bruise, Benny. It doesn't hurt to breathe, just when you poke at it."

"Sam, do you want these?" Anya had Sam's sweater coat and tunic top across one arm.

"No. Burn them. I won't even try to get the blood out of them."

Jake hung his jacket in the closet and stifled a yawn. It was after midnight and bed never looked or sounded better. He made his way down the hallway to the kitchen where all the lights told him someone was still up. Alex was leaning back in a chair, eyes closed, feet resting on another chair. His eyes snapped open when Jake entered.

"Hey, Alex. Get evicted from your house?"

Jake sank onto a chair and wiped the fatigue from his eyes.

"Abby did not want to bother you at work so I offered to wait up for you." Alex pulled his feet off of the chair and turned to face him. "She is asleep now and the doctor says she needs her rest."

"Abby?" Jake saw the look on Alex's face then jerked from the chair but Alex reached across the table and clamped a hand on his arm so quickly, it dropped Jake back into the chair.

Alex kept his hand on Jake's arm as though he needed to keep him tethered to solid ground. He then told Jake about the assault on Sam and how Benny patched her up.

"The guy kicked her while she was down?"

"Han. Tacu hu." Alex pointed at his side.

Jake was picking up bits and pieces of Lakota. Alex oftentimes conversed with Abby and Sam in their Native language, but Jake suspected Alex used his Native language when he wanted to keep outsiders in the dark. Jake could only assume Alex said "yes" and that Sam was injured on her right side.

"What about the baby? Benny isn't an obstetrician."

"Babies," Alex corrected him. "Sam said she feels fine but has an appointment tomorrow morning with her doctor." Alex finally released his grip on Jake and stood. "My job is done. I will go home now."

Jake watched Alex slide the patio door open, then closed. The golf cart started up and Alex drove the asphalt path back to the house in the back acres. Jake felt numb. He wanted to punch something, someone. What was Sam doing at the church? Why didn't she call the police or an ambulance?

He trudged up the stairs to the bedroom, stopping at the nursery door for a brief peek, then creeping into the master bedroom. He turned the light on low above the headboard casting just enough light for him to see. Sam was lying on her side facing the patio doors. He made his way around the bed and regarded Benny's handiwork. A gauze pad covered Sam's forehead close to the hairline. She was sleeping soundly, too soundly to awaken. He started to pull the covers up. Sam stirred and stretched, raising her right arm above her head and lifting the cami above her waist, exposing the bruise developing on her right side.

"Jezzus." Jake's outburst woke Sam. He lifted the cami higher as he knelt down. "Who the hell did this? Did you see his face? Why were you at that church alone? Why wasn't I called?"

She blinked but it appeared painful to do even that little of a movement. She reached up and stroked his face. To most suspects this was the face of a bruiser, a man who protected the weak and abhorred the oppressors, especially against women and children. To women, he had a rugged appeal. The strong, silent type. He grabbed her hand and kissed the palm.

"Jake, just for tonight, could you be a husband first and a cop second?"

Jake didn't have time to study his mental handbook on spousal reaction. He wanted to tear the town apart looking for the person responsible. He slowly rose from the bed and undressed in the walk-in closet, tossing clothes into the hamper and slipping into a pair of gym shorts. As he washed up in the bathroom, he splashed cold water on his face then looked at his reflection in the mirror. Controlled rage could best describe the look in his eyes. He braced his hands on the counter and took several deep breaths until he could feel his muscles relax.

He turned off the bathroom light, then the light above the headboard. Sam had her back to him and he couldn't tell if she went back to sleep. He slipped into the bed, slid his hands under her and gently pulled her over to his side of the bed, careful not to touch the bruises.

"I love you, Jake."

"Shhhh. Go back to sleep," he whispered as he gathered her in his arms. He could be the husband tonight, but tomorrow he would be the cop.

38

"If you ask me, he's too stupid to have killed her." Frank held his hand out for his phone messages.

"Since when are killers smart?" Scofield slapped two pink slips into Frank's hand.

"Doesn't matter. We didn't have enough evidence to hold him." Jake took one message from Scofield and scanned it.

"Thought he stole her ATM card?" Scofield gazed over his bifocals at the detectives.

Robinson lumbered up to the desk, swiping several pink slips. "We made a deal. If he showed us where he was when the body was dumped, we'd forget about the money. We got most of it back and we'll hound him for the rest."

Scofield took off his bifocals and waved them in the air. "Almost forgot. Sam's here and she's writing all over your whiteboard."

Sam stood back and studied the board. The dots were connecting too fast and furious for her not to share her findings. "About time you guys got back."

"Aw shit, Sam." Robinson got all fatherly on her and wrapped her in a bear hug. "I agree with Jake. You should have gone to the emergency room."

"Yeah, but you should see the other guy." Sam's attempt at a joke fell flat. She, too, had been shocked when she looked in the mirror this morning. Her eyes were ringed in black. When she removed the gauze pad, it looked as though someone had dragged her behind a truck on a gravel road. Alex had used more berry root paste on the wound before she left for the doctor. Jake had insisted on meeting her at the obstetrician.

"I got these from Benny this morning." Robinson stepped back and pulled photos from his pocket. They had been taken by Anya before Sam was cleaned up. "I'm glad we have some record of what was done to you."

"Jeez, Sam." Frank stood at Robinson's elbow, his eyes widened. "How's the baby?"

"Babies are fine." Now Sam had to deal with three men going all protective on her, five if she counted Benny and Alex.

"I want the DNA results," Jake growled. "I want the sonofabitch who did this."

"I told Benny to give them only to me." Robinson placed the photos on the table. "I don't want you going all vigilante on me."

"It really looks worse than it is. I'm feeling a little battered and bruised but I'll be fine. Now sit. It's show-and-tell time."

Robinson gave the board a cursory examination. "What the fuck?" He sank into one of the chairs. Frank did the same while Jake remained standing as though waiting to catch Sam should she collapse from exhaustion.

Frank glanced at the whiteboard, then looked as puzzled as Robinson. When Sam had walked in, all that had been written on the board was one victim, Donna Oberweiss, and the names of close friends, the manager/ex-boyfriend Ron, and Davey who had stolen her ATM card.

Sam had erased all of it and at the top of the board she had drawn a rectangle-shaped box with four vertical lines coming from the box, one line dotted. Below the dotted line on the far right Sam had written Donna Oberweiss' name.

"Wait." Robinson's gaze was immediately drawn to Marti Johnson's name.

"Sam, what is this?" Jake closed the conference room door, then leaned against it.

Sam tapped the marker against Marti's name. "I'll try not to make this too confusing, although my head is still spinning. The captain asked me to look into Marti Johnson's suicide. I was skeptical at first, but I had

Mister Johnson walk me through, in his words, how Marti spent that last morning. I asked to see her cell phone since the police report said she had received a call but it only lasted four seconds and they assumed it was a telemarketer. When I turned the phone on, one word flashed on the monitor—*destiny*. Then a picture of Forrest and Samantha appeared as the wallpaper so I thought nothing of it.

"Forrest asked me to sit in on one of his suicide support group sessions where I met Carrie Farnswood." Sam tapped the marker against Carly's name. "Carrie's twin sister was one week away from her wedding when she drove to the beach, calmly stripped and walked into Lake Michigan. She, too, received a phone call before leaving her house. I had Beast…"

"Who?" Frank said.

"Beast is our tech guy in the basement at Headquarters," Robinson said. "Go on, Sam."

"Beast checked the SIM cards. Both calls lasted four seconds and came from disposable phones. He wasn't able to get any information on them." Sam tapped the marker against Nina Logesta's name. "I was curious about other recent suicides so Chief Murphy let me look through some files in the archives. Nina Logesta was a former gambler in hock to the River Queen Casino. Junior hired her as a dealer as a way to pay back the money she owed."

"I remember that case," Robinson said. "Her body hung in that woods for six months before someone found her. She still had gambling problems."

"Not true. I spoke to her neighbor. Nina was clean for two years. Nina's roommate lied to the investigating officer."

"The roommate told you this?" Jake looked skeptical and he was doing a poor job hiding it.

"Flo Dempsey, the neighbor, was never interviewed. This surprised her because she had quite a bit to tell."

"Let me guess." Frank waggled a finger from one name to the next. "Nina also received a phone call."

"Right. Fiona Vasquez, the roommate, tossed the phone and gave Nina's clothes and other possessions to Goodwill, but Flo had Nina's cell phone number in her address book. Beast obtained a list of calls from the phone company. The last call to Nina came from a disposable phone and the call lasted four seconds."

"That's something the investigative officer should have looked into." Robinson pulled a pen from his pocket and grabbed a napkin from the credenza. "What was the name?"

"Sal Marino."

"That ass." Robinson scribbled the name on the napkin. "Somehow sloppy police work coming from him doesn't surprise me."

"I don't understand how they tie together." Frank said.

"And what do they have to do with Donna Oberweiss?" Jake added. "According to the phone company, she didn't make nor receive any calls from Collin Revere so we still can't connect her to the golf course."

Any other time Sam would have hesitated mentioning how she received her information, but her gift had been very useful in past cases, and these three men were used to her strange methods. "I spoke to Benny about Marti Johnson. He happened to have the bag of evidence from Donna's case. I touched her purse strap and heard the same word— *destiny*. That's how I first suspected the cases were linked." Sam took the marker and wrote in the rectangle box, *Morning Glory Clinic*. Then she explained her visit with Jackie and how she saw Marti's and Carly's pictures on the bulletin board, and how William Borden Junior confirmed that Nina had also been a client at Morning Glory.

"Wait." Jake pushed away from the door. "Who have you been talking to about these cases, Sam?"

"I thought of that this morning as my raccoon eyes stared back at me from the mirror. I showed Collin Revere Marti's picture hoping to connect her case with Donna's."

"That WAS you at the golf course that day."

Sam ignored Jake's comment. "I tried to speak to the owners of Morning Glory but they were allegedly not in. I left my business card but neither of them called me. So I found out one of the owner's wives sold her designer jewelry to the Center. I conveniently ran into her there."

"And probably hinted that her husband was a killer."

Sam recognized that look of disgust and frustration on Jake's face. Sam had a knack for putting herself in danger and someone she had spoken to or accused might have been her attacker.

"All I said is that three of the suicide victims used to be patients at Morning Glory. I never implied that they killed them."

Robinson clicked his ball point pen. "So you spoke with Collin Revere...and what are the other names?"

"The owners of Morning Glory are Matthew Bordeau and Austin Revere."

39

As though too weighted down by a massive forehead, Robinson's brows slowly sank, settling close to his eyes. His arms rested on the desk top to brace his entire body from descending into a career-ending sinkhole. "You like giving me heartburn, Sam?"

"I like tripping up a killer who thinks he's clever." Sam opened the window and tossed sunflower seeds onto the sill. Two mourning doves landed on the sill and cooed. "Hey Tonto, Cochise. Hungry?"

"Nice, Sam. Thanks for the shit you dumped in my lap and now on my windowsill. Murphy is going to have my head on a platter."

"Murphy's going to love it." Sam grabbed her cup of tea and sat down. They were lined up in front of Robinson's desk like three delinquent students in a principal's office. Jake had thought Sam had been on her feet for too long during her show-and-tell fiasco and insisted on getting her a cup of tea and sitting her down in a comfortable chair.

"There's no love lost between Murphy and the mayor," Frank reminded them. "With Revere being a huge contributor to Mayor Schuler's campaign, Murphy will encourage us to stick it to him."

"The mayor has obviously gotten ahead of the body found on the golf course. Other than a mention of the course you can't find any report in the newspaper of Connor Revere even owning the golf course," Jake said. He pointed a finger at Robinson's notepad. "Maybe you should add Mayor Schuler's name to your list."

Robinson almost chuckled but then stopped. "That snake of a chief of staff he has isn't above hiring someone to pressure Sam." Robinson leaned back, a squeal of protest from his custom-made chair. "So how is the killer doing it? Any clue?"

"It isn't possible to hypnotize someone to kill himself, is it?" Frank asked no one in particular.

"I asked Doctor Collier about it," Sam said. When Robinson's eyebrows lifted in question, Sam added, "He's my therapist. Anyway, he said you can't hypnotize anyone to do something harmful. It's impossible. But he did say women were easier to manipulate than men. That might explain why all of the victims are women."

"Were the women still clients of the clinic up until their death, Sam?" Jake asked.

"No. That's the puzzling part. Marti started going when she found out she was pregnant because she was desperate to quit smoking. She was through with her hypnotherapy in the third or fourth month of her pregnancy. Savannah, her daughter, is nine months old, so it's been over a year since Marti set foot in Morning Glory. Carly wanted to lose weight before her wedding and went through some weight loss program. Nina needed help with her gambling problem. Whether hypnosis was used in their programs or not, I don't know, because neither of the good doctors called me."

Jake cocked his head to study Sam in his typical FBI way. She felt she had just been dissected visually like a jigsaw puzzle, then put back together. "Did your attacker say anything to you?"

Sam paused and thought back to last night. She had made an effort at Benny's to remember details, but things had been a little hazy. Now that her memory was clearer, she was remembering more. "Yes, he did. He said, 'Keep your damn nose out of other people's business or the next time I won't be so gentle.'"

"You." Robinson pointed a finger at Frank. "Keep an eye on your partner because I don't like the look on his face."

"I'm fine," Jake said, even though the set of his jaw and the tense look in his eyes said different.

"I'll pull you off this case, Jake, if I even suspect you're out of line." The captain turned back to Sam as he typed a detailed report on his keyboard. The links to the victims were too complex to rely on his memory. "Well, I think someone at that clinic was still seeing or even dating these ladies. Maybe they have blackmail pictures and they chose suicide over exposure."

Sam was shaking her head even before he finished his thought. "Already posed that question to all the victims' relatives."

"They are the last to know," Jake reminded her.

"You two," Robinson pointed at Jake and Frank, "get over to that clinic and interview the two owners. If they aren't in, chase them down. If we have to, send a car and bring them into our fine establishment. The women were patients, how long were they there, when was their last visit, what kind of treatments did they get, were drugs involved?" His beefy hand made a rolling motion through the air. "You know the drill. Get them, or at least Revere's son, to go crying to his daddy. Then we'll all sit back and watch Mayor Schuler's head blow off."

Sam smiled a little too gleefully.

"Don't show your hand," Robinson warned. "Don't want to spook them, just let them know you are a little bit suspicious."

Sam handed a pamphlet and several sheets of paper to Jake. "I didn't think the bios on the pamphlet were enough so I did some computer searches on their two names. I printed out some additional background info."

"Thanks, babe." Jake opened the pamphlet to the two faces of their new suspects.

"And you." Robinson pointed a finger at Sam. "Go home and get some rest. Stay out of sight."

"Come on," Sam protested.

"He's right." Jake folded the papers in half and stood. "There's someone out there who's probably waiting for you to make a move. Now go home."

He sat near the window at Java the Hut watching the entrance to the Morning Glory Clinic. How many more bread crumbs did he have to drop before the dumb cops took a hint? Did he have to do their job for them? Obviously. He didn't doubt for a moment that their well-connected families would get them out of trouble. That's why he had an ace up his sleeve. He always was good at gambling. That's how he made a lot of his extra pocket money. Of course, he had to be alone at a blackjack table and he had to make sure the pit boss wasn't watching the table. He had no fear of the cameras. There were so few people manning them these days that it was easy to get away with just about anything. It wasn't wise to sit at the high limit tables. That's where they centered most of the surveillance. And he had to make sure he had a female dealer. They were the easiest to work his magic on. There were enough casinos in the area to spread himself around. Never hit the same place too often. Never look the same twice. Never flash around wads of cash. And never broadcast his talent. Once another player joined his table, he ceased his carnival act. For three years it had served him well financially. But he should be better off. He should be a multi-millionaire, living in a mansion. It should be his silver Mercedes parked in a reserved spot in the back of the building. It should be his fifteen room mansion on the shores of Lake Michigan with a pool in the backyard. He should have just shot them both but he wasn't a violent man. At least in his mind he wasn't a violent man.

He had tried a year ago to draw attention to them by making the dealer his first victim. But the dumb broad hung herself in an area where few people traveled so her body wasn't found immediately. It was just as well. Made the game more enjoyable.

What's this? He slowly straightened, lowered his cup of coffee. A dark sedan just pulled into the drive and headed to the turn-around. It may as well have CHPD emblazoned on the door. *Well, well. Now things are finally getting interesting.*

The sound perforated the air along the walking path. Sam stopped to listen. She remembered one time when she was small sitting on the floor in the kitchen. A black insect the size of a lightning bug had fallen over on its back. It had remained motionless, not struggling to right itself. Then she heard a click. The beetle jumped in the air. Another click and it landed on its feet. *Click...click.* As she stood on the path she wondered if those click beetles were around or were they extinct. The sun was setting as she continued her walk over a wooden bridge and deeper into the walking trail. *Click...click.* Could it be a locust? But locusts made a buzzing sound. Her gaze fell on a figure seated on a bench up ahead. She slowed her pace when she realized the sound was coming from his direction. *Click...click.* He was a shadow of a man, all black without any features. In his hand he held a small object. *Click.* A car key sprung from the side of the object. The key was narrow with a blunt end. With one finger he swung the key back into the slot. *Click.* He pressed something on the front of the key fob. *Click.* The key sprang out again. The faceless figure turned in her direction, but this time he was holding a bottle of water in his hand. He pointed the bottle at her. *Click.*

Sam jolted to a sitting position then grabbed her head. She didn't know which was pounding louder, her head or her heart. A small whimper was oozing from the baby monitor. Sam dragged her body up from the couch and swung her legs over the side. The man in the coffee shop. What was it called? Java the Hut. He was playing with his key fob. Was it just something her brain decided to weave into a dream or did he factor into the case? Another whimper, this time developing into a plaintive wail.

Abby appeared next to the couch. "Lie back down, Samantha. I'll take care of Dillon."

Sam obeyed, grateful for a little more time to rest her body. She was on the couch in the living room where a fire crackled in the fireplace. The sun was bright and shone through the windows in the Florida room. Sam pulled the afghan up and thought about her dream. *Click...click.* Why else would her mind be so focused on that one sound? More importantly, why the walking trail? If the victims had all attended Morning Glory Clinic, shouldn't she be seeing that building instead? There was a nature trail on the grounds of the clinic. But there were a number of walking trails in Chasen Heights. Then she remembered the last vision, with the man sitting on the bench. He had been studying his victims! He knew where they walked, shopped, probably knew their daily routines. Had the owners of Morning Glory or Collin Revere hired someone to keep an eye on their prey?

She heard the front door bell and was just ready to give up on napping when she heard the door open and Jackie's voice cooing at Dillon whose crying had stopped abruptly at seeing his Aunt Jackie.

"Where is my girl? My poor baby." Jackie maneuvered her way across the wood floors to the living room. "Oh my gawd!" Tears welled quickly and Jackie waved a hand in front of her face to try to dry her tears. "Sam, you poor thing." Jackie tossed her coat on a chair, plopped on the couch and held Sam at arm's length, studying all of the bruises.

"I didn't think I looked that bad until you came in."

"Who did this to you?" Jackie demanded. "Why did you go alone, in the dark, in that part of town? I should have been with you."

"There were people there, well, in the basement. I left early." Sam repeated the story about meeting with Forrest and Carrie, the attack in the parking lot, and her trip to Benny's.

"Benny had you on his autopsy table? How creepy is that." Jackie lifted stray hairs on Sam's forehead and winced at the scrapes and cuts spreading from the adhesive strips. "Do the police have a suspect?"

"Jake has a short list of suspects."

"Revere's father owns that golf course where the other body was found, right?"

"Right. And I've pissed off the mayor, but what else is new."

"I'd be worried about the Reveres. People with that kind of money can hire thugs to do their dirty work. Thugs who don't care about roughing up a pregnant woman." Jackie grabbed Sam's hand and sandwiched it between hers. "Now, what can I do for you?"

"I need newspapers from Reed University during the time those doctors attended. How are you at computer searches?"

"Honey, I'm like a bloodhound with claws."

40

"Gentlemen, I'm pleased you took time out of your busy schedule to see us." Frank's pastoral voice sounded like anything but interrogation.

Austin turned from the window. "Like we had a choice."

"Everyone has a choice." Frank set his business card on the desk in front of Matt. "We're here about three of your patients." Matt leaned back in his chair not giving the card a second glance. They were as preppy looking as their photos in the brochure, and smug.

"Clients," Austin hissed. "We never refer to them as patients."

Matt said, "This have anything to do with accusations that police consultant made?"

"We wouldn't have had to come if you had responded to her inquiry." Jake remained standing, already deciding he didn't like either of these two men. His gaze took in the décor. The office was nouveau rich in black and chrome with abstract paintings hanging on the wall that probably doubled as Rorschach inkblot tests. The gray and black area rug was plush under his feet. A counter along the corner wall looked more like a happy hour bar.

Frank took a seat in the upholstered chair in front of the desk. Austin Revere remained standing with an unwavering glare telegraphing his disdain. At least Bordeau had a trace of a smile on his face. Frank opened a file folder and placed three pictures in the center of Matt's immaculate glass top desk. "Nina Logesta hung herself a year ago. She was a client here for her gambling addiction." He pointed at the next photo. "Carly Farnswood wanted to lose weight before her wedding. As excited as she was about her wedding, she stripped and walked into Lake Michigan just one week before her nuptials." His finger jabbed onto the photo of Marti Johnson. "Marti set her infant in a high chair, heated a jar of baby food, made herself a cup of coffee, put on her shoes, walked out of the condo and jumped off the overpass several blocks away."

Austin studied the buff sheen of his nails as he spoke. "Are you insinuating we had something to do with their deaths?"

"We'd like to take a look at their files, see what type of treatment they received."

"Doctor-client privilege. You should know that, Detective." The last word rolled off his tongue like something distasteful. Matt slowly gathered the photos into a pile. "You would need a court order."

"I believe that so-called privilege ends when the patient is deceased but no problem," Jake said. "Our captain is working on that court order now."

"It would save time if you'd just tell us about those clients." Frank glanced briefly at Jake. "That way we won't have to take you back to the precinct for a little chat."

Austin snickered, a smug laugh punctuated by a slow, rhythmic clapping of his hands. But his smile faded as Jake opened the office door and ushered in two uniformed officers.

"What the hell is this?" Matt looked to Austin as though his smug laugh had rubbed the detectives the wrong way.

"You can drive over of your own accord to answer some questions, or we could have you escorted out the front door of your clinic. Take your pick." Jake checked his watch as though timing them.

Austin looked at Matt whose face showed panic. "I'm calling our lawyer." Matt moved to pick up the phone.

Jake nodded to the officers. "You can do that at the precinct."

"Where are our guests?" Robinson assembled his detectives in one of the conference rooms and closed the door.

"In the interrogation room waiting for their lawyer. They won't speak until he gets here," Frank said. Jake and Frank used the time to search for more information on their background.

"Let's get our ducks in a row before you dissect those two."

"What about the search warrant, Captain?" Frank tossed a stack of papers on the table.

"Can't get a judge to sign off. Austin Revere's father knows every damn judge in the city. What do we know about them?"

"No police record," Frank started. "Not surprising when rich families control the newspaper publishers. Matt and Austin were college roommates at Reed University in Chicago. Matt Bordeau studied psychology with a minor in art theory and practice, whatever the hell that is. Austin Revere also studied psychology with a minor in humanities. They both chose their graduate work in counseling psychology." Frank looked up from his notes. "Both were more into academics than sports. Other than speeding tickets, neither has been in any trouble. Both had originally entered college majoring in theater but they changed. Guess they figured there wasn't much money in theater."

"Austin Revere is separated from his wife, Emma," Jake reported. "They were married for two or three years, no children. Her family is also from money. Her father deals in antiquities, sort of Michigan's answer to Christie's in London."

"And he cheated on her?" Robinson asked.

"They cited irreconcilable differences," Jake said. "But no luck talking to the ex. There's some gag order in the divorce papers. Neither one is to speak ill or good of the other."

"He cheated," Robinson and Frank said simultaneously.

"Revere's father is well-connected, too, and must be pretty good at white-washing any family secrets because I couldn't find anything in any of the papers, except for the announcement of the separation, but that accompanied the typical 'we ask that you give us our privacy during these trying times' yada yada." Jake flipped over his page of notes. "The clinic was built three years ago and is completely paid off. They began selling franchises last year and the company is reported to be worth in the neighborhood of three hundred million."

Robinson let out a whistle. "Not bad considering the average salary of a psychotherapist is around one hundred and sixty thousand. They must have only high end clients." Robinson cranked his hand as if they weren't talking fast enough. "What about Matt's wife, the one Sam talked to?"

"When we called, she was pretty testy. Already knew we had her husband on the hot seat. She told me she has nothing more to say." Frank opened up a brochure Sam had left them and ran a finger down the page. "The franchises they sold have some pricey clientele spread from San Diego, L.A., Seattle, Las Vegas, Long Island, Marco Island, and everything in between. Patients pay according to their phobia. Guess if you have a sleep disorder or substance abuse problem it might take longer and cost more. Fear of flying or afraid of crowds, maybe panic disorders...wow." He closed the brochure and shuddered. "If I keep reading the list of phobias I'm going to start imagining I have every single one of them."

"No skeletons in the closets?" Robinson looked at each of them.

"Slate is squeaky clean," Jake said.

"No one is that clean. Find some college friends. There's gotta be someone those rich families haven't paid off."

The mouthpiece for Morning Glory sat calmly between Matt and Austin, staring with beady eyes over square wire-rimmed glasses. His bald pate shone under the bright lights of the room. Jake didn't want to piss them off too much by putting them in the box. Instead they were in one of the empty offices.

"How can we help you detectives?" The mouthpiece was known as Edmund Einhorn, Esquire. He used the index finger of each hand to signal the questions Matt and Austin were allowed to answer. Jake had no doubt that a call had been made to Collin Revere by the attorney and by now, Collin was on the phone reaming Mayor Schuler a new one.

Einhorn fit the Bordeau image from the gold watch and large square ring studded with diamonds to the silver hair at the temples where not one strand looked out of place. He lowered his head ever so slightly to peer at the detectives over his bifocals. His trimmed eyebrows etched slowly up his forehead. Austin and Matt didn't smile but their lips twitched now that their attorney had rescued them.

Einhorn took off his glasses and started to rub an imaginary speck off of them with a silk hankie. "We can answer a few questions as long as they don't involve specific clients," he clarified, as though he would also be responding.

Frank took a seat and opened a file folder. Jake leaned against a wall, more interested in what type of shoes the doctors wore. Neither of them wore deck shoes, but he didn't expect them to wear casual shoes to work.

"Nina Logesta, Carly Farnswood, and Marti Johnson. Were any drugs used as part of their therapy?"

Einhorn raised a hand. "I said no specific clients."

"Jeez," Frank said under his breath. "Do you use drugs as part of your therapy at Morning Glory?"

"Absolutely not." Matt was adamant about drug use as he explained that they believed in a holistic approach to therapy. "We use audio and visual tapes."

"Hypnosis?"

"Depends on what you mean by hypnosis." Matt opened his own folder, pulled out a pamphlet and handed it to Frank. "You have heard of the process of learning another language by listening to tapes while you sleep. The audiotapes we use work the same way by planting subliminal messages once the therapist places the client in a relaxed state of mind."

"Hypnotized."

"You make it sound as though we put clients into some trance and channel mysterious occult forces," Austin snarled. "We don't practice voodoo."

Einhorn made a slight motion with his hand, prompting Austin to snap his jaws tight. "If you are implying that Doctors Revere and Bordeau hypnotize subjects to do harm to themselves or others, it is completely impossible. I can assure you not one person has ever been encouraged or motivated to do something he or she would not do in his normal, everyday life."

If the attorney was trying to get Frank to address his comments only to him, he was out of luck. Frank kept his attention on the doctors. "But you must run your clients through some type of testing to see if they are receptive to your power of suggestion."

Austin leaned back in the chair as though removed from the conversation. It appeared to the detectives that Matt was the alpha male in the room. Perhaps Austin had been known to say too much on occasion.

"Of course. Some clients work best with group therapy, some one-on-one. Some are excellent candidates for hypnotherapy. Our holistic approach heals the mind as well as the body. Yoga, the use of mantras, tai chi, relaxation techniques. It isn't all swinging pendulums."

"Do you find women more receptive than men?"

"Probably. But you have to understand that women are more inclined to seek professional help whereas some men don't want to admit they need help or feel they are strong enough to weather their own problems."

"Did either of the three patients…"

"Clients," Matt and Austin said simultaneously.

Frank sighed. "Clients return after their initial session was completed?"

Einhorn whispered something in Austin's ear, then turned to Matt and did the same thing. "If you are asking if they dated any of their clients, the answer is no." Einhorn finished brutalizing his glasses and turned them toward the lights. Satisfied, he put them back on.

"Dating never entered our heads," Jake said, speaking for the first time and startling the three men. "Where were you two last night between the hours of seven and nine?"

Matt and Austin exchanged looks. Einhorn held up an index finger for each of them. "Why do you want to know that?"

Jake walked over and flung Sam's business card in front of them. "She left her calling card as well as a message about the three clients. Sam was assaulted last night on the east side of town, in the parking lot of the Family Christian Center."

Austin snorted. "Like we'd ever be seen in that part of town."

Einhorn flicked an index finger again.

Jake dragged his gaze to Austin. "She had also spoken to your father about the body found on his golf course who might be victim number four."

"You can't pin that…" Matt started.

"This meeting is over. Let's go." Einhorn rose and flapped his hands as though helping a duck and her ducklings across a busy street. "Next time you want to speak with my clients, you better have an arrest warrant."

"I doubt you would get your hands dirty. You or your father could have hired someone." Jake wasn't about ready to let it go. It was all he could do not to grab one of them by their scrawny necks and give him a sample of what Sam had gone through. "We're going to check phone records for calls made to and from your personal, business and home phones."

"Good luck with that court order, too, Detective." Einhorn herded his ducklings out of the room.

Matt pounded the elevator button as Einhorn checked his watch. "What the hell was that all about?"

"I haven't a clue," Austin replied.

"But the body was found on your father's golf course. Are you sure your father had nothing to do with harming that consultant?"

"Positive."

"I trust both of you have your noses clean. I'm a corporate lawyer, not a defense attorney."

"My dad will handle this. He's a good friend of the mayor's." Austin pulled out his cell phone and dialed.

41

Police Chief Dennis Murphy was contemplating a late lunch when he heard a familiar loud voice outside his office door. He opened a file folder and positioned it in front of him. Next he placed a stack of opened mail on the corner of his desk as an attempt to clutter his otherwise pristine desk. He had read Robinson's memo three times to make sure he had his facts down and wouldn't have to refer to the details on the suicides and how they might relate to the body found at the Lake Bluff Country Club. Knowing Mayor Schuler, Murphy assumed there wouldn't be a knock on the door. Schuler would barge in not bothering to be announced.

The door pounded open and a red-faced Schuler charged in. "I thought I made myself perfectly clear." He remained standing so as to establish his authority.

Murphy pulled off his glasses and leaned back in his chair. "This must be about the homicide at the golf course. It's still an open case."

"I thought I said to close it. Don't your detectives have someone in custody?"

"Had to release him. Not enough proof."

"But now your detectives are hounding Revere's son, trying to tie three closed cases to the Oberweiss murder."

Murphy showed him his palms. "Any good cop would have followed the leads."

Schuler's face turned crimson as he pointed his finger toward the window like some imaginary directional signal. "That pit bull the department uses as a consultant. I thought I told you to fire her."

"She's under contract. Only the Council has that authority." Murphy kept his voice calm and even. The hard part was trying to hide the glee from his face. He furrowed his brows in an attempt to look worried. "According to my captain at the Sixth, Sam Casey is working for the family of one of the victims." He lifted the report from the desk and waved it like a surrender flag. "Is there any truth to this? Three patients of the Morning Glory Clinic committed suicide. It's hard to sweep those under the rug."

"What loony bin hasn't had a slate of suicides? She's making more out of this than needed and I bet you put her up to this to discredit me."

"Hey, there's no love lost between us. You forget how she tried to paint me as a killer in that Embers Hotel case."

"If I remember correctly, she's the only reason you were exonerated."

"Only because I was innocent. Sam is more into finding the truth. She's just like her father. He didn't care who he skewered as long as the truth won out."

As though thoughts of the loss of Revere campaign money made him weak in the knees, Schuler grabbed the back of one of the arm chairs. "Well, there's more than one way to discredit the bitch. She spent some time in a loony bin herself, as I recall." He straightened as if his spine were refortified. "Perhaps a well-placed article on her history might take the focus away from Revere and his son."

"I'd tread lightly, if I were you." Murphy tossed his glasses on the desk. "Someone assaulted her last night, knocked her around a bit."

"Who can I send my thank you card to?"

"My detectives are looking at everyone Sam spoke to concerning this case. That includes the two Reveres and Matt Bordeau. She didn't talk to you or your chief of staff, did she?"

Schuler's beady eyes slitted. "Are you implying...?"

"She's not only pregnant but also a former cop. We protect our own and stop at nothing to find the perpetrator." Murphy imagined Schuler's pea brain was already drafting memos for damage control should the newspapers catch wind of the attack. "Tom Lukavich was real good at verbally assaulting people during the campaign. Do you really know what he's capable of when acting without your authority?" He thought it better to throw the suspicion on the mayor's chief of staff.

"I'm going to forget we had this conversation." Schuler turned and stomped out of the office. Murphy watched Schuler storm toward the elevator. As though on command, the doors opened. If he were wearing a cape, Schuler could have just as well whipped it around and disappeared in an explosion of smoke. Once the elevator doors closed, Murphy leaned back with a smile.

42

Plan ahead. If you had planned ahead you wouldn't have to rely on others to determine your future. Those words of wisdom were seared in his memory and the person who said them would be forever in his crosshairs. *Click...click.* It was such a habit now he barely realized he was doing it. It helped him to think. *Click...click.* When he fell into a rhythm it almost sounded like a metronome.

He watched her movements on the other side of the pond. Three times a week, rain or shine, she always jogged around the park ending with a slow stroll around the pond. The landscape was painted in fall colors and the brisk air required a jacket. She was dressed in a silver and gold warm-up suit with silver running shoes. As if to match her platinum hair, she had made a recent purchase of a silver Lexus. He knew she met friends for brunch on Wednesdays, volunteered at the hospital once a month, dropped off orders at the Art Center on random days, and liked to shop at the outlet mall in Michigan City, Indiana. With a Masters Degree in art theory *(what the hell was that?)* she preferred playing the social butterfly and attending functions that would get her name and face in the Sunday newspapers.

The small object at his feet barked, then whimpered. He saw a movie once about guys using puppies to pick up girls. It had worked well for him so far. Just walk into any Humane Society and offer to take a dog for a walk. Women like the cute, cuddly puppies. This mixed mutt looked like a poodle and a cocker spaniel. It had tight curly fur and large brown eyes.

The puppy sprang to life as the woman approached, its tail wagging furiously. It seemed to have springs for legs as it bounced up and down and yipped in a high squeal.

"That's it. Work your magic." It wasn't as though he needed help finding women. He wasn't a total dog. Just average. His was the face of a priest or accountant without any scars or tattoos that would make him memorable. "He was average, Officer. Average build, average height, average weight, brown hair, brown eyes, I think." That was always his problem. He was too average. Not GQ material, not rich enough.

The woman slowed to a walk. He knew every detail of her face as it exploded in his binoculars when he watched her daily from a block away. She was definitely a beauty.

"Awwww, look at you." She knelt down and held out her hand. "Can I pet him?"

"Sure. He's had all of his shots." *Click…click.*

"What's his name?"

"Timber. He thinks he's a wolf." *Click…click.*

She took a seat on the bench next to him. Timber followed, placing puppy paws on her knees and licking her hand. "Hi, Timber. I'm Crystal."

How like her to have some exotic name. "Do you have pets?" *Click… click.* He dropped the leash, then placed his foot on top of it so his hands were free.

She laughed, and god help him if it didn't sound like the tinkling of crystal chandeliers. "We don't have time for pets, unfortunately." She grabbed Timber's face in both of her hands. "Pets need a lot of attention, not owners who are rarely home."

He waited for that right moment, when her eyes met his, swam in the pool of darkness. *Click…click.* "Sure is a hot day. I bet you are parched." Her eyes met his. *Click…click.* Truth was the sun was low on the horizon and the temperature was dipping to fifty degrees. He watched her tongue move around in her mouth, trying to assess the dryness. "Could use something ice cold to drink." *Click…click.* He had her now. He could see it in the way her eyes were swimming. He pulled a bottle of water from his jacket pocket. "Here." He unscrewed the cap. "You feel like you just walked out of a desert." He handed it to Crystal but she hesitated, her tongue still trying to work up some saliva. "It's a fresh bottle."

"Thanks." She grabbed the bottle and drank long gulps, gasping at the icy liquid, although it was barely room temperature. She wiped her mouth with the back of her hand, color rising to her cheeks. "Sorry. Guess I was thirstier than I thought."

He gently placed a hand on her neck and leaned in. "Now, I have to tell you something and you need to listen very carefully." *Click...click.*

It only took five minutes to explain his instructions and for Crystal to repeat them. Afterwards he helped her to her car. She staggered a little as they walked but he pulled her close and laughed so onlookers would think they were lovers out walking the dog. It would have been so easy to convince her to climb into his van. This one he would love to have his way with but there would be telltale signs. Women have a way of knowing when they've had sex, whether the man used a condom or not, and then they would suspect there were some time gaps, pieces of their day they couldn't quite recall. For now it was far better to walk Crystal to her car, help her in, and tell her to close her eyes and rest for a bit before driving. She obeyed and closed her eyes. He unclipped her phone from the holder, checked her cell phone number, and wrote it down.

His victims usually slept for thirty minutes or so and woke up refreshed without a hint of meeting anyone on the walking trail, of petting a dog, or remembering anything he said. At least not until he made his phone call. And he always called.

"Wow, look who's home, Dillon." Sam watched as her son's eyes lit up and his hands and feet started pumping. He was sitting in a carrier on the coffee table in the study.

"Hey, sport." Jake grabbed fistfuls of fabric in much the same way he grabbed Davey before dragging him out of the booth. He lifted Dillon out of the carrier and up in the air. The baby squealed with delight. "What have you been doing?" He planted a kiss on Dillon's cheek.

"Napped too long for one thing. Doesn't want to go to sleep."

Jake took a seat next to Sam on the couch and set Dillon in his lap. "How are you doing?"

"Still have a headache. Would love to take a bottle of aspirin but I can't."

"Let me." Jake placed one hand on the back of her neck. Dillon watched, his mouth gaping in a wide yawn.

She felt fingers gently kneading her shoulders and working their way toward the back of her neck.

"What are those?" Jake nodded at the printouts on the coffee table.

"School newspapers from our suspects' college days. Jackie did the computer search for me."

He kissed the back of her neck. "Good. Anything to keep you home and safe."

Sam ignored his comment. "Anything new on your end?"

"Andy and Maury took over reviewing the videos from Bailey's. They are looking for any customers who looked like they were giving Donna a hard time." His fingers were on her scalp now, kneading and massaging the pain away. "What about you? Have plans for tomorrow?"

"If I'm feeling better, I promised Mom I'd go grocery shopping with her."

"Take Alex with."

"Alex is canning tomatoes."

"Then take Mister Taurus with you."

"I'll definitely be armed with Mister Taurus."

She closed her eyes and let the tension drift. The house was silent and outside only the hooting of an owl could be heard in the distance. Abby was on her laptop in her room answering emails.

"How are the nightmares?"

"I wouldn't call them nightmares anymore. They are more like dreams with great special effects." That got a chuckle from Jake. "The thing is Doctor Collier told me to think back to when this new version started. He wanted me to go through old newspapers to see if some headline triggered it. But when I went through the archives of previous suicides, there were photos from the Nina Logesta case, when her body was found. It was the same image that was framed by the car fragments in my dream. The date on the report is around the date the new dreams started. Someone was trying to tell me something back then."

"Hmmm."

Sam knew that hmmm. It used to mean skepticism. Now it meant skepticism with an open mind.

Jake leaned close and whispered in Sam's ear. "You know, there are other things I can do to make your headache go away."

"Unfortunately, your son won't cooperate."

"You underestimate my abilities."

Sam looked at Dillon resting against Jake's arm. He was sound asleep.

43

The morning newspaper hit Robinson's desk as though some monster fly were being swatted. Papers and notes scattered and drifted to the floor. Robinson gave a resigned look at the floor, then the figure looming over his desk.

"What the hell is this?" Mayor Schuler barked. "I thought I told you that no one was to speak to the press. All communication comes through my office. What part of *no one* don't you understand?"

Chief Murphy stepped from behind Schuler and grabbed the newspaper from the desk. "This is why you had me rush over here?" The headlines read *Police Cover-up* with an opening statement insinuating Schuler's relationship with the golf course owner was the reason more attention wasn't being paid to the murder of Donna Oberweiss. The reporter also managed to weave in the connection to Morning Glory and the two owners.

Schuler ripped the paper from Murphy's hands. "Where are your detectives on the case? I want them in here."

"They are out working leads." Robinson hefted his bulk from the chair and picked up the litter from the floor. "If you read further along in the article you will discover that it is the victim's family that was interviewed by the press. I have no authority to tell them not to exercise their First Amendment rights. They are leaving town soon and concerned that progress hasn't been made on Donna's case." He assembled the pink phone messages in a time-stamp order and set them under a paperweight shaped like a gun. He gathered up the rest of the papers from the floor and put them in a neat stack.

There was a hint of amusement in Murphy's eyes but he kept the smile from his lips. "You can always order the family to keep their mouths shut. That should read good in tomorrow's headlines."

"Are you sure it isn't your investigative consultant who is putting words into the mouths of the relatives? Have you no control over that broad?" Schuler turned to the chief for a reply.

"I would be careful how you refer to women, Mister Mayor." Murphy checked his nails, wondering if he were due for a manicure. "Sensitivity courses are mandatory in the department."

"Fuck that. Now what is happening with your number one suspect, that guy you picked up who had the victim's ATM card?"

"We cut him loose," Robinson replied. *Where have you been?* he wanted to say.

"What the hell for?"

"No proof."

"This the derelict who curled up next to the body because it was still warm?" Murphy asked.

"What?!" Schuler's mouth gaped. His cushy job as owner of a trucking company had shielded him from some of the horrors in the everyday life of a cop. "And you let him sleep in our jail?"

"Yeah, like it's the Ritz Carlton." Robinson flicked his eyes to Murphy who was secretly enjoying the naivety of the newly elected mayor. "You have had a tour of our jail, haven't you?"

"Forget it. But I'll tell you one thing." Schuler jabbed a finger at Robinson. "I better not see one more article about the body at Lake Bluff."

"It won't come from my office, just like today's didn't come from my office."

"Perhaps your press secretary should pay a visit to the victim's family," Murphy suggested. "They are staying in her apartment while they finish cleaning it out. A little explanation that this is an ongoing investigation and mis-information in the press might deter the apprehension of the killer could help."

Schuler narrowed his beady eyes at the chief. If he was trying to look threatening, he wasn't pulling it off. He looked more like Baby Huey having a temper tantrum. "Are you telling me how to do my job?" He shoved the paper under his arm and stalked out.

When Schuler was a reasonable distance away, Murphy said, "Someone has to."

"We didn't talk to the press, Dennis. Neither did Sam or the family." This time the smile did reach Murphy's eyes. "I know."

Why that crafty bastard. Robinson should have known Murphy would work behind the scenes, letting Schuler think the family was the leak when it was actually the chief getting in his daily *stick it to the mayor.*

"I feel like spaghetti." Sam studied the shelves of pasta noodles. "Or maybe lasagna."

"I have plenty of sauce in the freezer, Samantha." Abby tucked the blanket behind Dillon to support his back as he sat in the grocery cart.

Sam pulled a box of lasagna noodles from the shelf. "Is one box enough?"

"Get two just in case." Abby steered the cart around the corner and down the cereal aisle. She consulted her grocery list as they maneuvered around a young woman pushing a cart shaped like a car. A toddler was turning the steering wheel and pushing an imaginary horn. "We need oatmeal."

Sam grabbed a container of instant oatmeal and placed it in the cart. Dillon tried to turn behind him to see what was in the cart but he was sidetracked by Abby shaking rubber toy keys in front of him. He squealed and grabbed the keys. The quilted cart protector circled him like an island so even if he dropped them, the keys would land in the blanket.

"Oooh, the baking aisle." Sam eyed the brownie and cake mix.

"I need corn bread mix." Abby pointed toward the Jiffy mix on the shelf. "Get five boxes. I think we're running low at home."

"You don't think Jake believes you still make it from scratch, do you?"

"I think he has seen the empty boxes in the garbage. You know not much escapes your husband's eyes."

Three women prowled the aisle checking the price of olive oil and spices. One woman wiggled her fingers at Dillon as he shook the car keys.

Abby stopped to inspect her list. "We forgot green beans. I wanted to make a green bean casserole."

"No brownies?"

"I'll make them from scratch, Samantha."

Sam grabbed a bag of chopped walnuts. "For the brownies." During her first pregnancy, Jake had encouraged Sam to eat only healthy foods so Abby had refrained from buying any sweets for the house. That had lasted a few months until Sam's cravings got the best of her. Jake had learned the hard way not to deny a pregnant woman anything.

They made their way back to the vegetable aisle where a stock boy was emptying a cart of canned products. He worked quickly, ripping boxes open and slamming the cans onto the shelves at an amazing speed. Sam placed three cans of French cut green beans in the basket. "Do we have cream of mushroom soup at home?"

"Yes." Abby checked off the item on her list. "I think we have everything we need."

A frigid breeze drifted down the aisle and swirled around them, wrapping them in an Arctic chill. *Click...click.* Where had Sam heard that sound before? *Click...click.* Out of the corner of her eye Sam saw a man wearing a suit pushing a grocery cart containing potato chips, frozen dinners, and a twelve-pack of beer. He slowed to study the canned vegetables. *Click...click.*

The chill increased as he neared. Sam saw Abby straighten and a look of apprehension filled her face. The man was dressed for the office. He was average height with dark hair cut military style. As he rushed past, Sam felt cold fingers crawling up her spine. The chill wasn't the only thing that bothered her. "Mom." She tried to keep the fear from her voice should Dillon pick up on it.

Abby swooped up Dillon and the cart protector in her arms. "We'll wait for you in the van." She held on tight to her grandson as she rushed toward the exit doors. Sam pulled on gloves as she maneuvered the grocery cart down the aisle. She found the man in the next aisle studying the cans of soup. Sam slowed, focusing on the stuffing mix but keeping one eye on the man. She was close enough to see he was checking the contents of a can of vegetable soup. He placed the can back on the shelf and grabbed a can of chicken rice soup. He returned that can to the shelf, grabbed two cans of chicken noodle soup and set them in the cart. Sam proceeded down the aisle keeping her attention on the cans he returned to the shelf. He paused at the end of the aisle. *Click...click.*

Now she remembered where she saw him before. He was watching Tamara when Sam was talking to her at the coffee shop. But he hadn't looked the same. At the coffee shop he had been dressed in work clothes. And he hadn't had that much hair. Was he wearing a hair piece? Today he was in a suit and wore horn-rimmed glasses. He didn't appear to recognize Sam but that was fine. At the time he only had eyes for Tamara.

He left the aisle and headed toward check out. Sam hurried to the shelves of soup, grabbed the cans he had touched and placed them on the top basket to keep them separate from her groceries. She planned to go through the self-service lane so the cashier wouldn't leave her fingerprints on the cans.

Both she and Abby had felt the evil floating in the air as he had walked by. It had crept along the floor before circling them and been so strong that neither Abby nor Sam had to touch him to feel it. But there had been more than the frigid air. Sam had heard a whisper, soft at first, then gaining in volume as he drew closer. It had been the same word she heard when she touched Donna's purse and the same word that had flashed on Marti's phone—*destiny.*

44

Sam knocked before entering the conference room. She found Jake, Frank, and Captain Robinson seated at the end of the table, eyes glued to the monitor hanging from the wall.

"This the tape from the grocery store parking lot?" Sam asked as she carefully placed the small brown bag on the table.

"Yep." Frank had the remote in his hand. "This your guy?" They watched as Abby, carrying Dillon, walked to a brown van. She slid open the side door and then settled Dillon into his car seat. Once she closed the door and climbed in on the driver's side, a man emerged from the store carrying one plastic bag. The cameras were mounted on the roof of the building and caught the man from the back side.

"Yes, that's him. Did you get a plate number?"

"Didn't drive. Either that or his car is parked down the street."

"Clever," Robinson added with a shake of his head. "We have a glimpse of him when he's walking into the store but he keeps his head down so we can't even use facial recognition software if the department ever owned any."

"What about the cameras inside the store?" Sam asked.

"Don't use them." Jake opened the paper bag and studied the two cans of soup. "They have the cameras but they don't turn them on. They think just having them hanging there will deter theft."

"Fat chance." Robinson rubbed his hands together. "Okay then. Let's get those cans over to the crime lab and see if our boy's prints are in the system."

"What about the cameras from Bailey's Sports Bar? Maybe we can see if Shopping Boy's face shows up there," Sam suggested.

Jake gave a shrug. "Worth a try. The Baby Dicks are still working on them. Maybe this video gives them enough detail to work with."

◇◇

Some would say it was best to put the past behind you. Stacy had said that too many times. But what did she know? She had wanted fame and fortune as much as he had. That was the reason she married him. All the promises, all the potential. Stacy had even looked past his weight as he tipped the scales at over three hundred pounds. When convincing people to accept him didn't work, he had to look to himself. Trimming down to one-eighty should have done the trick but it hadn't. He hadn't been born with the proverbial silver spoon in his mouth. Nature had been cruel early in his twenties and seen fit to pluck the hair from the top of his head. Stacy's friends couldn't understand what she saw in him. In the end, Stacy started to wonder the same thing. His magic had worn off. The fortune continued to be elusive. Luckily they hadn't had any children to fight over. In the end she got the house, the car, wiped out their meager savings account and moved back to Boston.

Stacy had been the one bright moment in his life. Blonde, beautiful, vivacious. She could have had anyone. Actually she did want anyone but him, until he convinced her otherwise. It had lasted three glorious years.

Memories of those years weren't enough to bring one glimmer of a smile to his life. Put your past behind you? Not a chance. Especially now. He should be happy that the two men were mentioned in the newspaper, but they were still walking around free. The article made it sound like Revere and Bordeau were helping the damn investigation, not one mention that they were suspects.

He let the feelings wash over him. He reveled in vengeance, bathed in spite, and laid in bed at night working out plans in his head. He could have rented a nicer apartment. His job paid him a livable salary, but staring at a depressing one bedroom apartment filled with consignment shop furnishings kept his hatred simmering, kept him focused on his goals.

He splayed the window blinds and studied the pathetic lives scurrying on the sidewalk two floors below. The odor of coffee wafted through the walls, probably saturating the wood. Not a bad scent to wake up to. Could have been worse. Could be living above a greasy taco restaurant or fish market. Living above Java the Hut gave him a good view of the Morning Glory Clinic.

Sam sipped her tea at the island counter. Outside on the deck Dillon was bundled up in the stroller napping away while Alex stoked his pipe.

"This is very good tea, Samantha." Abby placed a steaming cup in front of Sam, then poured herself a cup.

"I bought a bag of the tea leaves from the Café Fleurs Grotte. It's called Li Zhi Hong. I'll have to take you and Alex there for lunch one day." Sam scoured the back counter with her eyes. "Any lemon squares left?"

"Of course."

Although Sam thought Abby looked more regal when her hair was in a knot at the back of her neck, she loved it when Abby wore it down as it was now. It hung to her waist and gleamed as though polished. There was just a hint of silver threads and Abby was not one to color the gray and silver from her hair.

"What are you working on?" Abby set a plate with squares of lemon pastries on the island counter. She grabbed her cup of tea and took a seat next to Sam.

"College newspapers from the school our suspects attended."

"Looking for skeletons?"

"Always." Sam motioned to a photo on the front page. "When you look at these two GQ poster boys, don't you just know they are too good to be true?"

"Where shall I drop him?" Alex cradled a sleeping baby in his arms as though he were a bag of C4 ready to explode should Alex make too quick of a move.

"Put him in the crib in the study and close the door. Hopefully he'll sleep for a couple hours." Sam smiled at how Alex had become the doting uncle.

Abby prepared another cup of tea and set a plate on the counter next to Sam. "Did you find out the name of that man?"

Alex returned and shrugged out of his jacket, placing it on the back of the chair. "This the man from the grocery store?"

"Yes. He had a very unpleasant aura. Don't think I have ever encountered anyone whose very presence was preceded by the coldest chill I have felt in a long time." Abby set a plate and napkin in front of Alex who quickly grabbed one of the lemon squares. "If he hasn't already committed a crime, I'm sure it is in his mind."

"Oh, he's already committed it," Sam said. "I heard the same word that I heard while investigating Marti's suicide and the body found at the golf course." Sam thought back to the man in the grocery store, his facial features, height, hair. "The thing is, I have the two owners of the Morning Glory Clinic at the top of my list but neither one was the guy in the grocery store. And even though he resembles the man in the coffee shop, he still didn't look quite the same."

Alex filled his coffee cup from the carafe, then grabbed another lemon square. "Probably a hired hit man. They camouflage their appearance. The rich don't want to get their hands dirty, like with you...*wapageya*."

"Well, they aren't going to scare me away." Sam wrapped her arm around Alex's shoulder. "He probably was hired. You make a great detective."

"No thanks. I can't do what you and your mother do. Few people can."

"But you give me good advice. Take this newspaper." Sam thumbed through the pages pointing at various pictures. "Those two psychologists were on the debate team, tennis, theatre, you name it. Way too picture perfect."

"That's all they put in school papers, Samantha," Abby said. "They aren't going to list suspensions and police reports."

"Your mother is right." Alex pointed at a picture of Matthew Bordeau and a female teacher, Viola Williams, who had been in charge of the debate team and also the Humanities Department. "If you want to find out the dirt on anyone, ask the teacher."

Sam took Alex's advice and spent the rest of the afternoon searching the *Chicago Tribune* archives on the computer to find references to Reed University. According to a *Tribune* article, Viola Williams had been fired from her job. The newspaper stated she had changed the grades of two of her students. The students claimed they didn't ask her to and she swore she had never and would never in her lifetime jeopardize her career by doing something so dishonest. The two students had been Matthew Bordeau and Austin Revere.

Sam did another computer search of telephone white pages, hoping Viola Williams still lived in the area. She didn't find any near Chicago, but did find a Viola Williams in Merrillville, Indiana.

Sam picked up her cell phone. "Hey there, Miss Jackie."

"Uh oh. I know that tone, girlfriend. What are you planning?"

"Busy tomorrow? I'd like you to take a trip with me to Merrillville, Indiana."

"Honey, if it's to do some shopping at the mall, I'm all yours."

"We can go there afterwards if you'd like."

45

"Can you tell me why it took us twice as long to get here? We took just about every damn back road plus circled the mall twice."

Sam pulled up to the curb and shut the engine off. "I had a feeling we were being followed."

Jackie turned in her seat. "Where? Who?"

"It was just a creepy feeling but I had to make sure to lose the tail if I did have one."

"You're just jumpy, sweetie. I would be, too."

They climbed out of the Jeep and waited at the sidewalk. Jackie studied the brick bungalow in front of them and the two women seated on the porch swing. "Let me guess. You wanted this sister with you to talk to that sister." The porch was set deep and held several Adirondack chairs as well as the swing. The women on the porch were just as curious about them as their unwavering stares followed their movement.

"I thought you might be able to get them to open up more." Sam had called ahead to make sure Viola Williams would be home and that she would be willing to talk to them. The sun burned its way through a morning cloud cover, but sixty degrees still forced the two women on the swing to huddle in a blanket. Sam pulled her own coat around her tighter as Jackie let her cape fly open, oblivious to the nip in the air. At least Jackie left her hooker heels at home and opted for more sensible boots. Jackie wanted to be comfortable for shopping afterwards.

"You must be that detective who called." Viola Williams had tight gray curls framing a face with expressive eyes and skin lined with wisdom. "This is my niece, Yolanda." The younger woman regarded them suspiciously, surveying them from head to toe as though calculating their worth and comparing it to her aunt's humble brick bungalow and her own faded jacket and jeans. She didn't wear a wedding ring nor any jewelry for that matter. Jackie on the other hand rattled like a coffee can of loose change from her charm bracelet to her dangling earrings and beaded necklace.

"Aunt Viola was due to take her nap." Yolanda clamped a hand on her aunt's shoulder.

Viola patted the young woman's hand. "That's all right, dear. I haven't had visitors in a while and I'm sure you are in need of a breather from my old lady whinings. Why don't you bring us out a pot of coffee and some of those cookies you made."

"Why, you'all don't have to go through no bother for us." Jackie waved her hand in a shooing motion. It surprised Sam how Jackie could change her dialect based on her surroundings.

"Come, sit." Viola motioned to the two chairs on either side of the swing. An electric heater was in the corner, blowing a welcoming warmth to the chilly porch. "I love the fall weather so I hope you don't mind if we sit out here for a spell."

The porch was roomy and covered with area rugs, decorative tables, Americana statues, and wind chimes hanging at the corners from hooks. Several bird houses hung from the maple trees in the front yard. The grass was immaculately trimmed and starting to turn yellow from the chilly nights. Scarecrows stood like sentries against trees across the street while other front yards sported goblins and fake tombstones in the front yards. There weren't any Halloween decorations in Viola's yard.

"Why that little heater certainly spews out enough heat so we don't mind it out here at'tall."

Sam avoided Jackie's eyes. She thought her friend was laying on the *I'm from the same side of town as you* dialect just a little too thick. "This is fine, Miss Williams. We won't stay that long."

Yolanda emerged from the house carrying a large tray. Her jeans hung on her slim frame and it was easy to see the resemblance between aunt and niece. She set the tray on the wicker table in front of the swing, then pulled a chair over to join them. It was obvious she wasn't about ready to let these two strangers interview her aunt alone.

"Are you in school, Yolanda?" Jackie doctored her coffee with cream and sugar.

"Sure. The school of hard knocks."

"Mind your manners, Yolanda." Viola passed the plate of cookies to Sam.

"She asked." The young woman turned to Jackie. "I have an Associates Degree in pre-school education and I can't find a job. They have laid off dozens in my field and so I have to settle for a part-time job at a retail store. A ten-hour a week pay check just doesn't cut it. And now our landlord wants to raise our rent. The damn roof has started to leak." She looked Jackie up and down from her leather boots to her manicured nails and cashmere sweater. Then glanced at Sam's coat and turquoise jewelry. "Sure looks like you two are doing just fine." Her gaze settled a little longer on Sam's forehead and the dark circles under her eyes. "Looks like you pissed someone off."

"She has a way of doing that," Jackie said under her breath.

Viola sighed with a shake of her head. "It's been a rough year. Yolanda worked so hard for that Associates degree. Couldn't afford to send her to a four-year college. She's a little discouraged."

"That's understandable. I own a boutique but it took years of savings to buy it. Every day is like feast or famine. But it takes time. I didn't get there overnight, honey."

Sam almost choked on her coffee. Jackie had been a high-priced escort when Sam had met her. Jackie could make thousands in one night just for having dinner with a dignitary from Dubai. She obtained Jackie's Boutique on a steal when the previous owner skipped the country with the IRS hot on his trail. But Jackie also had a great business sense.

Sam pulled the college newspapers from her tote bag and unfolded the first to a photo of Revere and Bordeau on the front page. She set the newspapers on the table so they were closer to Viola. "As I explained on the telephone, I have some questions about these two gentlemen."

Viola settled a pair of bifocals on her nose. "I remember those two. Hard to forget. They are the reason I lost my job."

Yolanda stared closely at Sam, as though examining an insect she had never encountered before. "Exactly what is it you do and why are you looking into my aunt's prior employment?"

"I'm an outside consultant for the Chasen Heights Police Department. I'm looking into several possible homicides and these two names happened to pique my interest. If I could clarify some of their history it might give me a better picture of them. I'm curious how they factored in to your dismissal."

"Don't you go upsetting my…"

Viola cut her niece off with the lifting of one hand. "Actually, that's the strange thing. I remember the two approaching me in my office. They tried to threaten me. Kept saying 'You are going to give us an A in our final grade.' I threw them out of my office and told them if they tried something like that again I would see to it they were expelled."

"Yet they did get A's," said Sam.

Viola nodded. "To this day I'm not sure what happened. Their entire course history was in the computers. There were records of all of their grades. At best they were C students yet I gave them a final grade of an A. There wasn't any proof they did anything. I would have sounded nuts if I tried to tell people what I really thought. Besides, their fathers were huge contributors to the college." Viola sighed and placed the papers down. "It's all water under the bridge now." She took time to sip her coffee and have a bite of a cookie before asking Sam, "What is it you need to know about them?"

Sam eyed Jackie settling back in her chair, silently sipping her coffee. Jackie's job of making Viola feel comfortable was over, although she still had a little work to do on Yolanda. But that would have to wait. "You do know they now run a very successful therapy clinic. They have sold franchises all over the country."

"Don't surprise me none," Yolanda said in a hushed tone. "With all that family money behind them."

"Well, if they are practicing magic, they have honed their skills, cause they sure tried to run their spells on me. I had heard they did so-called parlor tricks in their frat house using hypnosis. Harmless things like making a guy howl at the moon or streak across the stage during opening night of the Theatre Department's rendition of *Rent*." She set her cup down and leaned in, looking Sam directly in the eye. "I have never ever changed a grade or passed a student falsely, whether for money or bribery or any other reason. Students have to earn their way. I was tough, but I was fair."

"But they didn't believe you." Sam made it a statement, not a question. "They come from pretty rich families. Were you ever pressured to show them favoritism?"

"Never, other than comments from students like, 'do you know who my daddy is?' Didn't pay it no mind. They all were from rich families in order to afford that school, if you ask me." Viola leaned back as though exhausted by the memories.

Yolanda picked up on it rather quickly. "Now see what you've done bringing up that one horrible incident that prevented my aunt from ever being hired as a teacher again. Thirty years of a teaching career and she ended up stocking shelves at the local Dollar store. She finally quit last year cause she just couldn't stand on her feet any more. Are you finally done dredging up the past?"

"Not quite," Sam said in a voice more like *I'll stay longer if you keep up the attitude*. "Were there any friends our two poster boys hung around with who might know more about their unique gift?"

Viola opened the newspapers again and took her time studying the pictures and articles, tapping certain photos but saying nothing. Finally with a shake of her head Viola confessed, "Sorry. Could be anyone in the theatre or debate groups. Actually anyone in the school. They were very popular and, as you can see, they were a hit with the ladies, too. With their obvious popularity and family money in the university's coffers, who was going to believe an old lady?"

Jackie stopped chewing long enough to pay attention to the conversation. "Wait…how could they think you would give failing students high honors out of the goodness of your heart? Did they find a ton of money in your checking account?"

Viola was shaking her head even before Jackie finished her sentence. "The test scores were right, that was the strange thing. I saw those tests with the incorrect answers. Then out of the blue, in my desk drawer, were the same tests with all correct answers altered in my handwriting to show incorrect responses. I supposedly changed their correct answers to incorrect ones so I could fail them."

Sam had seen enough computer wonders from Tim, her young hacking friend, to know nothing is impossible. But these tests and scores weren't in a computer. "Very clever." Sam refilled her coffee cup as she contemplated how this could have been accomplished. "Were there any witnesses to conversations you had with Revere and Bordeau? Anyone who can verify what might have been said?"

"Good luck with that," Yolanda hissed. "That hag at the front desk claimed the two men never even stopped by. She had to have been paid off." She stirred her coffee viciously, as though the cup itself were a substitute for the hag.

Viola sighed again. It was an effort just to control her niece, but she meant well and Yolanda was having it much harder these days with the anemic economy.

"There must be some old girlfriends who can dish out some dirt," Jackie offered. "They can't all be on friendly terms. Like that one." She pointed one long talon on the photo of a girl who was in just about every club photo alongside Revere and Bordeau. "Look at the way she is stripping them with her eyes. Uh huh. She's got some stories to tell."

For the first time, Yolanda almost smiled, and she was attractive when she did. Long lashes, expressive eyes, clear complexion, and dimples that could turn any man's head. She just needed an attitude adjustment.

Viola settled her bifocals on her nose again. "Amber Daughtry. Her family is big in banking, but she's from Georgia somewhere. I remember because everyone said she had won Miss Georgia Peach or some such pageant."

"Probably bought and paid for," Yolanda whispered to her cup.

Sam cut her eyes to the young woman. "Do you have anything constructive to add to this conversation?"

"I'm just saying…" Yolanda put her cup down and scanned the opened newspaper. "Okay. If I were looking for dirt, I'd find out who the porker is who is throwing daggers at the two rich boys in just about every class picture. I read a lot of hate in those eyes."

Sam pulled one of the newspapers over and studied each of the photos. Jackie walked around the table and leaned over Sam's shoulder. "She's right. He's definitely a contestant for *The Biggest Loser* TV show. What do you think he tips the scales at, three-fifty?" Jackie asked.

"Gary Staples." Sam wrote the name down in her notepad. "He's from Danville, Illinois. Not quite a rich neighborhood. Must have received a lot of scholarships. Do you know anything about him, Viola?"

The older woman shook her head. "He wasn't in any of my classes. Looks like he majored in psychology, though, just like Revere and Bordeau. Then switched to accounting." She pointed a gnarled finger at one of the frat house photos. "All three of them belonged to the same fraternity."

"Good catch," Sam said to Yolanda, who finally broke out in a wide smile. Sam placed two business cards on the table. "Call me if you think of anything else. I also left a business card for Trina Miller. She heads up the day care center in the Three Oaks Golf Course Condominium complex in Chasen Heights. She's trying to juggle things on her own with the help of seniors who live in the complex. She's looking for someone with a degree in child care to help out full-time." On closer inspection Sam could see the porch was starting to sag and in need of repair and Yolanda had mentioned that the roof was leaking. "I believe there are condos for rent there. It would save you a fifteen mile drive each way."

"Oh, I would love to volunteer with those little ones." Viola suddenly saddened. "Oh, but living on a golf course would be way more than we could afford."

"No, Auntie. If I can get the job and then I don't have to drive to work, just take the elevator, think of the savings on gas alone."

Sam gathered up her coat and the newspapers. "Don't be afraid to ask the management office about the rental cost. It's far less expensive than you think."

Jackie threaded her arm through Sam's as they made their way back to the Jeep. "I suppose it didn't cross your mind that I own several of those condos, one of which is available."

Sam smiled.

46

It took Sam two phone calls to find Amber Daughtry. First was a call to the Daughtry Savings and Loan in Augusta, Georgia. Posing as the committee chair for the Reed University reunion newsletter, she discovered that Amber Daughtry-Reynolds now lived in Dallas, Texas with her husband who was a surgeon. The receptionist couldn't give out Amber's unlisted number but took Sam's and promised to pass the information on to Ethan Daughtry, Amber's father.

"Talk to me, people." Robinson parked one ample cheek on the corner of the conference table. On the whiteboard in front of him were photos of Austin Revere and Matt Bordeau. Surrounding those photos were pictures of the deceased.

"We tried interviewing some of the staff but they all have nothing but praise for the two. They both appear squeaky clean on the surface," Frank offered.

"No one is squeaky clean." Robinson turned to Jake. "What about bank accounts?"

"Nothing that even hints of any improprieties." Jake sifted through his stack of papers. "They aren't in arrears with any payments to suppliers. Payrolls have been met. No questionable deposits or withdrawals."

"What about lawsuits? There must have been some disgruntled patients that were unhappy with their treatments."

Jake started sliding papers across the table. "There have been several and they have won them all."

"Any sexual misconduct?"

"None, unless they just didn't come forward."

"No gambling or drinking problems? No DUI's, parking tickets, petty theft, maybe a damn fight with the neighbor?" Robinson splayed his hands as though waiting for incriminating evidence to fall into his lap. He turned his attention to Frank. "What about Bordeau's wife?"

"Just what Sam told us. Crystal Bordeau is a jewelry designer. Makes some pretty high end stuff. Too rich for my wallet." Frank pulled out a photo, then walked to the whiteboard and tacked it on with a magnet. The photo showed an attractive blonde, her hair pulled back in a ponytail, cutting roses from a bush by a large deck. "Amazing what zoom lenses can catch. They have a corner house in a subdivision by the lake."

Robinson swiveled his dark eyes to Jake. "I know that look, Jake."

"What's that?" Jake kept his eyes on the board, shelving the names in his mental file drawer.

"If it had happened to my wife or daughter, I'd want to be alone in a room with him, too. We'll find the guy who assaulted Sam, but we won't get the charges to stick if you go all Jack Bauer on him."

"Gary Staples. I remember him." Amber's voice sounded rich, or maybe the oil-rich Texas slang she had acquired made it sound rich. "What a loser."

"He seemed to be in tight with Austin and Matt, at least in some of the pictures. Was he in the same fraternity?"

Amber Daughtry laughed and Sam could picture a hand layered with diamond rings pressed against a thin neck draped in pearls. "He followed them around like a puppy dog the first year and they finally let him into the fraternity. Austin and Matt seemed to humor him for a couple years, then they had a falling out the last year. Austin and Matt couldn't have been closer if they had been brothers and Gary was like a third wheel."

"Do you know what the falling out was about?" Sam heard the clinking of ice in a glass and pictured a mint julep or mimosa in Amber's dainty hand.

"Between you and me, Austin and Matt tolerated Gary. Gary Staples was brainy, straight A's, honors, was admitted on several well-earned scholarships. But he couldn't afford to go to graduate school."

"What was he majoring in?"

"Business, I think, or accounting. Austin and Matt were going on to graduate school and had big plans to open up their own clinic. They had family money behind them."

"And Gary didn't."

"He had more problems than money. I'm sure you've seen Gary's picture. Austin and Matt only wanted to be associated with attractive people. They were big on image. They planned to only hire attractive people, only have the most expensive and tasteful décor. They even planned how their damn business cards would look. Gary, well, he was over three hundred pounds and looked like Baby Huey. Gary had served his purpose so once Austin and Matt got what they wanted from him, they tossed him like yesterday's paper."

Sam wondered whether Austin or Matt had tossed Amber aside. Maybe both of them did. "I understand Austin and Matt were pretty good at hypnosis. Do you know if they had anything to do with Viola Williams's firing?"

There was that tinkling laughter again, a sound Sam could only equate to Abby's wind chimes back home. "Those two were only average students so even I was suspicious of the straight A's. That's what I meant when I said he had served his purpose. They would never admit anything but my gut tells me, if they didn't do it, Gary did."

"Gary? Why him?"

"Because Gary taught them everything they knew about hypnosis."

47

Sam rapped on the door frame before entering. A visitors badge hung from the collar of her sweater. "Am I interrupting?" The room looked like a morgue. She hadn't seen that many sullen faces since the last Chicago Bears winless season. "There were 'Hi Sams' all around in a tone that sounded less than enthusiastic.

"Hope you got something mind blowing, Sam, 'cause we are just about out of bullets." Robinson stood and walked over to close the door. He took Sam's coat from her and tossed it on the back of a chair.

"Poor babies. Are you stuck?" Sam smiled as the three men growled. She pulled a picture of Gary from her tote bag. She had stopped by an Office Max and had the photo from the college newspaper enlarged. She placed it on the whiteboard next to Austin's and Matt's photos. "I like your little bullet magnets." Sam grabbed a red marker and wrote *Gary Staples* below the photo. The three men sat up a little straighter. Before they could ask, Sam told them about her phone conversation with Amber Daughtry and the fractured relationship between the three men. Sam saved the best for last.

"Everything Matt and Austin learned about hypnosis, they learned from the best." She tapped Gary's photo with the closed end of the felt tip pen.

"And where do we find Mister Staples?" Robinson asked.

"Hey, do you want me to do everything?"

"Hell, yeah," Frank said with a chuckle. "That's why the department is paying you those big bucks."

Jake studied the board with skepticism, trying to connect the dots. "Even if we found this Staples guy, what could he tell us? He's obviously not a current employee because I don't remember seeing his name on the list from Morning Glory."

"Maybe he can tell us how Austin and Matt could hypnotize someone to kill herself. Maybe there's some added step even my therapist is unaware of. Amber wasn't sure where Gary was living now, but she did confirm that he was from Danville, Illinois."

"Oh, hell. If he's still living with mom, he's our number one suspect." Robinson punched a button on the intercom and asked for someone to run a report on Gary Staples.

Sam spent the next thirty minutes filling them in on her conversation with Viola Williams and how Gary Staples, Matt and Austin might have been responsible for her losing her job. "She lives with her niece in Merrillville, Indiana and had been unable to get another teaching job after losing her job at Reed."

There was a rap on the door. Andy Brainard entered and handed a print out to Frank. "I made several copies," Andy said. Frank thanked him and closed the door.

The room was silent as everyone reviewed the report on Gary Staples. Gary had used his accounting degree to work for a retail business in Chicago. After three years with the firm, he opened his own accounting business, doing mainly tax accounting.

"He seemed to be doing good, although his marriage only lasted three years." Robinson flipped the last page over, not expecting the report to have ended so abruptly. "Staples dropped off the face of the earth right after the divorce."

"Can't be that unusual. Maybe he pitched a tent on a beach somewhere to drown his sorrows." Frank took another look at the photo of an obese Gary Staples. "Might need a pretty big beach."

"Hey. Ain't nothing wrong with a little meat on the bones," Robinson said. Although the captain tipped the scales way past two hundred, his bulk was mainly muscle.

"It's probably genetic," Sam offered. "I think it was rather crude of Revere and Bordeau to discriminate against someone because he didn't meet their financial and cosmetic requirements. Makes me want to lock both of them up."

"Okay, people." Robinson stood and stretched, a sign that the meeting was over. "Sam, stay home and rest. Frank, follow up on Missus Staples. I'm gonna have Andy and Maury continue with those tapes from Bailey's. Jake, try to pick up the trail on Gary Staples. Maybe he's buried in a grave somewhere, compliments of his two buddies."

There was another knock at the door, then Andy stuck his head in. "Can I show you something?"

They clustered around Andy's desk where a monitor displayed a still shot from Bailey's. He took a seat and pressed a button. "This didn't seem to be much of an altercation the victim had with a customer but I recognized the customer from the photos on your board." He touched another button and paused the video. "There."

"What do you see?" Robinson leaned forward, trying to take in all of the activity in the bar.

Jake pointed at the screen. "Isn't that Austin Revere?"

Go home and rest. "Yeah, like that's gonna happen." Sam studied the photo of Gary Staples. Even though his face looked bloated and his body resembled the Michelin Man, there was something about him that bothered her. She had hoped to join Jake and Frank to watch the good doctors sweat but something about the photo nagged at her. Instead, she found herself at Headquarters on the elevator to Beast's lair when Chief Dennis Murphy climbed on and made a cursory glance of her injuries.

Once the elevator started moving, he pounded the red button bringing the elevator to a halt.

"What the hell happened, Sam?"

"This?" Sam touched her forehead, then winced. "I would think the grapevine fed you all the information."

"Do you remember anything? What the guy smelled like? Liquor? Nauseating cologne like Schuler's chief of staff wears?"

"You think the mayor had something to do with it?"

"I don't know. He's pretty driven when it comes to getting what he wants so I wouldn't put it past him."

Sam had to admit. There was a long list of suspects. She suddenly felt light-headed and before she could reach for the railing to hold onto, Murphy grabbed her in a fatherly hug.

"Dammit, Sam. We are going to catch this guy."

Sam was having a hard time hating her nemesis. Ever since she saw the other side of Murphy after working to clear him of suspicion of murder, he was fast becoming a replacement for the father she lost when she was five years old.

"Benny put a rush on the DNA sample." She peeled herself away from him as Murphy set the elevator back in motion.

"I already spoke to Benny. I told him those results are for my eyes only. I don't want Jake shooting first and asking questions later." The elevator doors opened and Murphy exited as quickly as he had appeared.

The mayor and his chief of staff. The list kept growing. Everything had happened so fast Sam hadn't had time to think of the scent of aftershave or cologne. All she remembered was the smell of oil and dirt from the parking lot. Her attacker wore gloves. She remember that much. Expensive leather coat or a pullover? She didn't know. When she was a cop she could never understand why victims couldn't be more specific about details and now she understood. At least she remembered the deck shoes and that he wore a ski mask because the fabric scratched against her ear.

"Are you getting off or are you going to just ride the elevator all day?" Beast asked.

Sam looked up, startled that the elevator had arrived so quickly. "Sorry. I was lost in thought as usual." She followed him down the dimly lit hallway to his equally dimly lit office.

His gaze drifted from the dark circles under her eyes to the adhesive strips on her forehead. "Who did you piss off?"

"Jeez, why do people always think I'm the instigator?"

"Your reputation is known far and wide."

"I watch *CSI* so I know you can age a child to see what he would look like today. But can you take this photo and make him lose about one hundred and fifty pounds?"

Beast took the photo from her. "Wow. He's definitely due for a diet. Sure. When do you need it by?"

Sam had hoped yesterday would be a good response but she glanced at three different monitors, each clicking and spewing data. "Whenever you have a spare minute. Can you attach it to an email?" She handed him her business card.

"So, is this the guy who roughed you up?"

"I don't think so. I would have felt three hundred plus pounds slamming into me."

"After I put him on a diet, you may have second thoughts."

48

"This is really bordering on harassment, Sergeant." Austin Revere glared at the two detectives as he took a seat behind the desk.

Murphy had instructed them to harass the hell out of them and Jake was starting to enjoy it, especially if either of them had anything to do with assaulting Sam. "We have you on film at Bailey's arguing with the victim whose body was found at your father's golf course. You told Sam Casey you had never met Donna Oberweiss."

Matt, seated in a barrel chair near the desk, picked a piece of lint from his slacks. He leaned over and flicked the lint into a chrome receptacle Jake could only guess was a garbage can. Frank was trying hard to refrain from touching the fabric. Too costly for his pay check.

"Casey, that bitch." Austin said the last two words under his breath but it was still heard by the detectives. "My father's going to make sure the mayor fires her ass."

Jake placed a photo on the desk in front of Austin. It showed Austin gripping Donna's arm. "I will ask you again, how well did you know Donna Oberweiss? From the look on Donna's face, she didn't appear to want anything to do with you."

Matt rose from the chair and walked behind Austin. Jake wasn't too surprised at Matt's reaction. From what Sam had told him after her conversation with Crystal Bordeau, Matt expected everyone to carry the Bordeau image creed to their off hours as well.

"Don't say anything more. I'll call our lawyer."

"It's okay, Matt. I have nothing to hide. I remember that night. My steak was too well done. The cook had to re-do it twice and the waitress was a bit perturbed at me. What you are seeing is her reaction to my comment. I touched her arm and said, 'Listen sweetheart. When I ask for medium rare, I expect medium rare.' She didn't appreciate my response.

But as far as hitting on her, really. Does she look my type? I usually don't eat at a sports bar either but it was late and I wanted something quick. That's all there was to it."

Matt straightened and checked his watch. "Is that all you have, detectives? We have a conference call lined up with a company in England interested in purchasing some franchises."

"Damn, this place smells good." Frank eyed the pastries in the glass case.

After dropping off the picture with Beast, Sam called Jake and asked him to meet her at Java the Hut across the street from the clinic.

"Thought you were going home to rest," Jake said.

"I wanted to know how it went with the good doctors."

They ordered their drinks then found a table by the window with a good view of the clinic across the street.

"No pastry, Frank?"

"Nah. I'd spoil my dinner."

Jake gave her the shortened version of Austin's run-in with Donna. "Hate to say it, but I believe him."

"Yeah. Matt tries to keep Austin on a short leash. Austin seems to be the hot head of the two but I'm not sure either one would want murderer on his resume." Frank sipped his latte as he watched the foot traffic outside. "Place sure is in a great location."

"That's how I met Tamara. I saw her coming out of the clinic and befriended her. Asked her about her take on the clinic and the methods the therapists use. She claims hypnosis wasn't used on her."

Frank chuckled at that comment. "Unless they hypnotized her not to remember they used hypnosis."

"Find out anything more about Staples or his ex-wife?" Sam kept watch for Tamara, hoping she'd stop by the coffee shop so Jake and Frank could question her.

"We got sidetracked by the tape and had to poke at the two doctors a little more." Jake's eyes kept tracing Sam's forehead and the dark circles under her eyes.

"I ran into Murphy at Headquarters." Sam told them that Benny was instructed to only give the DNA results on her attacker to the chief. "Either he isn't sure what you would do or he wants to save the department from bad press should you go all ape on the guy."

"I'm mellow." But Jake hardly smiled when he said it and seemed to growl the words versus say them.

"There's Tamara now." Sam nodded toward the attractive woman walking toward the street on the clinic side. She wore a short skirt, boots, and a leather jacket. Sam remembered the smile, bright eyes and dimples, but they were missing today. People jostled past Tamara as she remained on the curb, oblivious to the green walk light. "Something isn't right."

"What isn't, babe?" Jake followed Sam's gaze. It was after four and the start of rush hour. Shoppers were hustling to the various stores in the strip malls while school buses were starting to make an appearance.

Sam could understand if Tamara were texting or reading something and not paying attention to the traffic lights. "What is she waiting for?"

They slowly stood in unison and watched as the light turned red. From a distance they could see a city bus barreling down the street. Tamara suddenly turned to watch the bus, then stepped off the curb.

"Is she…?" But Frank didn't finish the thought. He and Jake charged out of the cafe, their attention split between the woman breaking into a run and the bus gaining speed toward the intersection. Bystanders were oblivious to the impending collision and went about their daily routine. Frank reached Tamara first and tackled her to the ground, their bodies a tangle of arms and legs. They escaped with inches to spare as the bus driver laid on the horn. Jake waved his arms in the middle of the intersection to stave off traffic.

Sam dialed 911 as she ran out of the coffee shop. She couldn't believe shoppers and onlookers weren't giving the incident a second glance. If they had been crossing the street they probably would have stepped over Tamara's body without stopping to help.

"An ambulance is on the way." Sam knelt next to Tamara, expecting blood and broken bones but there weren't any injuries she could see. "Did you get hit?" she asked Frank.

He shook his head no. "Barely made it with inches to spare." Frank squeezed his shoulder. "I took the brunt of the impact with the pavement." He leaned close to Tamara's face and felt her breath on his cheek. She wasn't moving and her eyes stared trance-like. "Must be in shock."

"Tamara." Sam grabbed the young woman's hand. "Can you hear me? Does anything hurt?" A crowd started to gather around them. She wanted to scream at them, "where were you when the bus almost ran her over?"

Tamara's gaze didn't move but her lips mumbled something. Frank leaned in close. "What was that? Can you repeat it, Tamara?"

Sirens wailed in the distance as gawkers started to gather at the curb on both sides of the street. Shoppers were emptying out of stores, finding the tragedy on the asphalt to be more interesting than the sales. Bar lights from a cruiser and an ambulance pulsed as they approached. The vehicles screeched to a halt several yards away as Sam caught sight of a cell phone near Tamara's purse. She picked up both then moved away as the EMTs wheeled a stretcher over. Sam quickly checked Tamara's phone. The last call she received was five minutes ago, probably right as she was leaving the clinic. She picked up her own phone and called Beast.

"I need you to check the following phone number." Beast remembered enough about the previous requests not to ask her to explain. He placed her on hold for several minutes. She watched as the EMTs checked Tamara's vitals and hooked her up with an I.V. Jake was watching from a safe distance while Frank conferred with the EMTs. Additional officers had arrived and were pushing onlookers back and directing traffic away from the scene.

"Are you there, Sam?" Beast asked.

"Yes. What did you find out?" Sam listened for several seconds, thanked Beast, and closed her phone. She slowly scanned the faces in the crowd as she joined Jake.

"What's up, Sam?"

"I picked up Tamara's phone. The last call she received was from a disposable phone and it lasted four seconds."

Jake turned his attention to the clinic across the street. Was someone in the building watching what was happening? Had one of the doctors been the one who had called her?

Frank rushed over after briefing the EMTs on Tamara's close encounter with the bus. "You won't believe this." He caught his breath and looked as dazed as the injured woman had. "Tamara said only one word—*destiny.*"

49

Sam was too stunned to think straight. She wanted to march into the clinic and haul Matt and Austin back to the precinct. Jake convinced her to go home, which was just as well. All she wanted to do was hold Dillon. Jake and Frank were going to question some of the employees as well as Tamara's therapist to determine if anyone had been stalking Tamara.

Jake must have called Abby because she went all motherly on Sam, leading her to the couch in the living room, having the fireplace crackling and welcoming, pressing a cup of hot tea in her hand, then waiting for Sam's hands to warm up before settling Dillon in her arms.

"I'm at a loss, Mom. Things seem to be spiraling out of control and I'm no closer to the truth than the first day I spoke to Forrest Johnson. I know these cases are all connected but I can't figure out how the killer is doing it."

"It will come, Samantha. Give it time."

"How much time? After two, three, four more women die?"

Dillon patted Sam's mouth and babbled something unintelligible. She grabbed his hand and kissed it.

"Jacob called, said he would be working late and stopping with Frank for dinner."

"They'll probably go to Izzy's for an artery clogging burger. I hope you didn't make too much because I've lost my appetite."

Abby rose from the couch and patted Sam's shoulder. "You may not be hungry but I'm sure the babies are." She turned to leave, then stopped. "Jacob also said he called the hospital and spoke with the EMT who treated the victim in the ambulance. She doesn't appear to have any injuries other than shock. But he was going to keep a police officer outside of her room."

Good, Sam thought. Once the killer realizes Tamara was still alive, he may try something. Then a more horrifying thought crossed Sam's mind. What if Tamara tries to kill herself again?

"Maybe you should have had your shoulder checked out." Jake accepted the beer from Nancy and slid it closer to his side of the bar. They were at Izzy's, a local hangout for the boys in blue known for the best burgers and fried chicken in town. It had a large bar area with a number of wide screen TVs playing an assortment of sporting events as well as a cozy dining area in the adjoining room behind the bar.

"Nah. Nothing's broken. I'll probably have a bruise to match the one on Sam's right side but I'll live." He held up his own beer glass. "Nothing a little brewski won't cure."

They turned their backs against the bar and watched the Chicago Bears on the larger screen above the juke box. Someone with a few too many beers had unplugged the juke box so he could hear the game. They recognized a table of beat cops filling out squares on a large football pool for the next Bears game. Although locals who frequented the bar knew the police were regulars, as yet not one law-abiding citizen had complained to the press or mayor about this minor indiscretion.

"Don't know why the captain wouldn't let us haul their asses in again." Frank made a fist as the Bears scored a first down. "Who cares if the mayor has a coronary? There are already four people dead and one injured."

"We don't have proof. Nothing solid." Jake's attention was drawn to one off duty cop he didn't recognize but he knew the type. He had his three table-mates enthralled with a story of a collar. The three other men at the table were younger, new recruits, Jake figured. The storyteller had Pacino good looks, dressed in what looked like a cashmere sweater. The watch on his wrist flashed gold. It was at that point that the Pacino twin crossed his right leg over his left, the ankle at his knee. He was wearing expensive-looking deck shoes. When his pant leg rode up, Jake saw several deep scratch marks on the man's ankle.

"Any idea who that guy is?"

Frank tore his attention from the game. "The husky blonde guy? I think he's a friend of Andy's. Plays racquetball with him or something."

"No, the loud mouth. The dark-haired guy."

Frank caught sight of the shoes and scratch marks and clamped a hand on Jake's arm. "It could be a coincidence. Don't jump to conclusions." Frank's cell phone rang. When he checked the monitor, he said, "Shit. It's the chief. Those shrinks must have called the mayor again." He waved a finger in front of Jake's face. "Don't make a move til I get back." Frank walked away from the noise and out the front door.

In another adjoining room there were pool tables. Jake noticed one of the file clerks from the precinct sitting on a stool watching the players. He remembered her name was a flower of some type, maybe Daisy. He walked over and whispered in her ear. Daisy looked over at the table Jake was referring to. She smiled in agreement. Jake exited through the restaurant and out the back door.

Jake waited in the darkened back lot of the restaurant. He had asked Daisy to write a note asking the loud mouth to meet her in the back lot. Daisy was young and attractive. He doubted the cop would pass up an offer by a cutie with perky breasts. Daisy planned to slip into the ladies restroom and wait several minutes before returning to the billiard room.

Several minutes later the back door opened and the man stepped out. The door closed behind him and he waited for his eyes to adjust to the dark. "Hey," he whispered. "Where are you?"

Jake struck a match and lit up a cigarette. He glared at the cop through the smoke, then dropped the match on the gravel. "She stood you up, too, I see."

"Aw, man. That bitch." He pulled out his own cigarette. Smoking wasn't allowed in any restaurants in Chasen Heights. There were park benches outside the front entrance for patrons who wanted to smoke but usually only the workers used the back lot. Jake struck another match and lit his cigarette for him. "Thanks."

The cop caught Jake's unwavering glare through the smoke and unconsciously took a step back. Jake had at least six inches and sixty pounds on the guy. "Like your shoes. Must be cold wearing them without socks in this weather." Jake inhaled long and deep, wondering how this guy could know Sam.

"These? Well, they are comfortable." He snapped his gaze back to Jake. "Which precinct do you work out of?"

"Sixth." Jake let the smoke trail lazily from his nose. "You?"

"Third. Homicide. I'm sure you've heard of me. I have the best closure rate in the city."

Bingo. Jake's hand started to shake as he pulled the cigarette from his mouth and flung it into the dark. "That so?"

"Yep. No one has touched my record."

Jake could swear the guy's chest just swelled with pride. "Sal Marino. *Grab and slap*. That what they call you?" Jake felt his right fist open and close and his jaw tense. The last time he had punched something it had been a brick wall and he had broken seven bones in his hand. Sal's smile slowly faded. He had been the detective on the Nina Logesta case Sam had told him about. "Wasn't there something in the paper recently about you screwing up a suicide case? A hanging, wasn't it?"

"That bitch didn't know what she was talking about."

"What bitch was that?" All Jake could think of at that moment was slamming Sal's face against the brick wall of the restaurant, giving him a sample of what Sal had done to Sam.

The back door burst open and Frank charged out of the restaurant. "Yo, buddy. We gotta roll. Just caught a lead." He tossed Jake's leather coat at him and dragged him away. "Sorry to interrupt," he called out to Sal as he pushed Jake toward the sidewalk and toward the front of the restaurant where their car was parked.

"What the hell are you doing, Frank? He's the one."

"I know. The chief just called to tell me the DNA results. He has plans for Mister Marino and wanted me to make sure you stayed away."

50

She was still alive. He had to wait until his morning shift to check on her. This hadn't happened before. How would Tamara's mind deal with it? She was so pretty. He watched from behind the glass window as the nurse adjusted the I.V. drip. Tamara was still unconscious, although the doctors couldn't understand why. When she woke up, exactly what would she remember? Would she still be under his influence? This was uncharted territory, but he couldn't worry about it now. It was a sign that it was time to move to the final phase.

"Coffee, Sam?" Captain Robinson was treating Sam with kid gloves. Now she understood why Jake hadn't slept that well last night. He hadn't even gone to bed, just slept in the recliner in the study. She had to wait until this morning for Jake to tell her about Sal Marino. Another cop had been the one who assaulted her in the parking lot of the Family Christian Center.

They were lined up in the front row of the viewing room. On the other side of the one way mirror sat Sal Marino, clueless as to why he had been asked to stop by and to bring his union rep. Earl McKinley was a seasoned veteran of the CHPD with a flabby body and a brush haircut. Robinson had brought in coffee for both Marino and McKinley. With the microphone on they were able to hear that Marino thought this was all about the Nina Logesta case.

She watched Jake refill his cup for the fourth time. Robinson had sandwiched Jake between her and Frank as though fearful two people were needed to keep Jake from launching his body through the glass and into Marino. The door to the interview room opened and the look on Marino's face was priceless. Chief Dennis Murphy rarely did interviews so the fact that he was in the room made Marino nervous. He looked at the union rep who was just as apprehensive. Trailing behind Murphy was a woman in a dark pant suit and starched white shirt. Her no-nonsense hairstyle was short and peppered with gray and her friendly smile had a tendency to make people relax. They took a seat across from the two men. Murphy set three file folders and a tape recorder on the desk in front of him.

"That's Meredith Stowe, head of Internal Affairs." Robinson sat down next to Sam. "Now the show begins."

Murphy opened the top file folder and spent several seconds reading. He then brought out a Mont Blanc pen and set it next to the folder. Meredith calmly sat next to him, hands folded in her lap, her eyes roaming from the words in the file to the two men across the table. Marino leaned back and folded his arms across his chest.

The chief pressed a button on the recorder, stated the date, time, and the names of everyone in attendance. He didn't look at Marino. Instead he spoke to the file folder. "Where were you four nights ago, around eight o'clock in the evening?" He picked up the pen and waited.

"Probably at Izzy's. I usually stop off for a couple with the boys. They often ask me for advice on a case." Marino shifted his gaze to Miss Stowe but all she gave him was the same reassuring smile.

"Can anyone collaborate that?" Murphy scratched something on the report in front of him.

"Sure. The bartender, several co-workers. Reese Banks was one of them. He'll vouch for me."

"Where did you go from there?"

Marino finally looked at the one-way mirror, his eyes narrowed as though finally wondering who was in the viewing room. "Home. Can I ask what this is about?"

McKinley checked the time on his watch. If it had been anyone other than the chief of police and head of I.A., he would have been demanding to know what was going on and ushering Marino out of the door.

Murphy scratched more notes on the paper. "Did you go anywhere near the Family Christian Center that night?"

Marino froze but recovered quickly. "It's not in my district but I've heard of it. No, I wasn't anywhere near that part of town that evening."

Murphy picked up a color photograph. Meredith unfolded a pair of red framed glasses and put them on. He held the photo long enough to make sure the Internal Affairs Director had it embedded on her retinas. Then he set the picture in front of Marino and his union rep. "Do you know Samantha Casey?" The photo was one of the ones Anya had taken before Benny had cleaned up Sam's wounds. Her face and hair were covered in blood, as was her coat and tunic top. Murphy let the two men get a good look at the photo, then set another next to the first. This one showed the right side of Sam's body where a bruise was already forming.

"Don't think I've ever met her but I believe I have heard of her."

"What does this have to do with Sergeant Marino?" McKinley had finally found his voice but it came out forced, as though he hadn't read the playbook for dealing with the top rung of the ladder.

"Sam used to be a detective sergeant here at the Sixth. In working on a couple alleged suicide cases she came across one from your district." Murphy set aside the first folder and opened the second. "Nina Logesta was a case you had worked."

"I have never spoken to her about it, although I would have been more than happy to fill her in." Marino smiled, but it was more of a smirk as only one corner of his mouth appeared to work.

"She spoke with a former partner of yours, Reese Banks. Did he happen to mention that the case you quickly ruled a suicide she determined was incorrectly handled?"

Marino shrugged and turned to McKinley whose own shrug said he didn't have a clue.

"So you didn't follow Miss Casey to the Christian Family Center four nights ago?"

"Hey." Marino held both hands up. "I have never met this woman and no, I did not follow anyone to that part of town four nights ago."

McKinley cleared his throat. "Were there any witnesses who saw Detective Marino near that area?"

Murphy ignored the union rep, moved the two photos down and set a third one next to it. "Our medical examiner took skin and blood samples from under the victim's fingernails. Her attacker first slammed her face into the brick building. When she was on the ground, he kicked her. It appears she was able to scratch her attacker on his right ankle."

"I'm sorry, Chief Murphy, but is she accusing me? Because I have to tell you, it wasn't me. She's probably setting me up in order to discredit my investigation."

McKinley motioned at the photos on the table. "Why didn't she call the police or go to the hospital? Why the M.E.? Something sounds off here. Why didn't she file an official report?" His jowls quivered as he spoke and looked to Marino for acknowledgment that he was doing his job. Marino just stared.

Meredith slowly removed her glasses and set them on the table. "I'd like to see your right ankle." Her smile had been slowly diminishing since the first picture.

Somehow Marino was able to retain his composure. "Sure," he said with a smile. "Although I have to tell you. I have a cat at home." He raised his right foot, pulled up his pant leg, then pulled down his sock. "I have had numerous scratches from this cat. Got him from a shelter." He pulled his sock back up and set his foot down, confident his explanation was sufficient.

Murphy ignored the display as though it were of little interest to him. He placed the DNA report on the table in front of them, pausing to make sure the Director saw the results first.

McKinley saw Marino's name on the report, then glared at Marino.

"I didn't really want to get into this," Marino started. "Casey and I are having an affair."

"Seriously?" Murphy had to struggle not to laugh. If he had a shovel he'd throw it at Marino and tell him to dig his grave a little deeper.

"You're going with that excuse?"

Meredith motioned toward the photo of Sam's bloody face. "Are we to assume she likes it rough?"

"She was fine when she left me. Someone must have followed her from my car, probably her husband."

Murphy's poker face revealed nothing. "And the DNA under her nails?"

"Well." Marino flashed a half smile. "We weren't exactly in the traditional position."

The Director spoke right over Marino's last words. "When did the affair start?"

Marino tilted onto the chair's back two legs, confident his fast thinking had just got himself out of a jam. "Six months ago."

A smile tugged at the corners of Murphy's mouth. Meredith caught the movement and leaned back, returning her hands to her lap. "Was this before or after her son was born?" Murphy asked. Marino opened and closed his mouth, his brain trying to think fast. The front legs of the chair slammed down. "Sam gave birth to a son six months ago. Not exactly a time when a woman thinks of having an affair." Murphy sighed, tiring of all the lies. He gathered up the photos from the table and placed them back into their respective folders. "Oh. Did I fail to mention the woman you slammed into the brick wall and kicked while she was on the ground is fourteen weeks pregnant?"

Meredith remained silent but couldn't hide her disgust. Marino avoided her eyes and opted to glare at his union rep, waiting for him to do his job. "Sounds like a case of he said/she said," McKinley said.

Murphy opened a final folder, ignoring McKinley. "I spoke with Fiona Vasquez this morning."

"Who?" There wasn't a hint of confusion on Marino's face. He obviously didn't remember all of his conquests.

"She was Nina Logesta's roommate, the only witness you bothered to speak to after Nina's body was found. She was quite forthcoming about your relationship."

McKinley snapped his gaze toward Marino. "You slept with a witness?"

"The case was closed and, yes, we dated a few times. So what?"

"Sam Casey interviewed Flo Dempsey. Your relationship with the roommate obviously distorted your assessment of cause of death." Marino didn't have any response to that. "Add that dereliction of duty to your assault on a former police officer and…"

"You don't have any proof," Marino yelled, then realized whom he was talking to. "I want a hearing with the Board of Police and Fire Commissioners. We'll see who they believe."

"Your shield, detective," the Director said. "You left your gun and holster with the desk sergeant so I'll get them from him." She held out her hand.

"That's it?" Marino shot out of his seat. "You're just going to take that bitch's word over mine?"

"Sit down, Mister Marino." Murphy had already stripped him of his title. "And I believe the Director asked you for your shield." After Marino reluctantly slumped into his chair and tossed his shield on the table, the chief continued. "I don't like bad publicity any more than the mayor. Press gets ahold of this and they'll have a field day. Now, you can either have your day with the commissioners and all that publicity that comes with it, and I can pretty much predict you won't win this one. You will lose your job, it will be on your record and you pretty much won't be able to work in law enforcement again. Or, you can accept a one month suspension without pay, after which you will be transferred to the Second and work a beat."

"A beat? You're putting me back in a patrol car?"

"I'll let you sit here and give it some thought." Murphy turned off the recorder, gathered up his folders, and nodded to Meredith. Before he left the room he glanced at the mirror and made a motion with his hand. McKinley tossed a disgusted look at Marino and trailed after Murphy.

Marino had no sooner slammed his fist down on the table when the door opened and Jake walked in.

51

"I can't believe you are letting Jake in there with Marino. He'll kill him." Sam paced Robinson's office as the captain took a seat behind his desk.

"Frank is keeping an eye on him. He won't let things get out of control."

"Murphy's okay with this? He'll fire Jake and Marino will still have his job. That's just great."

Robinson pulled out a chair and pointed. He didn't want to tell her that Murphy practically gave his blessing and his only warning to Jake was not to leave any noticeable injuries. "Sit. If you think the chief doesn't know what's going on then you missed the little hand signal he gave when he left the room."

Sam sat down and tried to quell her fears. "What if they have to carry Marino out on a stretcher? What if he goes to the media or worse, presses charges against Jake? Aren't you worried?"

"Not in the least. I predict Marino won't have a mark on his body. At least we now know neither of the Reveres nor Bordeau assaulted you, but we still have to prove those suicides were homicides."

Sam's cell phone rang. She checked the screen. "It's Abby. Hi, Mom."

"Samantha, you received a photo faxed to you from Headquarters."

"That's Beast. He was going to work some magic on a photo I dropped off, make a suspect lose a hundred plus pounds."

"It's him, Samantha."

"Him, who?"

"There was a phone number on the fax so I called and asked Mister Boonstra to send the photo to Jacob's email address."

"Mom, whose photo?"

"The man, Samantha. The man we saw in the grocery store."

◇◇

Sam watched Sal Marino crawl out of the interview room. He wasn't on all fours but he may as well have been. His steps were timid, face drained of all color. Marino trembled as though the Ghost of Christmas Future had just visited him and the prediction wasn't pretty.

"I don't get it. He isn't bloody, nothing looks broken, cut, or bruised." Sam turned to Frank. "What happened in there?"

"If I tell you, he'll have to kill me." But Frank was too chatty to let it go. "Jake promised to show me how pressure on a certain nerve can paralyze someone, make him feel as though he were just zapped with a Taser. Damn it was priceless. As you can tell the ass had to wait in that room until he regained his composure. He was crying like a baby. Almost wet himself."

Sam turned to Jake, ready to interrogate him, but the photo on his screen stopped her cold. "Oh my god. Mom was right. That's him. Gary Staples was the man Abby and I saw at the store. Why didn't his prints on the soup cans identify him?"

"Doesn't have a record. He's never been fingerprinted." Robinson waited for the photo to spit off the color printer. They were gathered behind Jake's chair as phones and normal morning routines buzzed around them. Sam studied Jake wondering exactly how dangerous of a man she had married. Robinson snatched the photo from the printer. "Get this photo over to that clinic and find out exactly what those guys know about Mister Staples."

"Wait!" Jake grabbed the photo and studied it, remembering the film from Bailey's. "I remember him. I could swear he was seated at the bar the night Donna had her run-in with Austin Revere."

52

"I'm so sorry, Doctors." Olivia was flushed as she tried to bar the detectives from entering.

"Oh for crissakes." Austin waved Olivia away. "Call our lawyer. He should still be in the building. This is definitely harassment. We'll have your jobs."

Jake, Frank and Sam entered and waited for the receptionist to close the door. Jake placed a copy of the college newspaper on the desk. It was folded to a photo of Austin, Matt, and one other person. "What can you tell us about Gary Staples?"

"Who?" The two men leaned closer to the desk. "Hell. I haven't seen him since college," Matt said.

"I remember him. He was one of those hangers on. Always wanted to be with the in crowd. Followed us around like a lost puppy." Austin shoved the newspaper aside. "He just didn't fit in."

"And you didn't include him, I bet." Sam didn't have to think long and hard about life on the outside. "He wasn't from a rich family, wasn't the right image. And his size. Wow. Bet you were embarrassed to be seen around him."

"He was in our fraternity but he was a nuisance, too. Don't profess to know what we had to deal with. It isn't easy being from a well-known family." Austin glared when Frank barked out a laugh. "Hey, people took advantage of us, claimed to know us, try to make reservations or buy tickets using our name or just by mentioning our names. Can't tell you the number of times someone ran a key along the side of my Beemer."

"Poor baby." Sam didn't have one ounce of sympathy for these two. She placed a photo on the desk of Gary Staples after Beast had applied his handiwork. "Have you seen him hanging around?"

They each shrugged, a mirror image of each other. Matt asked,

"Who is he?"

"Same guy," Jake said. "Gary Staples minus a ton of weight."

"You're kidding." Matt picked up the photo and studied it. "I'll be damned."

Austin blinked slowly, his silence speaking volumes. Jake said, "But you knew that, didn't you?"

"What?" Matt swiveled his gaze to his partner. "What does he mean?"

Austin shoved his hands in his pockets and turned away from the desk. He didn't reply for several seconds, preferring to find something more interesting outside on the back lawn. He finally turned back to the desk. "He came to see me last year, just after we announced that we had sold our first franchises. He wanted in on the deal."

"Where did he get the money to buy a franchise?" Matt asked.

"Oh, no. Gary didn't want a franchise. He wanted to be a full partner in the business. Said we wouldn't be where we were if it weren't for him. I threw him out. Told him we weren't looking for a partner and everything we had we built on our own."

There was a knock on the door and then *Mister Esquire* in a three-piece suit pushed his way in. "All talking stops right now." Edmund Einhorn slammed a leather briefcase on the desk and snapped it open. Frank didn't notice the intrusion. He was too busy studying the lawyer's threads and the Corinthian leather briefcase. Sam pulled out a chair and sat down.

"Your clients are helping us figure out who has been framing them for murder," Sam announced.

"We are?" Matt snapped his mouth shut and looked at his attorney.

"Explain." Einhorn rummaged through his briefcase and finally found a gold pen and notepad. He took a seat in one of the barrel chairs by the desk.

Jake condensed the conversation thus far for Einhorn's benefit. He nodded toward the photo of a slimmed-down Gary Staples. "Sam saw Gary Staples the other day in a grocery store. She didn't realize who he was until Miss Williams, a former professor, identified him in the college newspaper. Sam had one of our computer technicians do a composite of Staples trimmed down. However, we have been unable to locate him either through IRS or DMV records."

"And you think my clients have something to do with his disappearance." Einhorn raised his hand when Austin opened his mouth to speak. "Don't say anything." He turned to the detectives. "Unless you have proof, this conversation is over."

"On the contrary," Sam said. "I'm not accusing them of anything. We need their help with the killer's M.O."

"Killer? I don't understand."

Jake reminded the attorney about the four deaths and the recent attempt on Tamara's life. "We have reason to believe Gary Staples targeted patients…"

"Clients," Matt and Austin said in unison.

"Clients of Morning Glory in order to discredit them," Jake continued. "The first death occurred a year ago, around the time Austin turned down Gary's plea to be a partner in the business. When her body wasn't found for six months and progress wasn't made on her case, he started targeting other clients of yours."

"What we can't figure out," Sam said, picking up the thread of the conversation, "is how he is able to, Number One, convince someone to commit suicide, and, Number Two, delay it until he calls them with some trigger word. I think that word is *destiny*. It is the one word Tamara Rios said after she walked in front of a bus last night. If it weren't for Jake and Frank pulling her out of the way, she would have been hit full force. She doesn't appear to have any serious injuries but the doctors say she is catatonic. I say she's still under Gary's influence. If Gary somehow programmed her to commit suicide, she may try again. You two need to de-program her, pro bono. The girl can't afford your steep prices on her salary."

"Wait. How can you be so sure all of these deaths are connected?" Austin asked.

Jake glanced briefly at Sam. His logic was beginning to waver but to try to explain how Sam gathered her information was still something he did not care to share. "It is still an ongoing investigation. The only common thread is that each of the victims received a phone call prior to committing suicide. Each call lasted just four seconds, all from a disposable phone so we couldn't I.D. the caller. Sam happened to encounter Gary Staples in a store. We ran his prints but he's not in the system. So if the doctors here aren't responsible then it has to be someone who is framing them."

"Is it easy to make someone forget the hypnotic suggestion as well as who did the hypnotizing?" Frank asked. "And to even wait months before implementing the call. You would think a victim would remember talking to someone, wouldn't you?"

Sam thought back to her dream, of the man on the walking path in the park, the car key clicker, the bottle of water. "Drugs." Sam looked at each of the doctors. "Why not a date rape drug, something where the victim doesn't remember anything that happened yet they are pliant enough for Staples to hypnotize and plant a one word trigger. Is that possible?"

Matt and Austin each slowly took a seat, Austin behind his desk, and Matt in a barrel chair next to his attorney. "I must warn you," Einhorn started.

"It's okay." Matt shut him down with a wave of a hand. "Rohypnol is the date rape drug, but the effect might be a little more, shall we say excited, than someone would want, if you wanted the victim to be pliant. Revitrol is a knock-off version. It has the same effects but isn't available here in the U.S."

"What about Midazolam Hydrochloride or Versed?" Austin suggested. "It's a powerful sedative/hypnotic in the same family as Rohypnol. Gary, for all of his failings, was a genius, a straight A student. He could have finished college and grad school together in three years if he wanted to."

"Gentlemen," Einhorn cautioned, "you are giving the police all the ammunition they need to arrest you just by admitting you know about these drugs."

"Oh for crissake, Edmund." Matt glared at his attorney. "We're doctors. Of course we are going to know a lot about drugs. We have clients who are dead and someone is trying to shut us down."

Einhorn checked his watch, but Sam wasn't quite done with the doctors. "What did Gary have on you at college?"

"What do you mean?" Einhorn asked.

Sam told them about Viola Williams and how the grades had been changed. "She lost her job."

"Don't say anything."

"What difference does it make now?" Austin told his attorney. "Yes, Gary taught us about hypnosis but we never used it anywhere but at parties. Gary came to us after Miss Williams was fired. Said he changed our grade for us, did us a favor. Now we owed him. We never asked him to do that."

"But you never came forward so Viola wouldn't lose her job."

"Gary said if we told anyone what he had done he would say we were in on it. That would have been hard to deny since there were witnesses that we had visited Miss Williams and people knew we were pretty good with hypnosis."

"But nowhere near as good as Gary," Matt added. "We tried to distance ourselves from him. Once we graduated, we never saw him again."

"Until last year." Austin shook his head as he studied Gary's photo. "So Gary picked our clients in order to point the finger at us and ruin our business?"

Jake said, "We think he kept trying to point the police in your direction. Even the argument you had with the waitress at Bailey's. He was there and witnessed it. It's possible he killed her hoping witnesses would remember your altercation with her making you the likely suspect."

"But she didn't commit suicide," Austin pointed out.

"Maybe his hypnosis didn't work on her. There weren't any drugs in her system," Frank started.

Matt waved him off. "Drugs were never Gary's forte. His hypnosis was effective enough to not only plant the suggestion but make them forget whatever he wanted them to forget." He remained silent for several seconds, his hand raised as though signaling a waiter. He turned to Austin and said, "Remember how Gary used a gimmick to verify his subjects were under? He would give them a glass of water and told them it was ice cold. One idiot gulped it down and scalded his mouth."

"Yeah, I remember. How about the time he gave that one girl a jalapeno pepper and told her it was a dill pickle. She ate the whole damn thing, then had to go to the emergency room." Matt turned to the detectives. "It was Gary's way of verifying his guinea pigs weren't faking it. He was very effective that way."

"Wow," was all Austin could say as the intensity of Gary's revenge hit him. "Then the body at the golf course, that was Gary's doing? To involve my father just to get the finger pointing at me?"

"What else would he use?" Sam asked, thinking back to the remote key Gary used. "I remember hearing a continuous clicking sound, like a metronome. When I saw him in the grocery store, he was using his key fob, clicking it in and out in a rhythm. I thought it was a nervous habit." Sam didn't want to mention that she also heard and saw it in her dreams.

"Yes. Gary was big on repetitive sounds," Matt replied. "Although all anyone needed to see were his eyes. I swear sometimes the guy never blinked. Do you really believe he's still in town?"

"We're pretty sure." Jake stood and grabbed the paper and photo from the desk. "He's clever and he's dangerous. And right now we don't know who his next victim is."

53

Sam convinced Jake to put more guards on Tamara's hospital room, should Gary try to prevent Tamara from talking when she wakes up. She promised Jake she would go directly home, but after she stopped at Java the Hut to unwind. Anger built as Sam remembered Marti and the other women and the way they had died. Their only fault was being involved with the Morning Glory Clinic. An image of Savannah came to mind and she had to fight back tears as well.

She studied the menu on the wall. What was it Tamara liked to drink? Caramel latte. Sam placed her order with the barista who had so much metal in his eyebrows it made her wince. She was wondering how many people in the café were there the night Tamara ran in front of the bus when she heard the sound. *Click...click.* She turned slowly. A man was seated in the corner wearing a beret and a button down sweater with patches, as though he were a visiting professor or artist from England. He was doing a good job of changing his appearance. He was holding the paper open with one hand while his other hand played with a remote key. *Click...click.*

Sam moved a few steps away and pulled out her cell phone. She smiled and told the metal eyebrows to add extra whipped cream. With her back to the faux professor she sent a quick text message to Jake.

I'm at Java the Hut. He's here.

Jake sent a quick text back.

Don't do anything.

He knew her way too well.

Sam accepted her latte and slowly moved toward a table by the window, weighing her options. What pretext could she give to stop and talk to him? *Click...click.* That sound was really getting irritating. But she didn't need a pretext. He made the first move.

The Professor stood. "Excuse me. Could I talk to you?"

Oh, shit. Sam was hesitant. She didn't have to fake that.

He pulled out a chair. "I saw you come out of the clinic across the street."

Was he using the same line she had used with Tamara? Sam looked at the chair, then at him. He took off his sunglasses and smiled. He had the lightest blue eyes, almost like looking through blue ice. Sam didn't know why but she felt herself smile back and promptly sit down. *Click...click.* The doctors were right. Gary used the remote as a metronome instead of a pendulum. Sam also noticed he never blinked and she could swear his irises were circling like some spiraling kaleidoscope.

"I don't mean to pry. Please, drink your coffee. It looks good."

Without realizing it, Sam's hand brought the cup to her mouth and she took a sip. How could he be that effective that quickly? Sam had always prided herself for being in control.

"Those men you were with, are they cops?" He took a sip of his own coffee.

Sam tried to focus, tried to mentally document what was happening. She had to try to keep her mind busy. "Yes, they were interviewing the owners of the clinic," Sam heard herself say.

"But they didn't arrest them?" The professor leaned closer, his eyes penetrating. *Click...click.*

"They aren't the ones the police want." Sam didn't want to tell him anything but the words were spilling out as though dancing on a string that he was pulling. Then something strange started to happen. She heard a drum beat, slow at first. It drowned out the clicking of the remote Gary held in his hand. The beat increased in rhythm and volume but Sam was sure she was the only one who could hear it. She was no longer in the café but on the back acres of her property, looking down on several figures pounding out a rhythm, breaking Gary's control on her mind. The images swirled and danced, then faded. She held Gary's gaze then smiled as she said, "You are."

"Gary Staples?"

Gary snapped his attention over Sam's shoulder. Jake and Frank had arrived.

"Gary Allen Staples. Why the name change to Gary Allen?" Frank asked.

Jake leaned against the wall preferring to study the suspect. There wasn't anything outstanding or remarkable about him. He could be a next door neighbor or delivery man. Definitely not in the class of the Reveres and Bordeaus.

"I had a life-changing event happen in my life, lost a lot of weight. New me, new name. Tried to shed the old persona I had developed." Gary had been very forthcoming with all of their questions. A little too cooperative in Jake's mind.

"Been to the Morning Glory Clinic lately?"

"No. Not for at least a year." Gary smiled, a man with little to fear. "Looked up some old college buddies, see if they needed help. But you knew that."

Frank lined up the photos of the victims. "Do you know any of these women?"

Gary took his time studying each photo then shook his head no. "Sorry, I don't."

"You never struck up a conversation with any of them, maybe in a park, on a walking trail?"

"No. Why, did someone say they saw me with any of them?"

Frank placed a photo of Tamara Rios in front of Gary, a photo of her in her hospital bed. "What about her?"

Gary glanced at it and tapped his finger on the photo. "Yes. I've seen her at the coffee shop a couple times. Brian behind the counter said she was the one hit by a bus the other night."

Jake saw their case starting to unravel, not that they had much of a case to begin with. He pushed away from the wall. "I understand you are pretty good with hypnosis."

"I had fun with it in my college days. Is that what Austin and Matt told you?"

"Viola Williams, too. The professor who lost her job because some test scores were falsified," Jake said.

"Bad break." Gary's comment may have sounded sincere but his smile said the doctors deserved everything they got.

"And that doesn't bother you in the least?" Jake would like to lock him up just because he was annoying.

"From what I hear their rich fathers paid her to change the grades so, no, I don't feel sorry for her."

"You've lived above the coffee shop since you moved to Chasen Heights?" Frank made a checkmark on his notepad.

Gary shrugged. "What's a guy gonna do? Wasn't left with much after my divorce."

"But you could have gotten a better job than security guard, what with your intelligence and degree. Accountant, then a top car salesman. That hypnosis must have come in handy convincing people to buy cars. And your ex-wife. What a babe. You snatched her even before you lost all that weight." Frank smiled, showing a lot of teeth.

"What can I say? I have a great personality." Gary finally shifted his gaze to Jake as if to say *your turn*. But Jake said nothing.

Frank picked up a set of keys Gary had placed on the table when he emptied his pockets. "Besides your apartment key, got a key here for your locker at work?"

"Got a search warrant?"

"Working on it. Would be quicker if you just gave us your permission but now we have to wait for the judge to return from a conference." Frank set the keys down and smiled his all-tooth smile. "You get to be our guest for a while."

"You never told me what the charges are."

Frank waved his hand over the four pictures dotting the table. "Why murder, my man." He paused, his hand over Tamara's picture. "And attempted murder."

"Guess this is where I say, 'I want a lawyer.'"

54

"He lawyered up already?" Robinson watched two officers escort Gary Staples to the elevator.

"Yeah. Has been going by the name Gary Allen and works as a security guard at Community Hospital. Been a stellar employee, no complaints, no arrests, not even a fucking parking ticket."

"Sam said he was working a number on her and it didn't take long. I can't even get her to get me a beer," Jake said.

"How did he do it?"

"That damn remote he clicks in his hand works like a metronome and then his eyes. Weirdest fucking eyes I've ever seen." Frank shivered. "Kinda Charles Manson-like but the lightest blue."

"You sure he didn't hypnotize Sam to put a pillow over your head while you slept?" Robinson let out a long sigh. "Send a couple uniforms over to the work locker and you take Carol and Hank with you to the apartment. Let's find some evidence."

"Where shall I start?" Carol Beemison set a silver case on the coffee table. She gave a cursory inspection of the living room while Hank Sobczak mumbled something that sounded like "what a dump."

"Take the bedroom, Carol. Hank, why don't you start in the bathroom." Jake had taken Gary's keys while letting their suspect cool his heels in a cell. It hadn't taken the captain long to get a search warrant. Two uniformed patrolmen were searching Gary's work locker at the hospital.

Hank pointed a finger at Frank. "If there's a body in the bathtub, I'm holding you responsible."

"Sure, blame me." Frank tugged on latex gloves then pulled the blinds open on all of the living room windows. "What guy keeps his apartment this neat?"

But Jake wasn't paying attention. He was too busy looking out the front window. A small table and one chair was against the window. A pair of binoculars was on the table. "An obsessive guy for one thing. Look at this view. He sat here, eating every meal, and seeing every person who walked out of the Morning Glory Clinic. That's one sick bastard. He was obsessed with Revere and Bordeau." Jake moved to the bookshelf where there were a selection of mysteries next to books on birds, wildlife, *Farmer's Almanac*, and *National Geographic* magazine. "Not a porn magazine in sight."

"Look at this." Frank held up a stack of completed crossword puzzles that were on a desk. "Who the hell works the *New York Times* crossword puzzle in ink? And look." Frank waved his arm in a sweeping motion. "No television. What guy doesn't have a television?"

Jake did a quick inspection of the room with his eyes. "No computer either. Do you see a laptop anywhere?"

"Maybe he has it at work. Or maybe it's in the bedroom." Frank's phone buzzed. "Travis here." He listened for several beats. "No photos, notes, or receipts for burn phones?" He glanced at Jake and shrugged. "Okay. Thanks." He shoved the phone back in his pocket. "Nothing in the work locker except a uniform. No photos of women, nada, nothing."

Jake started opening drawers in the desk. There was a tray of paperclips, pens, pencils, and rubber bands. Another drawer held a checkbook. Jake opened it to find a balance of a little over five hundred dollars. The remaining two drawers were empty.

"It's almost like he knew we would eventually be searching his apartment. The guy lived like a monk." Jake shoved the drawer closed and stood.

Hank strolled in carrying his case. "Place is clean. No signs of a struggle. No trophy collection of jewelry or panties. No drugs in the bathroom. Checked every hidey hole known to man in the kitchen and didn't find any weapons."

"Same here," Carol chimed in. "No stains on the bedding or drugs in the nightstand or under the bed." She held up a roller. "Did find this in the garbage can in the bedroom."

"A lint roller?" Frank cocked his head to study the hair. "There's all sizes and colors."

"Dog hair," Carol said.

"No water or food dish in the kitchen," Hank said. "Not even a bag of dog food."

"I checked his closet. It looks like he was cleaning the pant legs. There were a few hairs left on a couple pair but they are definitely dog hairs and a variety of them, too."

They stood in the living room mulling over what Gary Staples could be doing with dogs. And if he had dogs, where were they? Then Frank snapped a finger.

"Dog walker."

Hank rolled his eyes. "You think this guy has time to walk dogs when he has murders to plan?"

Frank slapped a hand on Hank's shoulder. "You've been away from the dating scene for too long. Women love cute puppies. Pick out a cute little puppy, take it for a walk, and the women can't resist stopping to talk to you. Works every time."

"The woman at the Humane Society confirmed it," Jake told Robinson. After leaving the apartment, they had shown Gary's photo to the receptionist at the Humane Society.

"Gary would come in periodically, no set schedule, and pick out a puppy to take for a walk," Frank added. "He'd be gone a couple hours. Puppy came back with all four legs and his tail still intact so Gary wasn't abusing them."

"Clever ass." Robinson saw a woman emerge from the elevator, briefcase in hand. Her clothes looked as though she had just driven three hours in a fetal position. Her sweater was two sizes two large, as if she had borrowed her husband's clothes. Either the elevator ride was windy or she hadn't had time to put a comb through her hair in days. It stuck out on all sides.

Robinson escorted Geraldine Berda to the conference room with the whiteboard in full display. "Counselor, so glad you could fit us into your busy day." Jake and Frank trailed in and took a seat at the table. Robinson closed the door and took up a position by the whiteboard.

"Yeah, yeah. I'm fine, you're fine, we're all fine. I'm all out of niceties for the day. Tell me about this flimsy case of yours." She set a recorder on the table and pressed the play button. Then she pulled out a fresh yellow-lined notepad and pen.

Jake had hoped Geri would be assigned the case. She was a no-nonsense prosecuting attorney and had a winning track record. He had worked with her on several of his cases.

Robinson went through the timeline of the suicides in detail. Geri listened, took notes, and didn't interrupt once. Then Jake took over, explaining Sam's involvement with Marti Johnson's case that led to the other cases. Geri didn't even flinch or lift an eyebrow at the mention of Sam's name. She was familiar with Sam's method of police work.

With all the cases explained, as well as Gary Staples' relationship to Austin Revere and Matthew Bordeau, Geri leaned back and sighed. "I don't know, boys. You don't have any witnesses putting Staples with any of these women. You don't have any witnesses to his doing his hocus pocus. There isn't a weapon a jury can see, feel, and touch. Drugs weren't used supposedly, but if they had been, they were well out of the victims' systems at the time of death because the toxicology tests came up empty. And of course," she paused to look at Jake, "I can't use Sam's deducing of the word destiny. Do you have any record of Staples buying any burn phones?"

"No." Robinson pulled out a chair and sat down. "We don't have squat and hope you can work miracles."

"I didn't major in miracles, unfortunately. If he was able to pull all of this off, he is one clever bastard. Right now Revere and Bordeau look like better suspects than Staples."

55

By morning the press had a field day with rumors and department leaks as well as speculations from security guards Gary had worked with. The press had a difficult time deciding where to camp, either at the police station or at the Morning Glory Clinic.

Tamara Rios came out of her catatonic state at eight in the morning without any recollection of the bus incident nor did seeing a photo of Gary Staples spark any revelations.

The case was at an impasse.

"Now what?" Sam asked. "The mayor is all over the air waves affirming how his campaign donor, Collin Revere, and his son had been a scapegoat regarding Donna's murder. Making sure the public knows of their innocence is all he cares about, not about Gary's victims." She placed her tote bag on the corner of Jake's desk.

Robinson eyed the elevator at the opposite end of the room. "If Staples walks, the press is going to keep demanding answers. The front page is full of those ladies' photos. Speaking of which."

Forrest Johnson emerged from the elevator and charged across the room toward the captain. "Is it true? You arrested the guy who killed my wife?"

"Take a deep breath, Forrest." Robinson waved him over. "Why don't you take a seat in my office."

But Forrest was too agitated to sit. "Are you going to be able to make him pay? Will the charges stick? The newspaper articles say the police don't have enough evidence."

Sam placed her hand on his arm. "Forrest, calm down."

"Calm down?"

There was a commotion by the desk sergeant as two police officers escorted Gary and a woman from the elevator. Sam glared at Gary, daring him to try his gaze on her again. All he did was nod and smile at her. She felt her tote bag move but before she could grab it, Forrest already had her Taurus in his hand and was moving toward the elevator.

"YOU KILLED MY WIFE."

"Forrest, no," Sam yelled. Within seconds, drawers housing guns had been opened and weapons leveled at Forrest. "Stop." But Jake grabbed her before she could place herself in harm's way.

Robinson approached instead. "Forrest, give me the gun. You don't want to do this."

Gary broke into a grin as his lawyer remained standing, face stern. Gary held his hands out, palms up, as if to say, *take your best shot.*

"Forrest."

"Stay back, Captain." The gun shook in Forrest's hand. "He killed my Marti. I don't know how he did it, but he did it." Tears streamed down his face as he grasped the gun with both hands. There was anger and hatred in his eyes and Sam wasn't sure he would listen to reason.

"Think of Savannah, Forrest. You yourself told me that was one thing Marti never wanted—to see her little girl shuffled from foster home to foster home, the way both of you were. What will happen to Savannah if you're in jail?" Robinson was close now. He held his left hand up to motion to his officers to hold off. Then he reached out and placed a hand on Forrest's arm. "Give me the gun, son. Think of Savannah."

Slowly Forrest lowered the gun, then broke down sobbing. Gary smirked. Sam wanted to wipe that smirk right off of his face. Once Forrest was sequestered in Robinson's office, the officers escorted Gary and his young attorney to the interview room.

"Why does he have a female attorney?" Sam asked. "If this goes to trial, he shouldn't even have a female on the jury."

Robinson handed Sam her gun as he heaved a sigh. "Lucky you didn't have a clip in there."

"It's in my purse, just not in the gun." Sam pulled out her cell phone and dialed a number.

Jake asked, "Who's the attorney?"

"Ain't no way Gary is going to put his spell on her," Frank said. "She's one of those ACLU civil rights lawyers. I think her name is Biddle or Kiddle something." The attorney was a fireplug, short and compact but moved with long strides, almost marching rather than walking. Gary followed behind dutifully. They watched as Gary and his attorney disappeared behind a door. The two officers remained outside the room.

Sam ended her call and walked over to Robinson's office. Forrest had his back to the door but Sam could see his back heaving as his sobs continued. "I called my therapist. He's going to come over and talk to Forrest." Robinson nodded and Sam made her way over to Forrest, pulled a chair over and sat down. "Who's Savannah with this morning?"

Forrest pressed a handkerchief to his eyes and took several deep breaths. There was little anyone could do to console him. "She's at the day care. Savannah has taken a real liking to this older black lady, she's a former teacher, I think."

"Viola Williams. She and her niece were going to move there. Yolanda was supposed to work with Trina."

"She just started. Savannah really likes them both. Couldn't believe she sat still for an hour while Yolanda but those beads in her hair. Savannah loves to shake her head back and forth and listen to the beads clink." Another sob escaped and Forrest tried to muffle it with the handkerchief.

"I asked a friend to come over and talk to you, Forrest. He's my therapist and he's very good. Those support sessions are helpful but I think you need some one-on-one, too. Okay?" Forrest nodded.

Sam left him to his thoughts and returned to Jake's desk. "I have a very unsettling feeling."

"Me too."

"About what?" Frank asked. "Is there something I'm not getting?"

Robinson joined their little cluster. "What isn't anyone getting?"

Jake said, "We may not have evidence on Gary, but we also don't have solid evidence on Revere and Bordeau. If Gary's goal was to ruin them, he didn't succeed."

"He may have put a cloud of suspicion over their clinic, but pretty soon people will forget and business will keep booming. No." Sam studied the closed conference room door, wondering what they could be talking about. "He has something up his sleeve. I could see it in his eyes."

The door to the conference room opened and *Miss Fireplug* emerged. Sam asked, "Has Gary used a phone since he's been here?"

"No," Frank replied. "Lois Biddle is like an ambulance chaser and volunteered her services. So Gary hasn't made any phone calls."

Biddle stomped over to Robinson. "Release my client. You have nothing to charge him with."

Jake eyed the cell phone clipped to her belt. "Did you let your client use your phone?"

"What? No."

Jake ripped the phone from its holder.

"Hey!"

Sam was on the phone to Beast before Jake had the phone log up on Biddle's phone.

"A call was made from your phone two minutes ago." Jake turned the phone toward the defense attorney. "Did you make this call?"

Biddle studied the list of calls dialed. "I…no."

Jake pressed the redial button and listened for several seconds, then pressed the end button. "Message only gives the phone number, not the name."

Sam repeated the phone number to Beast. Within seconds, he had the information. "Gary called Crystal Bordeau's cell phone."

"See if he can pull up the number for her residence."

"I don't understand." The attorney turned to Robinson for an explanation. "I didn't give him my phone."

"That you know of. He played you, just like he played all of his victims."

Sam scribbled the residence number on a notepad. Frank dialed the number from the phone on his desk. She could hear Beast pounding on his keyboard.

"The housekeeper said Crystal took a phone call on her cell and left. She doesn't know where she went." Frank hung up the phone.

Beast could hear the activity through the phone line. "Hey, Sam. I have a bead on her whereabouts. I just tracked her cell phone."

56

"Hi, Missus Bordeau. How are you today?" Olivia had always admired Crystal, but had a hint of jealousy, too. She had never let it show, though, because it was difficult to dislike a woman who was always nice and gave great presents. Today Crystal must not be in her usual good mood. She walked right past Olivia's desk without even a smile or a hello. Olivia watched Crystal climb the staircase to the executive suites. There was something strange about the way Crystal moved. Her face was void of all expression. It reminded Olivia of one of the clients they had who sleepwalked. She debated whether to call Matt and let him know that his wife was here. Olivia decided to mind her own business.

Less than two minutes later, Olivia heard the first gun shot. Several seconds later she saw the two detectives burst through the entrance and race up the staircase. As their feet hit the top stair the second shot rang out.

"Oh my god." Olivia started to shake as clients and therapists came rushing out of the back rooms. Then a third shot rang out followed by the most frightening sound of all—complete silence.

"What do you think?" Robinson rocked his chair back, the report on Gary Staples spread out in front of him.

Geraldine Berda tossed her pen on the desk and gave the detectives a reluctant smile. "It's not going to be easy but it helped that your tech guy pulled the last conversation from the victim's phone. The fact that Staples spoke that one word—*destiny*, to Crystal Bordeau should help. Frank's testimony that Tamara Rios said the same word could also be a plus. That's the good news."

"Good news?" Jake pushed away from the credenza.

"That means there's bad news?" Frank said.

"Aw, shit." Robinson stopped rocking his chair and leaned forward. "Hit me with it."

"It's still all circumstantial. Still can't put the smoking gun in his hand, so to speak, on the other victims. He's going to plead not guilty and damn confident he'll be acquitted. The judge laughed at my request for an all male jury as well as a male attorney. And." She turned her gaze to Jake. "You know I can't put Sam on the stand and have her testify to her mystic revelations, cosmic messages, or whatever the hell it is she does. And then there's the matter of Crystal Bordeau. Lucky for her she can't aim straight. The bullet only grazed Austin's shoulder and her husband will survive the bullet wound to his chest. She doesn't remember anything from the time she left her house until you two showed up at the clinic. She doesn't have a license for the gun and if Sam's therapist can't prove Crystal was under hypnosis, Crystal may end up serving more time than Staples."

"Damn." Frank whooshed out a breath. "What if she's still, you know, under hypnosis? What if she's programmed to try again? I'd hate to be her husband, not knowing when the next bullet is gonna fly."

"When are they moving Staples?" Robinson asked.

"Tonight. He'll be at the correctional facility in Michigan City until his trial."

57

Mother Nature saw fit to give the Midwest one last day of mild temperatures and sunshine. The winds last night had torn more leaves off of the trees and the weather forecast for tonight was frost. It had been a week since Gary's arrest. Sam's headaches were fading, although Jake had suggested she stay home and rest. But Forrest had called and asked her to meet him this morning. She couldn't let him down.

Her boots splashed through piles of vibrant colored leaves. Of all places to meet it had to be a cemetery. She pulled Abby's wool cape tighter as she clung to a stack of photo albums. Hidden Oaks Cemetery was one of the oldest in Chasen Heights. Crypts with stained glass windows and tall monuments were unheard of in the newer cemeteries.

Forrest wasn't hard to find. Sam only had to follow the giggles of a toddler. She found Forrest and Savannah sitting on a blanket in front of a tombstone with a carving of a woman and child on its surface.

"Hey, Forrest." Sam joined him on the blanket. She touched the beads in Savannah's hair. "Look at you, how pretty." Savannah smiled shyly and climbed onto her father's lap.

"I wanted to thank you, Sam, for all you did. When no one else believed me, you came through. In my heart I knew I was right. If Captain Robinson hadn't asked you to get involved, I think I'd still be making a pest of myself."

"Fortunately, by bringing it out in the open, we were able to solve other suspected suicides." Sam thought Forrest looked a bit more relaxed, although it would still take time for him to get over his wife's death. "I thought you might want these back." She handed him the photo albums she had borrowed.

Forrest pulled them from her grasp, then clutched them to his chest. He closed his eyes as though she had given him the last remnants of his wife. "Sorry." Forrest swiped at his eyes with the back of his hand and took a deep breath. "How are those other two women, do you know?"

Sam shook her head. "It's too soon to tell if the effects of Gary's hypnosis are still embedded in their subconscious. Tamara and Crystal will both be under a therapist's care for a while."

Forrest picked a rose from the bouquet he had placed on the gravesite and inhaled its fragrance. He stared at Marti's name for several seconds. Savannah reached for the flower so he made sure it didn't have any thorns before handing it to her.

"They said on the news that the case against Staples is weak. Other than the phone call to Missus Bordeau, they have little evidence to tie him to all the other victims. He could be out, if not soon, then in less than a year, if he has to wait to go to trial."

Sam couldn't find any reassuring words of wisdom to impart. Forrest was right. Gary Staples had been clever. How much more havoc could he unleash if he were allowed to walk free?

"Have you been seeing Doctor Collier?"

"Yes. He isn't what I had expected."

Sam could attest to that.

"I thought one of the first things he would have me do was get rid of all of Marti's clothes and any other fragments of her existence. But he said to hang onto everything until I could accept that Marti is in my heart and Savannah's eyes, and not in a dresser drawer."

"You're going to work every day?" Sam had feared that Forrest would become a recluse, locking himself in his condo and neglecting Savannah.

"Yes, Mom," Forrest added with a smile. He hugged his daughter close. "Gotta take care of my baby girl." His smile slowly faded and he stared off in the distance as a flock of geese took flight from a nearby pond. Somewhere someone was burning leaves as the scent floated through the air. "Do you believe in an eye for an eye?" He turned to Sam. Was that regret she saw in his eyes, or fear that she would be disappointed in him? "I thought it would make a difference. I thought I'd open my eyes today and see the world in a whole new light. But I don't."

Sam froze. He couldn't possibly mean what she thought. "My god, Forrest. What did you do?" She hadn't seen anything in the morning papers and she hadn't listened to the radio or television this morning. Jake had already left for work and Abby had taken Dillon to the park. Even her car radio had been turned off on the ride over. But it was impossible for Forrest to visit Gary Staples. Only his attorney or the police were allowed visitation before the trial.

Tears pooled and slowly etched their way down his face. He didn't bother to wipe them away. "The thing is, it didn't make one damn difference. It didn't bring my Marti back. I don't feel any different. Just the same pain and emptiness."

"Forrest, talk to me. What did you do?"

His gaze settled on her forehead where the cuts and scrapes were still healing. She hadn't bothered to conceal the black and blue still evident under her eyes.

"What would your husband do if he ever found the man who did that to you?"

Sam stepped off the elevator and watched the commotion around a television set near the captain's office. She saw Frank, Jake, Andy, Maury, Captain Robinson, and several file clerks watching what looked like a press conference. She had skirted around a reply to Forrest's question, remembering how Marino had looked when he exited the interview room after Jake had his allotted few minutes with him, with the blessing of Chief Murphy. When she had pressed Forrest again as to what he had done, his only response was, "maybe it's best you don't know." He had an appointment with Doctor Collier this afternoon. Hopefully, he would open up to him.

"What's happening?" she asked Sergeant Scofield.

He pulled off his glasses and waved them toward the cluster of people. "Someone did society a favor this morning. Our esteemed magician, Mister Gary Staples, was taking a shower when something more than water came out of the spray. Isopropyl alcohol. Plain old nail polish remover. Even if by some chance a jury finds him not guilty, I don't think he'll be a threat to anyone anymore."

"It blinded him?" Sam didn't know whether to be glad he wasn't killed or thrilled he could no longer look at a woman with those demonic eyes. "Do they know who did it?"

"Workmen were in the evening before fixing a leak in that same shower stall. They came in a plain white van, even had a work order, but checking it out today, the company doesn't exist. The men wore hats to conceal their faces from the cameras, I.D.'s were bogus. Only thing the camera caught were the tats on their necks. It was as though they wanted the camera to see them."

Could it have been a coincidence? Sam thought. Maybe Forrest had just wished Gary ill and karma took over. But then the word "tat" registered. "Tattoos?"

"Yep, of cobras. My bet is they were gang members."

Sam mumbled her thanks and slowly made her way to one of the conference rooms. Duke, the gang leader, was in prison in Terre Haute. Forrest had said he still runs everything from inside his prison. Duke had told Forrest if he ever needed anything just to let him know. It was the least he could do to make up for what happened to Bobby, his foster brother.

She stood in the doorway to the conference room, unaware she was staring at the television, the look on her face catching Jake's attention. He maneuvered through the group and walked over to her.

"Hey, babe. You okay?"

"Sure." She tried to gather her composure so Jake wouldn't get suspicious. She pulled him inside the conference room. "I wanted to ask you about Marino." Although Sam had only heard bits and pieces from Robinson and Frank, Sam had never asked Jake. "What would you have done to Marino if Frank hadn't dragged you away that night behind the restaurant?"

Jake cocked his head and studied her. "But he did drag me away."

"But what if Frank hadn't come out when he did?" *An eye for an eye.* Forrest's words kept coming back to her and playing in an endless loop as she waited for Jake's reply. For a brief second his eyes took on that ruthless glare, his thoughts back in that alley where he confronted Marino. Just as quickly it faded.

He kicked the door shut and pulled her into his arms. "That what this is about? I didn't bloody him up enough for you?" There was a chuckle in his voice as he said it.

"No, although I would have liked to have seen Marino try to pluck a pound of cinder out of his face. But seriously, what would you have done?"

Again, that deadly silence. Was she trying to convince herself that what Forrest had done was what every husband would have done? Abby had always said that Jake was an honorable man.

Sam wasn't sure either she or Abby knew him that well, especially when he replied, "I guess we'll never know."

Author's Note:

For more information on books, essays, and short stories written by S.D. Tooley/Lee Driver, visit her at www.sdtooley.com

CPSIA information can be obtained at www.ICGtesting.com
Printed in the USA
BVOW08s0958080316

439495BV00001B/26/P